BOOKLOVER

BOOKLOVER

J.E. BIRK

HeartEyes
Press

For Mom

Thanks for being my 4 a.m. milking partner and for gifting me your love of the romance genre. I hope this book makes you proud.
(P.S. You can skip the sex scenes if you want.)

WHERE JAMIE, ONE OF OUR HEROES, REALIZES HE MAY HAVE A BOOK KINK

"I can't be . . . who you need me to be," Raya whispered. Her voice traced and etched lines in my chest, as though her words were carving holes into my heart.

"I don't need you to be anything other than yourself," I whispered back.

She shook her head, tendrils of brown hair falling out of her short ponytail. I resisted the urge to sweep them away from her face. "You deserve more. You always have."

"Don't I deserve the one person in my life who makes me laugh? Don't I deserve the person I want to see when I wake up in the morning?" I reached for her, hoping that if I could only —

Something wet pushes into my stomach just as Brett is getting his head out of his ass and realizing how much he loves Raya, and a moment later a flash of black and white is knocking Brett's perfect grand gesture right out of my hands. "Darla!" I shout. I dive to rescue my e-reader from the hard cement floor of the barn where it's landed. Good thing I have a case on it.

Darla just stares at me, unrepentant. Of course she does—she's a cow. Chewing her cud and getting me to give up the hay I'm holding under my left arm are a lot more important to her than whether two fictional characters get their happily ever after.

Dad chuckles from a few feet away. "Jamie, I keep telling you not to read while we feed the cows," he says. "Remember that book one of them knocked right into a water bowl when you were a kid? You were crushed. Your mom and I hunted for months lookin' for a replacement."

I grimace as I finish handing Darla her hay. She tilts her head at me approvingly. "Oh, I remember that. It was that out-of-print book I loved that I found at the used bookstore." I cried for six days, and Mom and Dad never did find another copy. "You're right. I shouldn't be reading in the barn. But I need to leave for my book club meeting soon." I've already read the book we'll be discussing, *Lost Cause* by Alyssa Samuel, a few dozen times. But it's one of my favorites, so I wanted to give myself a refresher.

"That's right." Dad glances down at his watch. "You better get going. Don't want you to be late. Think you have time to come by later this week and help me out with the gutter cleaner? It's been acting up again."

I don't have time, actually. I have a test in a few days and a paper that's almost due, plus shifts at my on-campus library job. But I just paste a smile across my face and say, "Sure, Dad," because this guy really did once call twenty-two bookstores after a cow tried to eat one of my paperbacks. He nods and waves me out of the barn, and I take off before I end up sucked into another set of chores that make me late for my meeting.

Mom and my sister Lissie are both out somewhere, so I have the house to myself as I shower and get ready to go back to Burlington. I live in the dorms at Burlington University, but with all the help my parents need on their dairy farm it sometimes feels like I still live back at home with them. My roommate Jeremy reminds me of this, while I'm pulling on a clean pair of jeans, by texting:

do u still live with me? Haven't seen you in days. COME
HOME PLEASE

I quickly message back:

Be back tonight. I have my first book club meeting this afternoon

My phone rings as I'm packing up my backpack. "Did you
really join a romance novel book club?" Jeremy demands.

"Of course I did. I told you I was going to."

"That's cool, I guess. The one in that LGBTQ-inclusive bookstore on Church Street?"

"Yeah, Vino and Veritas." Jeremy and I are both bi, and it
didn't take us long to find V and V after it first opened. I was a lot
more interested in the store than Jeremy, though. I'm studying
literature and I plan to become a librarian one day after I get my
grad degree in library science. Jeremy's basically majoring in sex
and sleep.

"Maybe I should have joined too. Then I'd actually get to see
you. I don't understand why you want to talk about books on a
Saturday, though. Don't you get enough of that in class?"

"Nah. Most of the classes at Burlington U aren't exactly
focusing on the contemporary romance genre. The other lit majors
would probably laugh their asses off if they turned on my e-
reader."

"Huh. Aren't all books just books?"

Jeremy is naïve in the best possible ways sometimes. "Literary
snobbery is weird, bro. Anyway, I should be back on campus in
time for dinner if you want to grab some together. What are you
doing this afternoon?"

"I should work on my stats homework. But I don't wanna. I'll
probably see if Sheila or Robert want to hang out."

I remember Robert from an awkward morning-after a few
weeks ago. The other name doesn't ring a bell. "Which one is
Sheila?"

"I met her last night."

She'll probably be gone before I even get the chance to lay eyes on her. Jeremy and I are complete opposites in so many ways. I spend any free time I have reading novels about true love. Jeremy spends most of his free time trying to find his next hookup.

"I gotta go," I tell Jeremy. "I don't want to be late." It's a fifty-minute drive to Burlington from where my parents live in Morse's Line, Vermont, and I really don't want to miss this meeting. Plus, I don't like thinking about how much free time Jeremy has compared to me. His family lives almost three hundred miles away, in Connecticut, and they pay for him to go to school, so he doesn't even have a job. He can spend the rest of the day lying on the couch in our dorm room, studying or hooking up or reading or messaging or playing video games, with no fear that his father is going to call him and ask him for help with a broken gutter cleaner.

"Cool," Jeremy responds. "Don't get stuck behind any tractors." Then he hangs up.

I really hope I don't. That's how I ended up late to a philosophy class two weeks ago.

The drive back to Burlington is mostly interstate. I flirt with the speed limit while I blast old Green Day songs and scenery of melting snow and mud rolls by me. March has definitely come to Vermont. We call this time of the year "mud season" for a reason. Winter fades away so slowly here that the snow we've accumulated for months becomes one with the ground and turns into globs of coffee-colored wet dirt everywhere you go. The mud piles freeze and then unfreeze, depending on the day. At least we're past most of the worst temperatures of the winter. It's a full forty-seven degrees today—practically balmy, and stubborn slits of sunshine are doing their best to break through a strong cloud cover. Just the fact that we're above freezing temperatures is enough to have me breaking out in song with Billie Joe Armstrong. You really haven't lived until you've milked cows in subzero temperatures.

I can't wait for summer. Summer, in my opinion, is the very best time to be in Vermont. It's when the whole state seems to wake up and come to life after a dark winter of hibernation. Summer here is swimming in rivers, paddle-boarding and boating on Lake Champlain, eating maple ice cream at Bob's Creemee Stand, and green grass and hills as far as you can see. Winters in Vermont are long, so you have to drink in every moment of summer you can.

The only problem is that I haven't told Dad yet about the job offer I got for this summer. Every time I try to open my mouth and say something, I see his face the day Aaron left. I envision the hard, wrinkled lines of sadness that pulled at his mouth and eyes . . . and then my lips just freeze up around the words. I still have over a month before I have to make up my mind about whether I'm taking the position or not, but the weather right now is reminding me that a month is going to go by quickly. I need to grow up and talk to Dad soon.

Not today, though. Today I get to sit around and talk about one of my favorite books on the planet in one of my favorite places on the planet. I steer the car off I-89 at the Burlington exit and pass the street I normally take to get to Moo U, which is what everyone calls Burlington University. Church Street isn't far from the school, and it's only a few minutes before I'm pulling my truck into a parking spot a short walk away from V and V.

Church Street is a pedestrians-only street, and every time I set foot on it, I stop and take a moment to just stare at everything around me. On the rare occasions I came here with my family when I was a kid, Church Street seemed wild and magical. Morse's Line, where I grew up, is a super tiny town right on the U.S. border with Canada. Coming to the big city of Burlington was always an exciting adventure, especially if Church Street was involved. Right now I'm looking down a long, bricked street packed with stores and restaurants on either side. The iconic church that gives the street its name is a few blocks away, and I see more people moving in and around one another than I'd see in a year at the Morse's Line Quick Stop. Signs are everywhere advertising musical events, sales, and the beloved Burlington Farmers Market. Church Street has always felt like a place of wonder and possibility to me. I thought that feeling might shift or fade once I moved to Burlington for college, but it hasn't. If anything, it's gotten stronger.

I draw in a breath and pull in the scents of The Maple Factory, a bakery and cafe that features maple in almost everything they make. Their crullers are delicious, and the place just happens to be right next to Vino and Veritas, so that's convenient. I'm definitely grabbing a maple cruller after I'm done talking about Alyssa Samuel's plot lines.

I quickly move through the groups of people surrounding me and step into Vino and Veritas. V and V is a combination bookstore and wine bar, with the books on one side of the space and the wine bar on the other. I'm a few months away from being able to order much in the wine bar, and I'm not sure it's open for the day yet anyway, so I navigate through the entrance on my right-hand side and into the bookstore. The first breath I take inside of the store is almost as good as the one I just took outside. It's that wonderful mix of old paper and leather and vanilla that every good bookshop smells like. That smell is part of the reason I knew I'd love this place the first time I ever walked in. The look and feel of it was another. Vino and Veritas is full of leather couches, soft jazz music, warm-looking old wood, and books everywhere.

I could spend every hour of every day here, if only I had that kind of time. Which I don't. Because I'm a full-time student with a part-time job and a family that requires me to be on speed dial for dairy farm emergencies. It's truly amazing I even made time for this meeting.

I pull my tuque (French Canadian for "beanie"—living right on the Quebec border does things to your vocabulary) off my head and start heading toward the circle of couches and chairs near the back where the inaugural meeting of The Booklover Club is supposed to take place. I make a quick stop at a shelf of new titles because the store's got at least three that I've been meaning to read. I grab one of them, a nonfiction book about dairy farming, and I take a quick pause to wonder if my wallet can handle a bookstore binge. I'm still reading the inside of the jacket flap when I hear a voice behind me.

"Can I help you?"

I turn around and try not to do that *thing* Jeremy says I sometimes do, where I stand there staring at someone or something without speaking. In my defense, I think the problem comes from spending most of my childhood surrounded by cows. Sometimes I just forget how to people.

Especially when incredibly hot human beings are standing in front of me. Which is happening right now.

This guy looks exactly like Porter, one of my favorite book characters. He's in Alyssa Samuel's gay romance novel *Lost Key,* and right now I can't help but wonder if he walked right off the pages of that book and into this store. The Porter lookalike in front of me has sharp, angular cheekbones sitting under hazel eyes and dirty blond hair and eyebrows. He's got some scruffy wannabe-beard-but-it's-not-there-yet hair around his chin that's straight out of the Vermont tourist brochures. His head is covered by a pilling green tuque, and his skin is this olive tone that should be next to impossible for any white guy to have in Vermont in March. He's wearing a flannel shirt and jeans, which is pretty much the stereotypical Vermont uniform, but somehow on him it manages to look cool and unique.

And as if all that weren't enough? *He's carrying a stack of books.*

Some men dream of seeing their perfect lover strutting around in hot lingerie or tiny speedos. I dream of my perfect lover naked, with a stack of books strategically placed in front of them.

"I . . . uh . . . ." I try to remind myself that I'd like to be able to come back to this store again, so it would be great if I didn't make a total ass of myself in front of someone whose nametag suggests that they work here. Too bad I can't read it—it's gotten scrunched up in a crease in his flannel shirt. "I'm here for The Booklover Club?"

Up until now, the Porter lookalike has had a fairly neutral facial expression. Not angry or anything, but not really happy either. Now the corners of his mouth move up into an immediate smile and his eyes brighten with excitement.

"Hey, cool, man. I'm one of the founders of the group. Great to see more people are here for it. We'll be meeting right over there." He points to a circle of couches and chairs. "I'm just going to go grab us a cheese plate from the wine bar. I'll be right over."

I nod stupidly and put down the book I'm holding. He turns around, and now his butt is taunting me as it moves across the room.

I usually don't mind that I never have time to date. I figure I'll have plenty of opportunity for that once I get to grad school, which will probably be in a much bigger city with a much bigger dating pool anyway. And a lot fewer cows to potentially interrupt any plans I might have.

But right now, as I'm watching the guy-who-is-not-Porter walk away, I let myself wish for just a second that my life was different. Because it isn't every day that your wet dream appears in front of you carrying a stack of books.

2

WHERE BRIAR, OUR OTHER HERO, BREAKS HIS WINTER FUNK. MAYBE. AT LEAST A LITTLE.

It's gray outside. Again.

I'm starting to think that Vermont doesn't have any other colors. Louie, who was hired at V and V around the same time as me and is the person I talk to the most here, swears this isn't true. "You moved here at probably the worst time, Briar," he keeps telling me. "You got to Vermont in October, just in time for the deep freeze. Don't worry. Everything will melt soon, I promise."

I never thought I was one of those people whose mood was affected by the weather. I grew up just one state south of here in Massachusetts, and it's not like Springfield is winning any awards for "most sunny days in America." I'm also not known for being the most cheerful person alive anyway, weather notwithstanding. Still, lately I've felt like all the gray days this state offers up are starting to get to me. I've been even more short-tempered than usual, which is saying something. Last week I almost bit some woman's head off because she dog-eared a page in a book she hadn't bought yet.

In my defense, there is a special kind of hell for people who dog-ear books. *Still.* I know better than to snap at customers. I may not have the best people skills, but I'm not an idiot. I know Harrison Fletcher took a chance on me when he hired me to sell books at Vino and Veritas, and usually I do my best to make sure he doesn't think he made the wrong decision. But six months into my first year in Vermont, I'm beginning to wonder if I can survive the winters here.

And that's not something I want to be wondering right now. Because in almost every other category of life besides the weather, Vermont has given me something I never had before. Stable and fun job with decent coworkers: check. Apartment that doesn't completely suck: check. Healthy food on my table every night: check. The ability to talk about romance novels with people while I'm on the clock earning money: check.

That last one is something I never, ever imagined I'd have.

So I'm trying to forgive Vermont for its current inability to find some damn sun. Some days it's harder than others, though.

"Doesn't your first club meeting start in a few minutes?" Louie, who's standing next to me at the check-out desk, points to the clock on the wall across the room. Immediately my mind goes to the quote "How did it get so late so soon?" from Dr. Seuss. I've been reading a lot more kid lit since I started working here and Mr. Fletcher asked me to run story hours sometimes. It's making me realize how many great books I missed out on when I was a kid. I especially like the one about the dragons and tacos.

"Yeah. I was just about to start setting up." I glance over at the couches and chairs near the back of the shop by the coffee counter. So far only Mrs. Donaldson, the lady who first gave me the idea for this group and set it up with me, is there. "You think anyone will come?" I ask. I hope I don't sound as nervous as I feel. I've never tried to get a group of people together in one place before—especially not to talk about something like books. I'm going to feel like shit if no one shows up for our first meeting. I know a lot of our regular customers already belong to online book clubs and reading groups. What if none of them want to make an extra trip to talk about books with people who aren't behind a screen?

Louie puts a hand on my shoulder, and I make sure I don't flinch or move away. It's something I'm working on. "You might have a small showing for the first meeting. That's okay. It takes time to get things like this going. Whether you have two or ten people here today, it's still a great idea. Book clubs are just one other thing that can set our store apart from the other bookstores in Burlington and the online retailers. Harrison will be happy no matter how many people come today, Briar."

His praise fills me up almost as well as the maple donuts from the bakery next door. Louie's got this great knack for making me feel like I'm not really the loser most people have spent my life telling me I am. I never really feel like I fit in here in Vermont or at V and V, but sometimes I manage to at least get next door to that feeling when I'm talking to Louie.

He's about twenty years older than me, which makes him just old enough to be my father. There have been plenty of times when I've wished he was my father—and I guess technically he could be, since I have zero idea who my father is. But Louie's about a foot shorter than me with curly blond hair and blue eyes. No resemblance at all. Also, he's a fairly well-known local artist who really only works at V and V part-time for fun and extra spending cash. I can't draw a circle. So the odds that we're related seem pretty low.

"Okay, yeah." I nod. "At least Mrs. Donaldson's here, so I won't just be sitting in the corner talking to myself." Actually, my regular conversations with Mrs. Donaldson are what started this whole thing. She's this elementary school teacher in her mid-fifties who wears bright purple lipstick and comes in once a week to scour our used book section for any romance novel she hasn't read yet. One day she accidentally knocked over a stack of romantic suspense books, and we started talking as we cleaned up the mess together. She made a joke about how we should start a book club, and I mentioned the idea to Mr. Fletcher. The next thing I knew we were making Facebook posts and flyers. Mrs. Donaldson is amazing like that. She's got more energy than anyone I've ever met, despite the fact that she spends all day with screaming eight-year-olds.

"I'm here! I'm here!" Someone comes running into the store, the bells of the door jangling behind them. I recognize her as one of Mrs. D's friends, but I can't remember her name. "Did the meeting start without me? I hope not! I'm so angry with this Brett character!"

Louie grins. "Nope, you're just in time. I'll show you over to where the group is meeting. Briar, don't forget to grab the cheese plate we made up for everyone."

"Yeah, of course. I'll get these books back on the shelf, and then I'll start setting up." I pick up a stack of books that need to be delivered back to New Arrivals. Huh. Another person came. The Booklover Club really is going to start today, and people besides me and Mrs. D are going to talk about books. Together.

It always surprises me when things that I want to happen actually end up happening.

I'm thinking so hard about the questions Mrs. D and I came up with for the meeting that I almost run right into someone who's standing at the New Arrivals section when I get there. "Can I help you?" I ask right away. If Mr. Fletcher's taught me one thing, it's that customer service is what keeps stores like his in business.

The guy glances up from a copy of *Milked*, which I'm pretty sure is a history of dairy farming in America, and geez. This dude should warn someone before he looks at them. Because this guy's *eyes*. They're this super deep, intense, brown color, like the dark mahogany wood that's all over the store. They're somehow lively and incredibly serious at the exact same time. I manage to stop staring at them long enough to hear him say the word "club."

This guy wants to join my book club? I get to talk about *Lost Cause* for an hour while I eat excellent local cheese *and* those eyes are going to be there the whole time?

Vermont has officially made up for its own lack of sunshine. Still, I try to remain as chill as possible as I answer. "Hey, cool, man. I'm one of the founders of the group. Great to see more people are here for it. We'll be meeting right over there," I tell him as I point out Mrs. D and her friend. "I just need to grab us a cheese plate from the wine bar. I'll be right over."

He sets off for the couches, and I try not to trip over my own feet as I quickly move toward the wine bar to pick up the cheese plate for the club. Then I have to immediately double-back to the New Arrivals section because I realize I forgot to put the books down there. By the time I make it back to the wine bar, there are already six different people sitting with Mrs. D and Soulful Eyes, as I've started calling him in my head.

Holy shit.

Rainn's working behind the bar, getting ready for that side of V and V to open. "Hey, I was just looking for you over in the bookstore, but Louie said you'd come to me for the cheese plate. I saw a bunch of people over there. Are they here for your club meeting?" Rainn works in both the bookstore and wine bar, but mostly the wine bar, so he's one of the employees at V and V I know the least. He seems like a good guy, though. He can be kind of grouchy at times, but he's all sunshine when he's dealing with customers. I get that dichotomy on a deep level. He hands over the tray of cheeses Louie helped me prepare earlier. Each one is from a local cheesemaker and is a cheese we serve right here in the bar. I love the way Vermont businesses all lean on one another. "If they are, that's a great turnout."

"Yeah?" I say, trying not to sound too hopeful. I know my coworkers don't know my background, and I wonder sometimes how they'd feel about me working here if they did know where I come from and what I've done in the past. There's a part of me that feels like I have to spend every moment of every day here impressing them, just in case they ever do find out.

"Yeah, man. Great idea. And way to make it happen with Mrs. Donaldson." He grins. "But let's talk about important stuff. When I was over there, you were definitely occupied. Who's the guy who was staring at you by New Arrivals?"

I snort. "Right. Sure." It's a nice idea, that Soulful Eyes would be checking me out, but there's no way. I'm wearing a beanie and a flannel shirt. It may be the unofficial uniform of Vermont, but it isn't exactly fashion-forward. Plus I'm trying to grow a beard, and it sort of just looks like a hot mess right now.

"I'm not screwing with you. He was looking at you like he never wanted to stop." Rainn winks at me. "Go for it."

"Just give me the cheese plate," I mutter. Unfortunately, this is exactly the kind of pressure I don't need. It's going to be hard enough running the first meeting of The Booklover Club without worrying about whether I'm impressing Soulful Eyes. Still . . . . "You ever see him in here before?" I ask.

"Yeah. He comes in here a lot. He's friends with this girl Lexy who's a regular too; she's in the Pride Alliance at Moo U. I can't remember his name, though."

Probably a student, then. He definitely won't end up interested in me after he learns that I barely passed my GED. So at least the pressure's off. I grab the plate and make my way out of the wine bar and back into the bookstore, through shoppers and shelves and over to the couches.

"Briar!" Mrs. Donaldson claps her hands excitedly as soon as she sees me. "Look at our little crowd here. So many friends came to join us!"

"We're happy to have you all here." I try to smile as I set the cheese plate down onto the coffee table. Smiling feels a little bit easier when Soulful Eyes flashes me a bright grin. I take a moment to appreciate that he's more than just a beautiful set of irises. He's got hair as dark as his eyes, and it's stretching in waves and curls over the top of his head and down the side of his face. His ears stick out ever so slightly. He's got a long and lanky body, with some muscles peeking out of the sleeves of his t-shirt that suggest he's getting in a lot more physical activity than I am these days. I carry a little more pudge on me than he does, and normally I go for guys with a body type more like mine, but not this time. He's wide and tall enough to take up half of one of the couches, his feet peeking out from under the coffee table, and I can't help but wonder how much space he would take up in my bed.

Dangerous thought. I've already learned the hard way to leave romance and great loves to my books. Some people seem destined to have real-life love affairs right out of the pages of an Alyssa Samuel novel, but I'm not one of them. These days I make sure anyone who joins me in bed doesn't stay there for very long, and I have a feeling Soulful Eyes isn't a one-night stand sort of person.

"Yes, we're so thrilled you all came," Mrs. Donaldson echoes as I sit down next to her, directly across from Soulful Eyes. "Let's start by introducing ourselves, shall we? Just your name, a few facts about yourself, and why you've decided to join."

And *this* is why you start a book club with an elementary school teacher. She's already got an ice breaker going. If I were doing this on my own I'd just be sitting there, staring in silence at everyone, trying to figure out what to say first.

Plus, this little exercise means I get to learn more about Soulful Eyes. *Thanks, Mrs. D,* I tell her silently. She beams at everyone, and I say a prayer of thanks to the universe that I've got her by my side for this new venture.

"Briar will go first," she adds.

Right away I take back every nice thing I've ever said about her.

3

WHERE JAMIE FORGETS HOW TO PEOPLE AGAIN

It's probably not great that I can't stop staring at my new crush. At least I have an excuse right now. The woman next to him may as well have just chucked him right under a moving bus, and now the poor guy is attempting to stammer his way through an introduction of who he is and why he's here.

"Uh," he mumbles. "I'm Briar Nord. Just moved to Vermont in October. I work here at V and V. I started this book club with Mrs. D because . . . ."

He trails off. I see his eyes wander over to a quote that's hung in a picture frame on the wall on the couch above me: "There is only try and try again," from Orson Scott Card. He frowns. "Someone told me once that you always know a romance novel is going to have a happy ending, and after that I started reading a lot of 'em. I like that you always know a romance novel is going to end the way you want it to."

He looks up briefly before dropping his eyes back toward his lap. They meet mine, just for a second. Neither of us blinks until he looks away.

Briar. It's a cool name. I wonder if there's a story behind it.

Now that Briar's broken the ice, no one else seems to feel intimidated as they introduce themselves. There's Lilah, the other founder of the group. She insists we all call her Lilah, but I notice that Briar always calls her Mrs. D. There's Betty, who turns out to be Lilah's friend. She and Lilah are both teachers, and they each look kind of like they stepped out of a hippie commune somewhere. Betty's even wearing what look like hemp ankle bracelets. There's a smiling blonde about my age named Emily. She's Betty's niece, though you could never tell that from the polo shirt and pencil skirt she's wearing. There's also Bart, a local bus driver who tells us that he raises emus in his spare time; Lucia, an aspiring writer; and Cherry, a psychology grad student at Moo U.

I'll admit that when I signed up to join this group, I sort of expected it to be a bunch of middle-aged white ladies and me. That probably sounds stereotypical, but I know the target market for romance novels, and I know Burlington's demographics. I'm glad to see my stereotyping was way off. There are plenty of different ages, genders, and racial backgrounds in this group. There's a lot more diversity here than in most of my lit classes at Moo U.

I'm so busy thinking about the group makeup that I almost miss when it's my turn to introduce myself. Luckily I manage to notice when Lilah nods at me, letting me know I'm supposed to be talking. "Oh. Hi. I'm Jamie. I'm a sophomore at Moo U, and I study literature. I want to work in a library someday." Briar's mouth peaks up into something like a smile when I say that. "My mom reads a lot of romance novels, and one day I picked one of hers up and I really liked it." I shrug. "A lot of my fellow students are weird about this genre, and I don't always have a lot of people to talk to about my favorite books. So that's why I joined."

"Totally get it," Emily says, beaming at me. "Do you know how much romance novel sales increased after the invention of e-readers? Just because people didn't want other people to know what they were reading! Ugh! It's so insulting." She tosses her hair gently and flashes some teeth at me. She seems like a nice girl, and I should probably be flattered by this open flirtation. Too bad there's someone else in this circle I'd rather have hitting on me.

Maybe Lilah notices I'm a little uncomfortable, because she cuts in pretty quickly. "So! Let's get started, friends. Briar, what question did you think our group should discuss first?"

Briar pulls a piece of folded-up paper from the pocket of his jeans and smooths it out. "Uh," he says nervously as he glances down. He's really cute when he's nervous. "Everyone read *Lost Cause* by Alyssa Samuel, right?" We all nod, because in this group I'm not the only good kid who does his homework. Why would you ever join a book club if you didn't plan to read the books the group picked? "Let's just start off with thoughts about the book, then. Have any of you read Samuel's work before? What are your general responses to this one?" He clutches the paper a little more tightly in his hands, and I realize they're shaking slightly.

Sometimes I forget that I'm not the only person in the world who isn't great at peopling.

"I dunno." Lucia frowns. "I really enjoyed the writing itself, especially the setting descriptions. But this isn't the first book of Samuel's that I've read, and sometimes her characters just fall a little flat for me. Especially their dialogue and their interactions with one another. You know?"

I whip my head up like a cow's about to crap all over me. What? No way. Samuel has some of the best characters I've ever read. In any genre.

"I couldn't agree more!" says Bart, a.k.a. Emu Guy. "I haven't read much of her other material, but I thought some of her characters in this were highly unrealistic. Brett is willing to marry so quickly in the third act of the story despite the fact that he spends the first act of the book incapable of making a commitment to anyone or anything. There's no clear motivator for change!"

"No, you're wrong," I blurt out before I can stop myself. "Samuel makes Brett's motivations so clear. He just watched his best friend lose the love of his life. That makes him realize he's letting the person he loves slip away from him because he's afraid. It's subtle, but in some ways it's an even better character arc than when Porter has to figure out his shit in *Lost Key*. Sorry not sorry, but his character arc is *great*." I throw as much emphasis as I can on that last word.

Every head in the circle is staring at me now. Oops. Looks like I've forgotten how to people again.

"If only my third graders were that passionate about literary characters," Lilah says, but she's smiling. "No, don't apologize," she adds as I start to open my mouth. "That's exactly the energy I was hoping to have in this group."

"I appreciate your passion," Lucia agrees. "But you're completely wrong," she adds bluntly, and Betty snorts out a laugh. "The character work in this book is straight-up lazy. Now, if Samuel had . . . ."

I try to pay attention to what she's saying as she's ripping my analysis apart—really, I do. But it's tough, because now Briar is kinda sorta staring at me.

He's trying to pretend that he's not. He keeps nodding at everything Lucia's saying, and then everything Bart says while he's agreeing with Lucia. But his eyes keep drifting back over to me, like they're magnetized in my direction.

Great. He probably hated *Lost Cause too*, and now his brain is working overtime trying to figure out how to prove that I'm wrong about Samuel's character writing.

Other people weigh in on the debate. Most of them seem to agree more with Lucia and Bart. Emily agrees with me, but that's no real surprise, and Lucia doesn't even try to hide her eye-roll as Emily gushes about how much she thinks I'm right.

"Briar? What did you think?" Lilah turns to look at him, and suddenly everyone's eyes are on him.

At least I have an excuse to full-on stare at Briar now.

He crosses his arms over his chest and frowns. "I think if seeing your best friend watch the love of his life die doesn't force you to make some changes, nothing else would," he says quietly. "The character creation and arc here work really well for me. But sorry not sorry, *Lost Key* is better than *Lost Cause*. Porter's fucking amazing." He definitely looks in my direction and sends me the tiniest smirk when he says *sorry not sorry*.

Wait. Is Briar flirting with me?

Even more important: Is he a hardcore Alyssa Samuel fan too? I wonder if he realizes he looks exactly like how she describes Porter.

Lucia glances back and forth between us. "This isn't an Alyssa Samuel book club, is it? Did I miss that detail on the sign-up sheet?"

"Nope," says Lilah cheerfully. "But now you know I wasn't the one who picked our first author. And apparently Briar's not the only one here who's an Alyssa Samuel fanboy." Everyone laughs, and I blush slightly as more eyes move in my direction. "So, moving onto the next question. Let's get into setting."

Cherry starts talking about allegory and allusion, and I do my best to focus on what she's saying.

But it's tough. Because Briar's eating a piece of cheese. Very, very enthusiastically.

Looks like I'm not just turned on by hot guys carrying stacks of books. I'm also turned on by hot guys who love dairy and enjoy reading the same authors as me.

Fifty minutes of heated discussion about plot and theme development later, Lilah pronounces the meeting over. "I need to get going; I promised my grandson I'd take him to a Mites hockey clinic. I always said I'd never cheer for any kind of violence in the world, but then he became a hockey fanatic. I suppose it could be worse—he could have chosen football." She shudders. "Let's choose our next title, then? I'm guessing the group would like to see it be something other than an Alyssa Samuel work?"

I don't say much as they select a romantic mystery by an author I've never heard of. One of the reasons I joined this group was to widen my reading a little more. It's a total coincidence that the first book they chose happened to be by one of my favorite authors.

Or luck, I think as I glance over at Briar again. He's eating another piece of cheese and murmuring to Lilah about something.

Everyone drifts away from the couches, talking excitedly about things like paperbacks versus hardcovers. I pack up my backpack as slowly as possible while Briar tidies up the leftovers from the cheese plate our little group demolished.

Okay, so maybe I don't have time to date. Everyone in Morse's Line and my dorm hall at Moo U knows that. But I should be able to find time for another friend, right?

"You really like *Lost Key* better than *Lost Cause?*" I finally blurt out, and Briar looks up at me in surprise. My social skills are just getting better and better today. But Briar grins, just a little, and suddenly I'm not worried about whether I'm a better conversationalist with cows than with people.

"Yeah," he says. "I almost picked that one for us to read first. But I thought maybe we should start with one of her bestselling titles. You know, follow the crowd and all that. You prefer *Lost Cause?*"

"I like both books a lot. Porter's one of my favorite characters. Just depends on what I'm in the mood for, I guess. If I want brooding, I go for Porter and Lance. If I want drama, I read Raya and Brett."

"Sounds about right." Briar hands a leftover piece of sharp cheddar across the table to me. I take it quickly, because no real Vermonter in history has ever turned down a good piece of sharp cheddar. "So you get to talk about books at Moo U all day Monday through Friday? And you still wanted to come talk about them more on a Saturday?"

"Well, not *all* day," I tell him. "I wish. The college wants us to be well-rounded or whatever, so right now I'm also taking a biology class I'd never take voluntarily, and I'm trying to figure out what the fuck Emmanuel Kant is talking about for my philosophy class. But yeah. It's not a bad life. The only shitty part will be actually getting into a good grad program for library science and then finding a job once I'm done. The world isn't exactly experiencing a shortage of librarians, you know?"

"Good point." Briar stands, the cheese plate still in hand. "You come in here a lot?"

"Yeah. Only every second that I can. I'm kind of surprised I've never seen you here before. I'm addicted to books. And those stupid maple crullers they sell next door."

"Well, I've only worked here since October. And the maple donuts are better." He shrugs.

That I cannot let stand. "No way, man. You might—emphasis on *might*—be right about *Lost Key* being the better Alyssa Samuel book. But I will die on the hill that the cruller next door beats the donut any day of the week."

"Oh yeah?" Briar's wearing a full-on, uninhibited smile now, something I haven't seen on him once all afternoon. "Want to take this debate into the field? My shift's over soon."

Did he just ask me to get food with him? Here I thought I was going to have to stammer through some more shitty small talk before I figured out how to tell Briar I wanted to talk more or hang out or whatever, and he managed to invite me to get something to eat with him about two minutes into the conversation. It doesn't get any better than this. A Porter lookalike who wears flannel like it's Gucci and eats cheese like it's his religion—and he wants to *do something with me*. No way I'm saying no.

Except just then my phone buzzes in my pocket. Because of course it does. I already know what this text message is going to say before I even unlock my screen.

911, reads the text from Lissie:

Downer cow. Dad wants to know if you can come back home and help?

Have donuts with hot, Porter-lookalike Briar, or drive an hour to help my father try to save a cow that's so sick it can no longer stand and will probably end up dying anyway? For most normal twenty-year-olds, this choice would probably be a no-brainer. But I'm not normal. I'm the guy that can't even people with others correctly because I learned to talk to cows before I learned to talk to humans. And I'm pretty sure I know which cow is down: Juniper, one of Lissie's favorites. Twelve-year-old Lissie isn't big enough yet to help Dad out with a cow that can't stand up, and there's no way I'm going to expect my mom, who has osteoarthritis, to do it.

"Shit," I mutter. "I have to . . . ."

"No, it's cool," Briar says quickly. The smile has completely disappeared from his face. "You've got things to do. No big deal."

"Oh, it's like a sixteen-hundred-pound big deal," I say as I quickly text Lissie back. *OMW*. Briar's eyebrows go up in confusion. "My parents own a dairy farm," I clarify. "Sick cow. I'm really sorry, but I've gotta go. I do come in here a lot, though. Raincheck on the cruller? If you don't realize that it crushes the donut, you haven't had enough of them."

"Sure," Briar says, but his mouth stays in a straight line. "Or maybe after our next meeting or something. See you around, Jamie." He heads away from the table, his back toward me.

In my hand, my phone buzzes. At least I can people somewhat respectably when I need to, because I resist the urge to throw it across the room in front of the entire bookstore.

4

WHERE BRIAR MEETS AN OLD FRENEMY

"It looks like the first meeting went really well!"

Louie is beaming as I come back to the checkout counter after dropping the remnants of the club's cheese plate with Rainn. "I think so," I tell him.

"I know so. Everyone was smiling as they walked out the door, and I got orders from all of them for that new book you chose. Well done, kid."

I wince internally, the way I do every time Louie calls me *kid.* It's not so much the word itself as the memories that attach to it. Gina's boyfriend, the one who ran off to Florida with her, used to call me that. That word doesn't have much meaning to me anymore that isn't negative.

But Louie seems to like calling me that, and Louie is a good guy, so I just nod. "Yeah. It went well." It went *great,* actually. So many people showed up. The conversation we had was exactly what I wanted it to be—exactly what I always dreamed conversations in book clubs and other places like college classes sounded like. The type of conversation I'm not normally in. Everyone was pumped to come back again for our next meeting, and like Louie said, the store got business out of it. Mrs. D thwacked me on the back before she left and said she couldn't wait to "debrief and discuss the agenda for our next endeavor." So far The Booklover Club is a win all around.

So why do I feel so fucking depressed right now?

It's not like me asking Soulful Eyes—*Jamie,* I remind myself—to get food with me was anything more than a weird impulse anyway. The guy called out my donuts; I had to put a stop to that. I don't date, so it wasn't even a date in my head. More like a chance to show up a cute dude who is fundamentally wrong about his maple baked goods.

A dude who just happens to like the same books as me and wear a Future Farmers of America t-shirt in a way that is somehow simultaneously unironic and incredibly hot.

But whatever. It's not like "sick cow" is an unreasonable excuse for someone to bail on you in northern Vermont. Mr. Fletcher's called out of work before because something was wrong with one of his partner's chickens. And even if the guy was blowing me off, what do I care? I just met him. It wasn't a date. I wasn't even thinking things through when I asked him to go next door. The words just came out.

Whatever. I can't worry about this right now. I've got books to put away before my shift is over.

I go through the motions of finishing up my shift while Rainn comes over to the bookstore to bicker with Louie about our next window display, and I do my best to think about anything but Jamie. Inventory numbers. Sale titles. Author names.

Maybe the problem is that I don't have a lot else to think about. My life in Vermont may be everything I always wanted, but there's not a lot to it. I work as many hours at the bookstore as I can, and when I'm not there I'm up in my small apartment, reading. I'm not really a part of this place. Not completely. Not yet. And since I've never really felt like a complete part of anywhere I've lived, I don't see that miraculously happening here anytime soon. I never exactly planned to be the Boo Radley of Vermont, but it's a role that works for me. Most of the time.

Until someone like Jamie crowds into my field of vision and

then disappears from it. Now all of the sudden my life is feeling as gray as the Vermont sky is five days a week.

I put in an order for a copy of the new mystery the group picked for our next club meeting, and then I wave goodbye to Louie, who's closing up the store tonight. I'd love to just stay at V and V all night, but they're hosting an open mic night in the bar area. Open mic nights make me twitchy. Too many people and too much potential for small talk in between performers.

So I force my feet out of Vino and Veritas and onto Church Street. I carefully work *not* to look up at the bakery next door as I walk by it. I even manage to hold my breath until I'm safely out of the vicinity. No good can come from sniffing that maple-y goodness right now.

Buses in Burlington don't run all that often, so I end up waiting about twenty minutes at the bus stop on the other end of Church Street for my ride. I peer at the sky, where a thin sliver of sunlight is doing its absolute best to cut through the mass of gray there. But that gray isn't budging.

Vermont weather sure is fucking stubborn.

I live in the Old North End neighborhood of Burlington, which isn't far from Church Street at all. I can walk to work when I feel like it. My bus ride is short, and soon I'm trudging up Adams Avenue, toward the large pink house at the very end. When I first met my new landlady here, I thought I was hallucinating. The place is the color of a five-year-old's birthday cake, and it's got eggplant-purple trim. Who paints an old house that's been converted into apartments to look like an Easter egg?

It turns out that Edna Krysnicki does.

"I thought the neighborhood needed more color," she told me seriously as she showed me around the building. And I guess she's not wrong. The Old North End sounds like a cool name, but it's one of the lower-income neighborhoods in Burlington. Most of the buildings here are more run-down and could use an update. Lots of the houses are divided into smaller apartments, so people tend to spill out in every direction of the properties the same way that the wood breaks away from the edges of window frames on some of the houses. It's nothing like the New North End, where Louie lives in this perfect mid-century modern rancher with his own perfect yard and his hot partner, Sam.

Still, I'd rather live in the Old North End than the New North End any day. This neighborhood reminds me of where I lived with Gina in Springfield. It feels real. It feels normal.

The pink house has more than ten small studio and one-bedroom apartments built into it, so I'm used to seeing people hanging out on the large porch that wraps around the front of the monstrosity. What I'm not used to is seeing someone I know sitting on the steps of that porch. I stop, dead in my tracks, as I hit the bottom of the driveway.

I stop. And I stare.

"Luke?" I say, incredulous.

"Briar!" He throws his arms open, like he wants a hug or something. "Surprised to see me?"

Actually, I'm just surprised it took him this long to find me.

We end up at the tiny table in my four hundred square foot studio, which is at the very top of the house. The eaves of the ceiling hang low, and we both have to duck to avoid hitting our heads when we first walk in. Despite the size and height of this place, it's been my escape from the world since the minute I moved in. The perfect respite. It's the first place I've ever lived that was just mine: no roommates, no pseudo-stepfathers, no bunkbeds. Just me. The moment Luke steps in the door behind me, though, it feels like a cage. Still, I know I don't have any other choice but to let him in and gesture him over to the tiny table in the center of the room. The last thing I want is to be seen out in Burlington with Luke. The last thing I want is Luke talking to anyone else I know.

"So?" he says as he sips on the beer I've just handed him. It's a microbrew from a nearby brewery that's popular with the locals. Louie gave it to me as a thank you after I helped him and Sam move some furniture. It's definitely going to be wasted on Luke, who spent most of our teenage years espousing the virtues of Bud Light, but there's no way I'm trying to have this conversation unless both of us have some alcohol in front of us. "How'd you end up here?"

"I was planning to ask you the same thing." I take a sip of the malty, slightly bitter beer, relishing the different flavors that roll over my tongue. There's a reason Vermont breweries are so popular. "How did you find me?"

"Almont." Luke gestures his bottle at the ceiling. "Not a bad place you got here."

Almont. Of course. I should have known that Luke would run into Almont at some point. Those two were always tight back when we were kids.

I never should have told Almont where I was going. I never should have told anyone. But Almont was the one who got me out of a garage and into his guest room, and he was the one who put me back in touch with DeShawn. I couldn't just disappear on him without telling him that I had a plan.

"Almont said DeShawn sent you up here."

DeShawn didn't "send" me anywhere, but I get where the language comes from. It's a pretty recent development for either Luke or me to have any say in where we live. "DeShawn put me in touch with my new boss, yeah. Helped me get a job." DeShawn, my former social worker, went to college with Mr. Fletcher. He heard about Mr. Fletcher starting a store and reached out to him about me because he knows how much I love books. It was just another in a long line of great things DeShawn has done for me over the years, though I know he doesn't see it that way. He's made it very clear that he feels responsible for me ending up on the streets back in Springfield. He isn't, though. My dumbass choices belong to nobody but myself.

"Good deal, bro." Luke moves his beer bottle across the table like he wants me to clink mine against it, but I don't bring my bottle up to meet his. Luke being here is nothing to celebrate. Luke has never been more than two steps away from any of the bad decisions I've made in my life—including the one that landed me on the streets and should have landed me in jail. I could have happily gone the rest of my life without seeing him.

Too bad that's not how life in the world of Briar Nord works.

Luke studies my dull studio, with its cheap and stained furniture. All of it was left here by the previous renters, and I was grateful for every piece. Meanwhile, I study him. He's thinner than he used to be. Probably still doing meth, at least once in a while. He's wearing a Red Sox cap over dark black hair that seems to be thinning, and his teeth look browner than the last time I saw him. His coat looks new, though, and the jeans he's wearing aren't too beat up. Luke knows how to get shit when he needs it.

I'm worried he's here because he thinks of me as another place he can get shit.

I decide it's time to get down to business. "So what are you doing here, in Burlington?"

"It's a nice place," Luke says, deliberately not answering my question. "How much do you pay?"

I take a sip of beer and stare. He stares back.

Eventually he shrugs.

"Whatever, man. Fine. Let's get down to it. I've been between jobs, yeah? Fucker I was working for at the lumberyard fired my ass." He shakes his head in disgust. "Bitch never liked me."

She's just joined a long line of bosses who don't "like" Luke. Luke seems to think it's a crime for an employer to expect their employees to be on time and sober every day.

"Anyway, I'm bumming around Springfield and I see Almont, and he mentions you're up in Vermont now at this bookstore, right? Says it's all fancy and crap."

My memory pings back to the day Mr. Fletcher agreed to hire me over a phone call. Almont and I got on his laptop and started looking at pictures of Vino and Veritas, and I couldn't stop talking about how great the place was, with its wine bar and expensive-looking furniture. Now I realize that Vino isn't fancy by a lot of Church Street shop standards, but it still feels like the most luxurious place in the world to me.

Not that I'm telling Luke any of that. "I mean, it's just a bookstore. But it's nice enough."

Luke smirks. "Right. Nice. Nice enough to have *nice* stuff in it." He leans across the table. "I did some hunting around online, Briar. That store you work for? They've got some stuff that's *more* than nice sitting around there. Including the original diaries of some dude named Justin Morgan. And guess what?"

I don't have to guess. Because I already know what he's about to say.

Vino and Veritas mostly sells new and gently used books, but Mr. Fletcher also trades and sells some rare and vintage books. There's a safe in the storage room, and all of them are locked up tightly there. Mr. Fletcher showed me the safe when he took me on my first tour of V and V. "Most people wouldn't believe this if I told them," he said. "But some of these books together would be worth more than the entire stock in the store." Someone checks the safe every night at closing, just to make sure it's locked tight. Every now and then Mr. Fletcher goes in and out of the safe to take out a book or add another one, but he and his mother Audrey, who co-owns the shop, are the only ones who know the combination.

The book Luke's talking about is some incredibly rare edition of the diaries of the guy who first bred Morgan horses. He's from Vermont, and everyone here seems to have a weird hard-on for him. His name was Justin Morgan. I've heard Mr. Fletcher talking about that book with Louie. "I'm still looking for the right buyer for that one," he said. "But when I find them, we're all opening a bottle of the good wine together."

That's because the book is worth twenty thousand dollars.

Luke's talking excitedly now, his beer bottle dancing in his hand. "That fucking thing is worth a ton a money! At least twenty gs, bro! Do you even know what we could do with twenty gs?"

The sad part is that I do.

I wouldn't change much, actually. Maybe rent a larger apartment that's not quite as pink. But I'd stay in Burlington. I'd keep working at the bookstore. This town may be gray as fuck, but it's the closest thing to home I've found, and I'm not in any hurry to leave. I wouldn't spend any of that money on drugs, like Luke probably would, or a new car, the way Almont would.

Nope. That money would be for my savings account. The savings account that currently has a balance of $265.41. The savings account that is way too small to bail me out if I'm ever dumb enough to end up on the streets again, like I did in Springfield.

I swore when I moved up here that I'd save every single cent I could and put it into that account, just to make sure I never ended up in that kind of position again. It was my most important promise to myself. But it turns out that saving money, even when you have a regular job you like, isn't that easy when you live in a city like Burlington. Rent costs. Electricity and heat cost. Food costs. And that's sort of the problem. It isn't much easier to save money here than it was in Springfield.

Which means I can always end up back on the streets here, just like I did there. The bookstore could have a few low months. I'd get laid off, and I might not be able to find anything else fast enough to keep my place. Or Mr. Fletcher could realize that I'm actually shit at talking to people and finally fire me. Or Edna could decide to raise the rent just a little too much.

Twenty gs . . . even just a small cut of that would change my savings account forever. Maybe I could finally sleep at night without thinking about the cardboard boxes and broken couch springs I slept on for three months.

But.

But.

"I'm not stealing from Mr. Fletcher, Luke." I set down my beer bottle and cross my arms over my chest. Sometimes you have to look more powerful than you feel. "He's been good to me." Great to me, actually. Everyone in that store has. "Anyway, I know the book you're talking about, and I don't have access to it." That's true enough. I have no idea what the code to Mr. Fletcher's safe is, and I have no intention of asking for it.

"Hey now." Luke puts his own beer bottle down on the table with a *thunk.* "No one's asking you to do the stealing, okay? I know that ain't your thing." He would remember that. When we were kids, I was always the one who kept lookout while he was the one who stole the candy bar or the hubcap or whatever it was he wanted to take that day. I could always tell it gave him a rush, taking something that didn't belong to him. Keeping lookout just made me feel dirty. "You don't have to take shit, Briar. You can just pass some info, maybe leave a door unlocked, keep watch. You know how it is."

I know how it is, all right. I know that I took a bus for five hours to get as far from Springfield, Massachusetts as I reasonably could. As far from Hope House and Luke—and Gina, wherever she is—as I could. And still, somehow, Springfield found me here.

"Sorry, Luke." I stand up, setting my own beer bottle down onto the table. "I can't help you."

Luke eyes me for a moment, and then finally takes the hint and stands up too. "Yeah? You sure? It's a lot of money, my dude."

Mr. Fletcher once told me a story about how he was convinced he was going to die at forty-two because that's when his dad and grandfather died. But instead he ended up starting a store with his mother and falling in love with a chicken farmer. It's the kind of story right out of a book, it's so unreal in its beauty and perfection. I could never be the one to crush any part of Mr. Fletcher's happy ending. "No, Luke. Like I said. No access."

And even if I did have it, I wouldn't give it to you.

Except.

Except there's my story too, and I don't know what the ending is yet. Do I get to stay here, in my tiny apartment in this giant pink monstrosity? Do I get to keep selling books and talking about other people's happy endings?

Or do I end up like I did in Springfield? Do I end up with another shitty ending for myself?

I know Luke's being real when he tells me he'd do all the work. It's how things always went when we were younger. If I did get the safe code and I gave it to him, it'd be just like back when I was his lookout. No actual dirt on my own hands. I could just stand there, quietly, and wait for the money to get shared.

And then I'd finally have enough money in my bank account to sleep at night.

"Huh. Too bad." Luke shrugs and starts making his way toward the door. "But you know, I'm staying in Rutland right now with some girl I met. It's not that far of a bus ride from here. Maybe I'll take a trip back up here again sometime? Just to make sure you still don't have access?"

I should tell him to get out of my apartment. I should tell him I never want to see him again. I should tell him the same thing I wish I'd told him every single time he talked me into pulling some shit with him back at Hope House: *No. I'm not in. Leave me the fuck alone.*

But I don't say any of that. I don't.

All I say is, "Whatever, man. Have a safe trip back."

5

WHERE JAMIE IS EXHAUSTED AND REALLY NEEDS A CRULLER

There are days when I seriously consider giving up milk. This is one of them.

Not that I could ever do that. I love milk—so much that I've developed a mild lactose intolerance from basically pouring gallons of it on my breakfast cereal every morning. And it's not just milk I couldn't give up. I love ice cream. Sour cream. Cheese. All kinds of cheese, even cottage cheese, which Jeremy says tastes like sadness. Dairy is in my lifeblood, and everyone in my family ingests it like we'd die if we had to stop.

But if anything is ever going to put me off dairy, it would probably be this week. First there was the downer cow that led to my missed cruller with Briar. Then there was a broken milk pump Dad needed help fixing, two separate milkings I ended up doing because Lissie had guitar recitals this week and Mom and Dad needed to go to both of them, and now I'm standing in a field helping Dad fix a barbed wire fence that a tree came down on last night because apparently the tree is in on the cosmic joke against me too.

All of this is on top of my job at the Moo U library and the six-page paper and lab I have due this week and the philosophy class tomorrow that I haven't done any of the reading for. I'm pretty sure I also have a quiz coming up, but right now I can't even remember for the life of me which class it's in.

I love my family's cows. But right now I really, really, really don't like them.

"Can we hurry this up?" I pass a pair of pliers over to Dad and pull my cell phone out of my pocket to check the time. "I've gotta get back to Burlington."

"We're getting there." Dad focuses on the wire he's twisting back into place. "Rush and you end up doing things twice. You know that."

I know that because I've heard him say it a thousand times. I also know that every second he spends taking his time is another second I don't have to get ready for my class tomorrow.

Dad's not exactly the most efficient person where time is concerned. He believes in doing a job well and right, which is great and all, but sometimes it means that a job which should take thirty minutes ends up taking ninety. Aaron and I used to rock-paper-scissors for the jobs that we knew would go especially long.

Aaron. It's been a while since I thought about him. Usually I think about him at least once a day, so I guess that just shows how busy my life has gotten this week. I wonder if he went to law school like he was planning to. I hope so. Maybe he's writing a paper or arguing a case in a mock trial somewhere. He probably is. And he's probably not worrying about Lissie texting him with an emergency or wondering if Dad's going to interrupt one of his classes for a fence job.

But then again, he also missed our family Christmas this year. He missed Dad's turkey and Mom's pumpkin pie and Lissie playing carol after carol on her guitar after dinner. I wonder who he spent Christmas with. I wonder if he was lonely.

I tried texting him a few times after the big fight last summer, but he wouldn't answer me. Finally he texted back:

I can't talk to you right now. So sorry, Jamie. Will text when I can.

That was it. Then radio silence since August. Mom or Lissie would tell me if they've been in touch with him, so I know they haven't. And there's no way Dad has reached out to him. Frank Morin is nothing if not proud, and he'd probably give up this farm before he passed an olive branch over to my brother.

"Dad, I've got class tomorrow," I tell him, trying to up the urgency in my voice. "I need to finish some reading."

He frowns at the fence post in front of him. "Maybe you should've taken a smaller course load or reduced your hours at the library this semester. You're always taking on too much."

If I didn't love this man so much, I'd strangle him with some of the barbed wire that's next to me. Taking on a smaller course load would mean dragging out my time in school even more. Reducing my hours at the library would mean giving up time in a job I love, the kind of job I hope I'll have for the rest of my life.

The more obvious solution, of course, would be to stop taking on so much at the farm. But Dad doesn't mention that. Because that's not even an option in his head. How could it be? We don't have the money for him to hire full-time, consistent help. Mom works at the high school two towns over, and she basically has another job here, but her arthritis problems mean there's a lot she can't do in the barn. And Lissie helps as much as she can, but she's still in middle school.

I wonder if Aaron realizes how much harder things got for me the second he walked away from Tiny Acres Dairy.

"So," Dad asks. "How are things with that book club you joined?"

And this is why it's hard for me to stay mad at my dad, even when he's taking twelve years to reattach barbed wire to a fence post. Because he cares about every part of me, even the parts that are nothing like him. He thinks it's cool that Mom and I read romance novels together, even though he'd rather be reading *The Monthly Herdsman*. He's always supported me wanting to become a librarian, even though I know he worries that I won't find a job. When I dated a guy for the first time, I brought him home and

Dad told me that "he's a nice guy, even if he is useless in the barn."

(Which, to be fair, poor Sean was. He was even afraid of the baby calves. We didn't last long.)

"We've only had one meeting so far, but I really like it," I tell him. "I might try to get Mom to come with me sometime. One of the people who started it is a teacher, like her. I think they'd get along really well." We both know that won't happen anytime soon—Mom is way too busy with school and the farm to make extra trips to Burlington—but she would love that group, and she'd love Lilah. "Actually," I tell Dad, "I think Mom would like the other guy who founded the group too. He's into an author that Mom and I both really like."

The corners of Dad's mouth tip up slightly. "Your mom would like this guy, huh?" he asks. "Just your mom?"

I can't help but blush. "Maybe not just her," I mutter. "He did ask me to get a cruller with him. I dunno."

"You didn't go?" Dad *finally* finishes up what he's doing and hands the pliers back to me. We begin to pack up our tools with the kind of weird choreography that happens when you've done the exact same task with someone else about three hundred times.

"I couldn't make it," I mutter. *Because you had a downer cow,* I add in my head. A year ago I probably would have said those words out loud. I might not have even tried all that hard to hide the resentment laced into them. It might have led to an argument, depending on Dad's and my moods.

But I don't say things like that out loud anymore. Not since the night Aaron and Dad were both in a bad mood and Aaron drove off for good.

Tools and wire in buckets, we start trudging our way back through the fields toward the barn. The ground is soft and muddy, sucking at our boots every few steps. It's a slow slog. Slow enough for Dad to keep the conversation going.

"You haven't mentioned going out much," he adds. "I think you should get that donut."

"Cruller," I correct. "They're better!" I insist when he starts laughing. "But yeah, maybe I will. I probably should. I've just got a lot going on right now." I haven't slept more than five or six hours a night in a while, and I'm feeling more worn down than usual. But no way am I complaining about sleep to a man who's averaged five hours of sleep a night his entire adulthood.

Dairy farming can be a tough life. Especially when you're running a small dairy like ours that specializes in having not enough money and not enough people to run it.

"I keep telling you," Dad says as he walks toward the wide entrance of the east side of our barn, "you're taking on too much."

He steps inside, where cows are mooing anxiously. They want to be fed. I'll probably end up helping him pass out some hay to them before I finally get back into my truck and drive to Burlington. Where I have hours and hours of work to do before I can finally crash.

"I know," I mutter to his back. "Believe me, I know."

Mom's cooking stew when I finally make it into our old farmhouse forty-five minutes later. You eat a lot of beef when you've constantly got a freezer stocked full of it, and the smells of seasoned meat and blended vegetables fill the wide space of our open kitchen with the giant table in the center of it. "Honey, can you stay for dinner?" Mom asks. She's bent over the pot, stirring intently.

"I wish." I sidle up next to her, leaning into her for a side hug. "I've got to head back. Way too much work to do tonight, and I've got classes tomorrow, and . . . ."

"Oh, Jamie." Mom cups her hand around my cheek. "You look exhausted, sweetie. You didn't have to come up today, you know. I could have helped Dad with that fence."

She would have tried, too. And probably messed up her hip—the one that needs to be replaced at some point soon—even more while she was working with Dad. That's why I didn't hesitate to say yes when he called and asked if I could come up.

"It's fine." I shake my head and pull out of her grip, walking over to the fridge to look for a soda. "Where's Lissie?"

"I'm trying to figure out why algebra matters." Lissie, my incredibly dramatic twelve-year-old sister, walks into the kitchen from the den and sits down at the table, dropping her head loudly onto the tabletop. "I'm going to fail seventh grade," she says into the wood.

"You are not." I pull two cans of seltzer out of the fridge and walk over to sit next to her, bumping one of the cold cans into her forehead.

"Ow. What are you doing here, anyway? You've been here like a bajillion times already this week. And don't you have some paper due that you were complaining about a few days ago?"

"A paper, Jamie?" Now Mom, all five feet two inches of her, manages to look almost menacing as she crosses her arms over her chest and glares at me. "Jamie! School first, always!"

"Sure, right." I send her back an even gaze. I'm not ten anymore, even if that look makes me feel like it sometimes. "What do you expect me to do when Dad calls? Just ignore him? Or when Lissie texts about a downer cow? Tell her to pick it up herself?"

Mom's look softens. She covers the stew and sits down in a chair at the table next to me and Lissie. In our family, genes seem to pass down on gender lines. Mom and Lissie both have the same dirty blond hair and light blue eyes. They're both short and round at the edges. Meanwhile, the Morin men all have the same dark brown hair and brown eyes, and Dad and Aaron and I have always run on the skinnier side. Right now, sitting in between them, I look like part of the *one of these things is not like the other* puzzles that Aaron and I used to like.

"I'm sorry this has been so hard on you," Mom says, placing a hand over mine. "Have either of you heard from him at all?"

"I keep messaging him." Lissie plays with her can of seltzer as she stares at the table. "Even though he doesn't answer. What a jerk."

Mom frowns. "I know you're mad, baby. And you have every right to be. But remember that he's still your brother. He's hurting. He isn't ignoring you because he doesn't want to talk to you."

"Are you sure? Because it definitely feels that way." Lissie shoves at the can. "He gets in a fight with Dad and stops speaking to the rest of us. And now Jamie's basically dropping out of college to help out here and Aaron doesn't even care."

"I'm not dropping out of college," I say at the same time Mom says, "No one's dropping out."

"I'm just saying that he's being a pretty crappy brother."

"Language," scolds Mom.

"What? That's barely even a bad word. And it's the right one." Lissie stands and stretches. "He already missed some of my biggest recitals this year and Jamie has to miss all of them now because he's so busy. And I get that whatever happened between Aaron and Dad was bad, right? But I didn't do anything to Aaron. I thought he loved me more than that." She snatches the can from the table and turns to leave the room. "I'm going back to my stupid algebra problems," she calls over her shoulder.

Mom rubs at her forehead with the palm of her hand. "I don't know what to say to her anymore about her brother," she mutters.

I don't either. The truth is that Lissie isn't wrong about any of this. Aaron fought with Dad and then dropped the rest of us like we were poison. Even Mom. The woman who has lived for her children since their birth suddenly had one of them disappear out of her life. I know that has to hurt her more than she lets on.

"What is there to say?" I shrug. "He's not coming back."

"That's not true," Mom says sharply. "He just needs time."

That's what she's been saying since August. That we all just need to give him time. *He'll be back. Give him space, let him be. He'll start talking to us when he's ready.*

I believed her in August. I held onto hope through September and October.

Now, in March, my hope has faded like the snow that's slowly disappearing from the pastures around the barns. Every day I wake up to find a little more of it gone. One day, I know, I'll wake up to find that none of it remains.

"I have to head back to campus, Mom. I love you." She packs up some stew for me, and I hug her goodbye, hard. She needs to be reminded that I'm not going anywhere. Neither is Lissie. Mom may have lost one kid, but she won't lose either of us.

It's already starting to get dark by the time I aim my truck back down the interstate toward Burlington. The Avett Brothers are singing about how no man can save you or enslave you as I pass exit signs etched with memories. First comes the exit Aaron and I used to take when we'd bring Lissie swimming in Lake Champlain on summer afternoons. Then there's the exit that goes to Jenny Summerville's house, where Aaron got his first handjob and I discovered exactly how much I like guys. Next is the exit that could take me to Silver's Diner, home of world-famous milkshakes, where Mom and Dad used to stop every time we needed to go to Burlington. Aaron and I would both always order the Peanut Butter Lake Monster.

I need to go back to my dorm room. I need to read philosophy and start writing papers and reports and study for a quiz. I need to do a lot of things.

So it's a mystery to the entire universe, particularly me, why I find myself turning onto the street that will lead me to the Church Street Marketplace.

Right to Vino and Veritas.

6

WHERE BRIAR IS WORRIED HE ISN'T VERMONTY ENOUGH

"Are you okay there, Briar?"

Louie's talking to me from across the Fiction and Literature section, where I'm completely zoned out in front of a shelf. I'm not exactly worker of the year right now—lately it's been taking me hours just to re-shelve a few books. "Yeah. Sorry, Louie. I'm fine."

"No need to apologize." Louie crosses the space to pick up a pile of manga volumes next to me. "I'll get these back where they go. You sure you're feeling all right, though? You were staring at that shelf like it had personally wronged you a few moments ago."

It wasn't the shelf that I couldn't stop staring at. It was the book that has the short story "Brokeback Mountain," by E. Annie Proulx, in it. I've never liked that story very much, but it has one of my favorite quotes in it: "I wish I knew how to quit you."

In my head I'd started listing all the things I wish I could quit.

The list was long.

"I'm good, I promise. Just didn't get enough sleep last night." I flash Louie a quick almost-smile, and he frowns for a moment before he finally takes the hint and walks away.

Thank goodness. I'm not really used to people asking me

things like whether or not I'm okay. Most people probably have no problem with answering questions like that—maybe they even answer them honestly. For me, though, that kind of question always feels like it's coming from a multiple choice test I have no chance of ever passing.

At least I'm off soon. Normally I don't look forward to leaving Vino and Veritas. This shop, with its soft music and millions of words circling each other, is the place I feel the safest. But ever since Luke showed up in Burlington, I've felt more and more claustrophobic inside of Vino and Veritas. Like the walls are pushing in, forcing me closer and closer to the safe in that storage room.

I saw it yesterday. I had to go into the storage room to grab a box of picture books for the kids' section, and there it was. Dark black, paint peeling and fading on one side. It doesn't look like anything special from across a space crowded with books. It's just a safe, after all. Anything could be in there. Wills. Maybe old family heirlooms that aren't worth one penny.

Except that I know exactly what's in the safe.

Fuck Luke Presserly. He's been nothing but an asshole since the first day I met him at Hope House. He was supposed to be the kid who showed me around the place. He was my new room-mate, the bottom bunker to my top bunk. Within three hours of meeting him, I was already learning where he stole candy bars and how much money he made selling them to other kids.

I've been trying to quit him ever since. I guess maybe there are kinds of quitting like E. Annie Proulx's: the kind where you don't really want to quit the person, because you know that quitting would just make you feel even worse inside. But in my life, that kind of quitting has only ever existed in stories. The kinds of quitting I've always needed to do have been from people like Luke. People who I knew I needed to quit because it would lift weights from my chest that I forget are even there most of the time.

But just when I thought I had quit Luke for good, he showed up in Burlington. At my tiny little table in my studio apartment in my bright pink house, hundreds of miles from where the two of us first met.

"I'm not a big fan of that story." The voice behind me is one I shouldn't recognize that easily, because I've only heard it one other day in my entire life. But I'd know it anywhere.

I turn around and there they are—those eyes. Still and thick, like water you can tread in for hours. It's Jamie. In the store, on a day the club isn't even meeting. "Which story?" I ask curiously.

"'Brokeback Mountain.' That's the book you were looking at, right? The one with that story in it?"

My eyes widen. There are more than two hundred books on the shelf I'm staring at right now—he could tell that's the one I was thinking about? "It's not my favorite either," I tell him. "But I can never exactly explain why when people ask me. I mean, Proulx's an incredible writer."

"It's the ending," Jamie says simply.

"Huh?" I feel like I'm not catching up to this conversation as quickly as I should be. Then again, Jamie had time to prepare for it. He's the one who walked up behind me.

"You like knowing that the endings of your books will be happy. But that story's literary fiction. Authors aren't allowed to be predictable like that in literary fiction. It's against the rules of literature or whatever. That's why I don't like a lot of literary fiction—and why I didn't like that book. I spent the whole thing terrified one of the main characters was going to die." Jamie shudders. "That's why we both like the romance genre, right?"

He's exactly right, of course. Someone was paying attention to what I said in our last book club meeting. "Give me some Alyssa Samuel any day of the week instead," I reply hesitantly. "So . . . what are you doing here? Did you need to pick up a book or something?"

Jamie frowns, and I realize how dismissive that probably sounded. "Not that I'm not glad you're here," I add quickly. "Because I am. I mean, I'm always glad that the store has customers. And it's nice to see you again. Not that it's nice just to see you. It would be nice to see any of the book club members. What I mean is—"

I'm clearly drowning here, but Jamie's nice enough to throw me a rope before I go too far under.

"It's nice to see you too," he interrupts. "Um, you want to have that cruller versus donut battle we missed out on the other day?"

Before I can even answer, Rainn's somehow standing next to me. It's one of those days when he's picked up a shift in the bookstore to help us out, and he's been doing inventory with me and Louie. "Briar, I'll close up," he says, taking the book I'm holding right out of my hands. "Go with the nice man." He smirks as he pushes me toward Jamie. "You know you can't miss out on a good donut."

Jamie's eyes brighten, and I have no idea what my facial expression looks like as I find my coat and follow Jamie out of the door of Vino and Veritas.

"See? Cruller wins all day long."

Jamie breaks off another piece of the pastry in his hand and passes it over to me. We're sitting at a counter next to a giant glass case filled with maple-covered baked goods, and I can't stop thinking that the cruller and the donut are both losing right now to Jamie's mouth: watching him push that cruller in between his lips is definitely the best thing happening in this shop right now.

"It's good, don't get me wrong," I agree. "But this donut just melts in your mouth, you know? I can never eat enough of them." I pick one up off the plate in front of me and pass it over to him. Our fingers brush against each other as he takes the donut from me, and I don't feel the immediate urge to pull away.

It's nice.

"I could eat everything in this place," Jamie agrees. "Have you tried their ice cream?"

"I haven't had that yet. Can't bring myself to eat cold stuff while the Vermont winters are freezing me out of every piece of clothing I own."

Jamie laughs. It's a sort of quick, high-pitched sound, not exactly what I would have expected from him. I like it. "That's right. You just moved here, didn't you?"

"In late October."

Jamie winces. "Wow, man. You even missed the best of the leaves. You haven't seen what Vermont has to offer yet. Unless you're into winter sports, I guess."

"I'm not. Kind of want to try skiing, but it's expensive." And every penny I would spend on renting skis and boots and buying lift tickets is a penny that wouldn't go into my savings account.

"Yeah, it can be." Jamie nods. "One of my friends operates the lift at Smugglers' Notch on weekends, and sometimes he gets me passes and stuff. That's the only way I can afford to go. Maybe I'll invite you to come with me sometime." He pops another piece of cruller into his mouth. "If you admit that the cruller wins, of course."

"Sell out my favorite donuts in the world over some skiing? Never." I study the jeans, heavy work boots, and tight Henley shirt Jamie is wearing. "You just come from another sick cow?" I ask.

"Not a sick cow this time, luckily. Fence repairs. My dad called and asked for my help."

"Where does your family live?" Hopefully that's an okay question to ask. Small talk isn't exactly my jam. If this is even small talk anymore, now that we're discussing families and cows and where people live and whatever.

"About fifty minutes north of here, in a town called Morse's Line. I stay in the dorms, but I go up there whenever Mom and Dad need me." Jamie shrugs and concentrates on sipping at the tea he ordered.

"I guess that's not a bad job to have while you're in school. Kind of a commute, though."

"Oh, it's not my job. Not really, anyway. I work in one of the libraries on campus. It's my dream job, basically." Jamie's face lights up with happiness. "I got assigned to the Beeder Library, which is one of the best at Burlington University. Do you know we have one of the biggest collections of books originally published in Vermont?"

The crazy part is that I do. "Mr. Fletcher's mentioned that," I tell him, smiling. "He buys and sells vintage books once in a while."

A quick flash of Luke's face runs through my head, and just like that I'm not smiling anymore. Luckily Jamie is concentrating on some piece of cruller that's falling down his chin, and he doesn't seem to notice. "It's like the best place to work, ever," he says around a mouthful of crumbs. "Hopefully I don't have to quit."

"Why would you have to quit? I thought it was your dream job. Don't you want to be a librarian someday?" Now I'm worried I missed something Jamie said while I was focusing on his mouth.

Jamie sighs. "My dad's needing more and more help on the farm lately. I'm kind of screwing up in some of my classes. Between the library and the farm and school I'm just . . . running out of hours in the day, I guess." He groans. "I should be reading a philosophy book right now. Whatever. I don't really want to think about that. So do you like Vermont? Even though it's cold as balls?"

"The cold is the worst. I'm not a big fan of the gray either," I add, and Jamie nods. "I love the bookstore though. Working there is pretty great. I just . . . ."

"What?"

I can't believe I'm about to tell some hot guy on what may or may not be a date this, but before I can stop myself, I do. "Sometimes I'm not sure I'm supposed to be here, you know? Like maybe I'm not Vermonty enough or something."

Jamie snorts. "Right now you're wearing flannel and a tuque. Which is exactly what you were wearing the last time I saw you."

"That's just practical. It's been fucking freezing for six months. Why do you call hats tuques? I thought that was a French-Canadian thing."

"Morse's Line is a border town. Some of the phrases bleed over. Seriously, though, why do you think you don't belong?"

I think about my little apartment here, and how the only other person who has ever seen the inside of it is someone I hate. Someone who wants me to be the worst part of myself again. "I don't know. I'm not exactly making friends here, I guess?"

"That guy who told you to get a cruller with me seemed nice enough."

Rainn is pretty great. So is Louie. So are lots of other people who work at V and V. And of course Mr. Fletcher, who took a chance on me just because DeShawn asked him to. "They're not the problem," I mutter. "This is all me."

"Don't say that. You started a book club and ran the first meeting like a champ."

"That was mostly Mrs. D."

"Disagree," Jamie says mildly. He frowns. "I think you might be suffering from flatlander syndrome, Briar."

"Excuse me?" I almost spit out the sip of coffee I'm in the middle of taking. What the fuck did he just say?

"Flatlander syndrome. Look, I love Vermont, and most of the time the people here are pretty cool, but we can also be kind of . . . insular, I guess? Sometimes we treat people like they'll never really belong here or something if they weren't born wearing work boots and flannel. In Morse's Line, you hear the word "flatlander" sometimes. It's what we call anyone who's from out of state."

I can't help but laugh at that. "Seriously? How have I never heard that before?"

"We don't say it to people's faces or anything. We're not total assholes, and it's not like we're out to drive new people away from the state or something. But it's part of this low-key attitude we can have that we've got something figured out here other states don't. I mean, I love Vermont's mountains and all, but who are we kidding? Our highest peak is like four thousand feet. I remember learning in school that there were mountains out west that are over fourteen thousand feet high and wondering if I'd be a flatlander out there."

"I guess you would be," I mutter

"Maybe. Anyway, it doesn't sound like your coworkers are treating you like an outsider or calling you a flatlander or whatever. But you've managed to convince yourself you don't belong with the rest of us anyway. Flatlander syndrome."

I frown and twirl the spoon in my coffee cup. "Maybe. Or . . . maybe it's more like I've never belonged anywhere I've been."

And kill me now, because I can't believe I just said something that cheesy to Soulful Eyes. Jamie's cool about it though. He doesn't laugh in my face or ask the server for the check or even smirk at me. He just nods. Then he takes another sip of tea and hands me another bite of his cruller.

"That sucks," he says softly.

And then he says: "Maybe this could be the first place you belong. Eventually. Like I said, your coworkers seem pretty cool. So do Lilah and the other people in The Booklover Club. Maybe you just need to get to know them better."

Maybe. But the problem there is that once you get to know someone better, they want to know things about you. Like where you're from, and what your hobbies are. What you've done in the past.

If I spend enough time with Louie or any of the other people I work with, they're going to want to know those things. How am I supposed to answer them? Will they even still be able to look at me once they realize who I really am?

"Yeah, you're probably right," I say shrugging off Jamie's comment. "Sorry to get all weird and emotional on you. Must be how stupid gray it was again today. All day."

"I'd say you get used to winter here, but it's more like you learn to count the days until summer." Jamie grins. "We're getting close, at least. Spring break's coming up next week. It starts the day of our next club meeting." He leans back and stretches. "They really shouldn't call it spring break here, though. Not when it's happening in Vermont. We'll get lucky if the weather hits fifty-five or sixty degrees." He shrugs. "Still, I can't wait. A whole week of no fucking school. A whole week of only worrying about work and the farm and whatever else I want to do. Hey!" He sits up in his chair. "You should come to the maple festival with me!"

Only in Vermont could those words seem remotely normal. "Uh, there's a maple festival here?"

"Yeah! Well, not here in Burlington. I mean, there probably is one in Burlington at some point, but that's not the one I'm talking about. The one I go to every year is up in the county where I live, in another town near Morse's Line. We always do it around the end of maple season. You can get maple everything there. Cotton candy, donuts, maple cream . . . ."

Now I'm sitting up too. "There's a thing called maple cream?"

"Hell yeah, there is." Jamie stands. "You gotta come with me. It's next weekend, at the beginning of spring break, so I won't even have to abandon you to go read philosophy like I do right now. You can have me all to yourself."

His eyes are filled with a weird innocence I'm not used to seeing. It's a look that I've never seen when I've stared in the mirror, and it's becoming one of my favorite things about Jamie. He hasn't had the light in his eyes dimmed yet. He hasn't quite realized how shitty the real world can be.

I want to keep swimming in that light. And if I get to try some of this maple cream stuff along the way, I have a feeling that won't suck either.

"Okay," I tell him. "I'm in. But only if there are more donuts."

7

WHERE JAMIE JUST NEEDS TO BE SOMEWHERE ELSE

By the time the second meeting of The Booklover Club comes around, I'm a little worried I'm not going to be able to stay awake for it. It's been *a week*. Papers due, quizzes I had to study for. One of my coworkers at the library got sick, so I had to cover their shifts. Mom called two days ago when the gutter cleaner broke again and Dad needed help fixing it, so I drove up to Morse's Line for that. I barely managed to squeeze in the time to read the book we'll be discussing at the club meeting today, and it came at the cost of some very precious rest.

For the first time, I'm starting to wonder if joining this book club wasn't the best idea. I love reading romance novels, and I'm tired of not having anyone to talk about my favorite books with. But I'm also just *tired.* And like I was telling Briar last week, something is going to have to give in my schedule. I can't keep doing everything I've been doing. And I really, really don't want to give up my library job.

But I also *really* don't want to give up The Booklover Club. Because, see also: Briar.

Our impromptu donut/cruller competition has basically been the only thing keeping me going this week. When I was ready to throw a wrench across the barn a few days ago, I saw Briar's expression as he bit into that maple donut, and then I held tight to the wrench. When I thought I was going to break down in tears at two in the morning while I was writing a lit analysis paper, I started to imagine walking through the booths at the maple festival with him. I imagined bringing him to a maple cotton candy booth and watching him twirl the threads of syrupy-goodness around his fingers.

Yeah, it's probably not a good idea to start falling for a guy you just met, especially when you barely have time to read the book for his book club. But like Emily Dickinson said, "hope is a thing with feathers." And I need some feathers to lift me out of the funk I've fallen into this week.

At least today is the official start of spring break at Moo U, so I'm going to get a small reprieve from the chaos of my normal life. Too bad I'll probably spend most of the week just catching up on all the assignments I'm behind on.

I also may need to use the time to find a new roommate, because I'm going to kill Jeremy if he locks me out of my own dorm room one more time.

"Jeremy!" I pound on the door to room 304 loudly, because fuck that stupid sock hanging off the door handle. I've had like three hours of sleep and I just finished a shift at the library. I need to get my stuff or I'm going to be late for the club meeting. "Dude, I'm late! Lemme in. I need my stuff."

The door slides open a crack and tufts of Jeremy's blond hair peek through. He opens the door a little wider, and now I can tell he's shirtless. His face is red and his hair is mussed and untamed. It screams the words *I just had all the sex.* "Buddy, I know you're not trying to be a mood killer, but you won't believe what's happening in here right now."

If I had a few more hours of sleep, I might laugh with him and make some crack about how sorry I am to cramp his style. But I haven't had much sleep at all, and right now I hate my roommate just a little bit. Partly because he has a sock on the door almost every other day and partly because the only things he ever needs to worry about are getting laid and getting to his classes on time.

And most of the time he doesn't even seem to bother with the last one.

"Just get me my red backpack," I grumble. "And be done before I get back. I need my bed. For sleep. Fuck the stupid socks."

"Oooh, someone's touchy." Jeremy disappears for a moment and reappears with my backpack in his hand. "But seriously, later on I gotta tell you about *what is happening in here right now,* because—"

I slam the door right in his face. I'm not proud of it. But it happens.

There is a chance I am jealous of just a little more than Jeremy's schedule. Because it is also true that I haven't gotten laid since last summer, and I'm pretty sure Jeremy is in there with more than one person. The giggling I'm hearing from inside 304 definitely sounds both male and female.

Meanwhile, I'm crushing on a guy who I can't even spend one hour with before I have to rush off to a philosophy textbook. And all the time I'm spending with Kant and Descartes lately is doing *nothing* to assuage my libido.

So, unfortunately, I'm crabby as fuck when I arrive at Vino and Veritas thirty minutes later. It doesn't help that Briar isn't at the couches yet. He's helping some customer over in Health and Sexuality. A very hot male customer, who has the leg muscles of a marathon runner and super excellent cheekbone structure. Briar is handing him a paperback and laughing.

I'm not usually a possessive person, but it's all I can do not to growl across the room.

"Hey!" Emily plops into the seat next to me, flashing a row of perfectly white teeth in my direction. I mentally roll my eyes.

"Hi," I mumble as I massage my right temple with one finger. I have a low-level headache sitting there that won't quite go away.

"How was your week?" she asks. "Man, mine was crazy! The

coffee shop I work in was super busy, and somehow I ended up getting invited to like three different baby showers—I can't believe I know that many people having babies, can you? And . . . ."

Please shut up, please shut up, please shut up, I find myself chanting in my head. Emily's a nice girl, and all she's trying to do is have a conversation with me. But my head hurts. And Briar is still talking to the prick with muscular legs.

I hate him. Whoever he is, I absolutely hate him.

"Hey, everyone." Briar himself finally appears on the couch in front of me. Emily stops talking long enough to chirp a hello at him. "Are you okay, Jamie?" he asks. His eyebrows cross together as he frowns.

"Yes, son, are you alright?" Bart puts down the newspaper he's been reading and Lilah, Betty, and Lucia settle into seats around us. Cherry isn't here yet, but I'm sure she'll arrive just in time to stare at me too.

"I'm fine," I say as smoothly as possible. "Just a little headache."

"Oh, then you need some of my oils!" Betty says, and her voice is just so *loud* that I wince. "Here, let me find some . . . ."

"You sure you're okay to do this meeting, honey?" Lilah asks. She manages to not sound like a screeching owl, which I appreciate.

"I'm fine," I tell her, flashing her the best smile I can, even though it's probably terrible. Then Cherry appears, and soon I'm rubbing some kind of scented oil across my forehead, but at least it seems to help a little, and then, thankfully, Bart prompts us to start talking about the book.

I can't say this title will go down in history as one of my favorites. I'm really picky about mystery writing, and I found it too hard to suspend disbelief for a lot of this one. In what world does a secretary at an accounting firm end up acquiring nuclear codes? But I did like both the heroines in the book, who fall in love with each other right as they're both about to potentially die. Not everyone else in the group liked them as much, though.

"That Carly," says Betty, and I swear she *tsks* her tongue for just a moment. "I wanted to like her, honestly, I did. But she's so gruff sometimes. And the way she acted around Mel's family! As though they were weren't good enough for her!"

I'm trying to find the energy to disagree when Briar does it for me. "I don't think that was her problem," he says. "The problem was that she wasn't from that town. She didn't know anybody or feel like she belonged. Mel was the only thing keeping her there. The way she acted was a front, you know? She was afraid that everyone would reject her, so that was her coping mechanism or whatever. She didn't want to be a . . . flatlander, I guess?"

Lilah gasps. "Let's not use that word in this group," she says seriously. "I strongly dislike that term." She huffs and tucks her infinity scarf closer around her neck. Cherry looks like she is dangerously close to laughing. "Where on earth did you hear that word?" Lilah demands, like Briar is one of the students in her classroom. "Has someone been calling you that since you moved here? Who do I need to have a talking-to with?"

"Uh, sorry Lilah," I interject. "I'm the one who told Briar what the . . . f word is." Cherry openly snorts. "He was just talking about feeling out of place, and I was trying to explain about how Vermont does that to people sometimes . . . ." Everyone is staring at me. "I mean, I wasn't *calling* him a flatlander or something!"

"I didn't realize it was such a terrible word." Briar leans over to squeeze Lilah's hand. "I won't use it here anymore. I promise."

"Thank you." Lilah adjusts her scarf again. "I think we've worked hard to become more open and inclusive here in Vermont. Words like that have the potential to undo so much."

"Are you feeling like an outsider, son?" Bart asks Briar.

Briar frowns. "No one's treating me badly or anything. It's not like that. Moving here was just an adjustment, I guess. And your weather sucks." Half the group laughs, and the other half nods in agreement.

"It's hard to feel like I belong anywhere sometimes, I guess." His gaze drops to the floor, and I wonder if that's the most Briar's said about himself to anyone in Vermont but me since he moved here.

"I get it. I felt the same way when my fiancé asked me to move up here with him. But at least you can throw on a winter hat and look like you fit in," Lucia tells him. "Try being Latinx in Burlington, Vermont. Brown skin does not blend in with this uber-white background."

"I don't see color," Emily says, and Bart looks at her sharply.

"Then you're a fool," he says, not unkindly. "Because the whole world does. Do you know that my family's been in Vermont for three generations, and people here still ask me if I'm from New York or Connecticut?" He shakes his head. "We all see skin color. Even babies do—so say the scientists. Pretending you don't see it just makes it harder for us to reckon with it."

"At least once a week someone asks me if I speak English," Lucia says.

"I get pulled over at least once a month," Bart adds. "People can't handle a Black man driving a BMW in Vermont. Gives 'em all kinds of ideas."

"You own a BMW?" Lucia asks. "I thought you were a retired bus driver."

"Bus drivers can make investments," Bart replies mildly. He looks over at Briar. "Son, stop staring at the floor like it's the most fascinating thing you've ever seen. You hear what we're telling you? Sometimes a person isn't destined to fit perfectly somewhere. Doesn't mean it still can't be their home."

"Well," says Betty, "I for one am horrified to hear that so much racism still occurs here on such a regular basis. Makes me all the prouder to have protested for equality at the capital last month!"

"Betty, love, you assumed our new gym teacher at the school was the gardener when you met him," Lilah reminds her with a sigh. "Let's not get too far up on our high horses here."

My horse is feeling pretty low right now. I assumed Bart wasn't from Vermont when I first met him. And I used to use the word flatlander all the time without even thinking about it. Around the gentle pounding of my headache, I'm realizing that I've never worried very much about what my place in Morse's Line—or Vermont—is. Even when my family drives me crazy, I've always known that *they're* my place. And this ridiculously cold, cow-filled, maple-loving state we live in has always felt like home.

I can't imagine what it would feel like to have people assume I don't belong here. I can't imagine what it feels like to think that I've never belonged anywhere.

"Look," says Lucia. "I don't need this to turn into some kind of self-help group for white people to work through their issues with race, okay? You all have Instagram for that. I'd like to go back to talking about the book now. Briar, don't piss off Lilah by using that word anymore."

"I'd also prefer if we could avoid 'piss off,'" Lilah responds primly.

"Sure, fine." Lucia sighs. "And Briar? If it helps? The first time I met you, I assumed you'd grown up on some kind of goat farm a few towns over or something. So maybe you're fitting in better than you think."

Briar finally looks up from the floor. "A goat farm? Really?"

Lucia shrugs. "I think it was the wannabe-beard."

We have to stop the discussion not too long after that, because everyone's laughing too hard to keep talking.

"You still don't look great, man," Briar says.

I'm trying to pack up my backpack after the meeting, but it's taking me forever. My headache's back, swirling against the side of my head in a consistent thumping pattern. All I want to do is find a quiet space to sleep for a day. Maybe a week. But I have a bad feeling I'm going to find that a sock is still on my door when I get back to my dorm.

"I'm tired," I tell Briar honestly. "Thank fuck it's spring break.

I just need some sleep. But I can't even go back to my dorm, because my roommate's having some kind of orgy in there. And if I go home, my dad will find fifteen things I need to help him with before I can go to bed."

Briar nods and hoists himself off the couch. "Come home with me then."

"What?"

"Come back to my place. I'm off work. I live in this tiny studio, but I don't share it with anyone. You can take a nap, and I'll read or something. C'mon. You look like you need a rest." He holds out a hand in front of me. "C'mon, Jamie," he says again. "The flatlander goat farmer is offering you a bed. Maybe even some aspirin if I can find any in my cabinets."

I take his hand.

"For the record," I tell him. "I never thought you were a flatlander when I first saw you. Or a goat farmer."

"Oh yeah? What did you think, then?" Briar's smiling now. I like when he smiles. It's a rare enough occurrence that every smile is special somehow, like a gift he's just handed me.

"I thought you looked just like Porter from *Lost Key*," I tell him.

"No shit, really? Porter's hot as fuck, man."

"Hell yeah, he is," I murmur.

Briar grins a little wider. And then he leads me out of the store.

8

WHERE BRIAR MAKES EXCELLENT USE OF HIS APARTMENT

"So," I tell Jamie as we start our walk down Church Street, towards the bus stop. "There's only one rule you have to follow if you're going to visit my apartment."

"What's that?" Jamie asks as he rubs at his forehead. I've got to find this guy some aspirin, and fast. It's really bugging me to think that he might be in pain.

And that is not really a thought I've ever had about another person before. Not even Paul. I can't examine that too closely right now, though. First I've got to discuss the importance of etiquette when visiting a house that looks like a bottle of Pepto-Bismol. "No making fun of the paint color," I tell Jamie.

"Huh?" Jamie stops in the middle of the street, right in front of an Urban Outfitters. "What's wrong with the paint color of your apartment?"

"Let's just say my landlady likes things to be unique. I almost didn't rent the place because it's kind of the color of a marshmallow Peep."

Jamie's face scrunches into a strange pattern. "You mean like those little bunnies and chicks that people think taste good and give out at Easter?"

"Yeah, those. The bright pink ones. People think those things taste good?"

Jamie shrugs. "My sister does." He sighs. "Briar, right now I wouldn't care if your house was neon orange and made of cotton candy. Just as long as it has a place for me to lay down."

"School's really that hard? Or is it the farm again?" I ask him. We're ambling down Church Street at a snail's pace, because the bus isn't going to be here for a while anyway and I'm not about to rush a guy who looks like he might keel over at any moment.

"School. Been working a lot of shifts at the library. And the farm . . . ." Jamie shakes his head. "I gotta talk to my dad," he mumbles, more to the sidewalk than to me.

"About not working there so much?"

"Yeah. Or maybe not working there at all anymore. I got an offer to work at the Rawlings library on campus this summer, running their interlibrary loan program. That position would look so great on my grad school resume."

"You're going to take it, right?" I resist the urge to reach out and grab Jamie's elbow, because his meandering walk is getting more and more meander-y. It's definitely time to get this guy a place to lie down. "That seems like way too good of an offer to pass up."

"It is, for sure. Except summer's when Dad needs the most help on the farm." Jamie sighs. "I can't figure out how to tell him that I don't want to work with him this summer. Or maybe any other summer ever again," he mumbles.

I should probably bow out of this conversation right now—because this is definitely not my area of expertise. I haven't even seen Gina in almost a decade, so the last memories I have of negotiating with a parent involve getting the breakfast cereal I wanted. But it's pretty clear Jamie's just shared some deeply private and important shit with me, and I'm not about to let him think I didn't care or something. "That really sucks, dude. There's no one else in the family who can help?"

Jamie snorts. "That's a fucking long story."

We walk in silence for a minute. I've got long stories of my own, and I'm not the kind of guy who forces other people to spill theirs.

The light on Church Street is moving into duskiness, and the colors of a distant but vivid Vermont sunset are turning the sky behind the stores around us a pinkish-yellow color. Logically I know that Massachusetts probably had pretty sunsets too, but I don't remember noticing them. The first time I ever remember noticing a sunset was my second night in Vermont. I was walking through Burlington, trying to get to know the city a little, and I ended up on a hill overlooking Lake Champlain. The sunset turned the water this perfect shade of purple, and I almost burst into tears it was so brilliantly beautiful. "Do you think Vermont's sunsets are prettier than sunsets in other places?" I ask Jamie.

Jamie shifts his backpack up farther on his shoulders and squints into the sky. "I haven't seen a lot of sunsets in other places," he says mildly. "Farmers don't get out much, you know?" He grins at me. "But yeah. I always kind of figured they were."

And then the weirdest thing happens.

His left hand brushes up against mine.

My right hand brushes up against his.

There's this fizzle and *crack* in my brain, as though something in Jamie's skin reacts with something in mine.

I haven't held hands with anyone since I was a little kid, and I'm not even sure I did then. Gina wasn't exactly the handholding type, and Paul definitely wasn't.

But my hand keeps brushing up against Jamie's as we walk. He's still squinting up at the sky, which is slowly dimming in color as the light around it fades. We walk by a restaurant that's playing classical music from outdoor speakers, and the notes seem to bump into the sky and the street and then our hands, and before I even realize what I'm doing I'm curling three of my fingers into Jamie's, and then our fingers are attached.

Together. I'm holding his hand in mine, and we're walking down Church Street.

Together.

It's nearly dark by the time we get to my apartment, but there are plenty of streetlights there to ensure Jamie can make out the color of the thing. "You weren't exaggerating," he says. "You swear I can't make fun of this? 'Cause I've got *jokes*, trust me. And I've only been looking at it for like three minutes."

"Nope," I say. I walk up the front steps, Jamie just behind me. His hand slipped out of mine when he stood behind me to get on the bus, but I can still feel the sensation of the callouses on his first and second finger where they pushed into my palm. "That's the rule. If you live here, you get to make fun of it all you want. But outsiders just have to pretend it's completely normal."

Jamie grins. "Sure, okay. I'll pretend this thing is some chill shade of beige or whatever. But tell me that the inside doesn't look like this."

"The walls in my place are white."

I decide not to mention that the building's hallways are chartreuse.

Jamie snorts a little at the green hallway walls, but he doesn't say anything else on the trip up three flights of stairs to my attic apartment. When we step through the doors, he lets out a little sigh.

"This is fucking awesome," he says softly.

I grin at him. "It's like four hundred square feet, and you can't even stand up on the far sides of it."

"Yeah, but there are no roommates fucking all over it. And no cows."

I laugh, but Jamie doesn't. He's looking back and forth between the couch and the bed, but his eyes keep landing dreamily on the bed. "Lay down," I tell him. "You can use the bed if you want. The couch isn't that comfortable. I'll get you some water. And I think I have some aspirin in the bathroom."

Jamie's eyes are looking more and more glazed over, like he's drunk or something. And I'm guessing he is: drunk with tired. I've been drunk with tired before, and it's no fun.

"You sure I can use the bed?"

I nod. "You need some sleep. And you'll sleep a lot better there than on that couch—trust me. I think that thing is older than I am."

Jamie laughs, and I find him a glass of water while he chucks off his sneakers and lays down across the top of the floral comforter I found at a thrift shop. The thing is ugly as sin, but it's soft. "You can get under the covers," I tell him. "Get comfortable." *Lose the pants*, I want to add. But I don't. When do you cross the line from helping out a friend to openly hitting on them? I've got a feeling it happens when you tell them to take off their pants.

I rummage around the medicine cabinet in my bathroom until I manage to find a bottle of aspirin that isn't past the expiration date. But by the time I get the bottle back to the bed, it's pretty obvious Jamie isn't going to be using it anytime soon. He's passed out on his back, buried under my sheets and comforter. His curly brown hair is flopping all over his forehead and face, and his Burlington University sweatshirt and his jeans are draped over his backpack on the floor.

Which means Jamie Morin is in my bed, wearing nothing but underwear and a t-shirt.

I've never had a guy in this bed before. I've had sex since I moved to Vermont, but it hasn't been the type of sex you have in a bed. More like quick moments of tension release in bathrooms or behind bars. In fact, I'm not sure I've been in a bed with a guy since Paul.

Those aren't exactly memories I like to cling to.

For a few seconds I feel completely out of place in my own apartment. What am I supposed to do now that one of the hottest guys I've ever spent time with—a guy I just held hands with—is fast asleep under my cheap comforter? I told Jamie I was just going to read while he slept, but where am I going to do that? I usually read in my bed, because the sofa in this apartment really is about as comfortable as a pile of rocks.

"Lay down with me," Jamie murmurs.

"Huh?"

His eyes never open as he speaks. "Lay down, if you want. You might be tired too." He pats the blanket lightly with one hand, his eyes still closed.

I shouldn't do it. It's a bad idea. Me laying down in a bed with Jamie Morin is never, *ever* going to be anything but a bad idea.

But it's like my body isn't listening to a damn thing my brain says as I shuffle around the apartment, turning off lights and finding my old, tattered copy of *Lost Key*. It might be strange, rereading a book I've already read about a thousand times, but *Lost Key* is one of my favorite comfort reads. And right now I desperately need a comfort read.

Because *Jamie Morin* is in my bed. And I'm about to lay down next to him.

I lay down across the covers, still clothed, because that seems like a *slightly* better choice than taking off my pants, too. I flip on the bedside light on the table next to me, carefully turning the lamp to the side so that it won't keep Jamie awake. "Bed's so comfy," he mutters.

His hand is on top of the covers, tucked into the top of the bedsheets. As he drifts off, and the sound of light snores begin to fill the apartment, I let myself move my own hand across the bed and lay it on top of his.

Just for a minute, I tell myself. *I'll only lay here like this, with my hand on his, for a minute.*

But Jamie's snores are quiet and soothing, and my eyes begin to close before I think of moving my hand again.

———

The light outside the apartment is completely gone the next time I open my eyes, and the light from the lamp next to me feels harsh in the room. I quickly turn it off.

And that's when I realize: I've ended up under the covers. And I am very, very much not alone there.

Jamie's arms have come around me at some point, and he's basically spooning me in the middle of the bed. His hard dick is pressing directly into my ass. My dick can't help but respond, and soon it's like concrete rubbing into the zipper of my jeans. All I want to do is reach down and touch it while Jamie's cock is nestled into me like this. All I want to do is jerk off while I imagine Jamie slowly easing inside of me, whispering soft words into my ear, just like Lance always whispers into Porter's ear in *Lost Key*.

I'll admit that a lot of my jerking off happens while I'm reading sex scenes from my favorite novels. But I usually don't think much about those scenes when I'm actually with another person.

"Jamie," I whisper, because I'm only human, and I'm not sure how much longer I can stay still in this position. And the last thing I want is for Jamie to wake up and feel like he's been taken advantage of or something.

"Hmm?" Jamie mumbles. His voice is filled with the fuzziness of sleep, and then he's nuzzling his lips up against my neck. They're chapped and a little dry, and the rough sensation of them against my skin is somehow the hottest thing I've ever felt. My dick bumps up against my zipper, reminding me that it can't take much more of this. "Jamie," I say, a little more loudly.

"Briar," Jamie whispers. "Fuck, you feel good right now." He pushes into my back a little harder, his dick a statue now against my jeans. "I didn't mean to start cuddling you in my sleep," he whispers, "so tell me to get the fuck off you if you want. But also, if I took off my clothes right now, and you took off yours, we could reenact that scene from *Lost Key* where Lance and Porter fuck for the first time." His lips settle against my neck again, and I realize just how very not-asleep Jamie Morin is.

I would wonder how long he's been awake, except I really don't care.

Because I was just thinking about that exact same scene.

"Lance undresses Porter in bed," I say, and my voice sounds rough in my own throat. "Undoes his jeans first, right?"

"Yeah." Jamie's voice sounds a little hoarse too as he moves his hands down the front of my body and stops in front of the zipper of my jeans. "You want to be my Porter, Briar? You want to whimper in my arms when I touch your cock for the first time?"

I've had plenty of sex in my life, so I'm as surprised as anyone when I almost lose it in my pants just hearing Jamie Morin say the word *cock.* It's something about the way those consonants sound as they move over his tongue and lips. My dick twitches in my pants again. "I'll fucking whimper for you," I tell him.

"Good." Jamie begins to slowly ease my zipper down. I hear the sound of every single piece of moving metal deep inside of my eardrums. "You remember how that scene goes, right? Lance and Porter end up in bed together, but Porter still has his clothes on. Lance undresses him, and then he wraps his arms around Porter and fucks into him so slowly that Porter begs him to hurry." Jamie's murmuring every one of these words into my ear as he eases my pants down my body. I help him out by kicking them off my ankles. Then his hands are at the waistband of my boxer shorts. "And," Jamie goes on, "the entire time, Lance is whispering in Porter's ear, telling him what he's about to do. Porter almost goes off like four times just waiting for Lance to get inside of him."

My dick's rock hard now, and I moan as I arch my body forward. I've never had a person talk to me like this before. I've never had someone use words to set my entire body on fire.

Jamie wraps his hands into the opposite sides of my boxer waistband and begins to tug. "Briar," he says, "I'm about to take this underwear off of you. Then I'm going to take mine off, too. I want you to feel every fucking inch of how hard I am when I touch your cock for the first time."

He edges the waistband of my shorts down, letting it catch on the tip of my dick. I'm so hard it almost hurts as he pulls my underwear over the head and my dick springs back against the edge of my stomach. "Don't cum yet," Jamie whispers. "Lance doesn't let Porter cum until he's all the way inside of him. Remember?"

Hell yeah, I remember. I remember reading that scene in the book over and over, thinking how incredibly hot it was. I remember jerking off to it at least twice.

My underwear is around my ankles now. I reach down with a hand to pull it all the way off. Now I'm naked from the waist down, and my t-shirt is still on. Next to me, Jamie has managed to somehow get his own underwear off without ever moving me out of his arms. He leaves his t-shirt on too.

Then he's nestled up into me, both of us naked as fuck except for our shirts. That's how Porter and Lance fucked for the first time in the book, too. I remember thinking how strangely hot it was, the idea that these guys were moving together so intimately with their t-shirts still covering the top halves of their bodies.

The apartment isn't cold, and we're both under the covers, but I shiver slightly. Jamie wraps his arms a little more tightly around me. "You want this?" he asks, and there's a different edge to his voice now. Serious. Almost concerned. "I honestly never meant to climb up on you while I was sleeping. I just woke up like that. If you want me to stop . . . ."

"Oh hell no," I say, laughing. "Lance wouldn't stop now, and neither are you."

Jamie laughs too, and the feeling of his breath lingers across my ear and cheek.

"I'm going to touch your cock now," he says, and he's back to using that voice that makes me think of Lance: deep and demanding and sexy and uncompromising. "I'm going to wrap my fingers around it, Briar. And you're going to fucking love it." He nibbles gently at my earlobe.

"How the hell did you get so good at this?" I say, though the words come out more like a moan. "It's like you're a sex aficionado in a twenty-year-old body."

Jamie laughs. "I read a lot of romance novels, remember? And this scene we're acting out is one of the hottest ones I've ever read."

Then he wraps three fingers around my cock, and it's all I can do not to scream.

Jamie's rutting gently up against my ass crack, reminding me exactly what comes next in this scene. My cock feels like it could explode at any minute, and Jamie's fingers dance gently all around it, like they're playing out a pantomime.

"Now." Jamie's voice is gentle but stern. "You're going to tell me where the lube is and where you keep your condoms. Then I'm going to rub lube all over my hands and I'm going to get that perfect hole of yours ready for my dick."

I tell him that the lube and condoms are in the bedside table next to him, and he does exactly what he said he would. His fingers conduct a symphony inside of my hole, one at a time, until he's got three buried inside of me at once and I'm squirming in his arms, begging for him to hurry up and fuck me.

"Are you ready for my cock, Briar?"

I recognize those words from straight out of *Lost Key*. That's what Lance said to Porter just before he sank inside of him for the first time. And I remember what Porter said back, too. I laugh.

"Fucker, I think I was *made* for your cock. Get inside of me. Now."

I feel the head of Jamie's cock first, as it nudges inside of my hole, and I whimper so loudly that Jamie grabs hold of my earlobe with his teeth. His right hand is still moving up and down my cock, and I'm not sure I'm going to keep myself from going off before he makes it all the way in. Jamie stops, his tip just barely inside me, and goes perfectly still. "I could just stay like this," he says in my ear. "Lance does that, you know. He just sits there for a minute, barely inside of Porter, driving him wild."

I let out a moan that I think Porter would be proud of.

"But Lance must have the patience of a saint," Jamie goes on. "Because you're so fucking hot and tight around me right now,

Briar, and I just need to be inside of you. All the way inside of you."

"Do it," I whisper in a strangled voice. "Fuck me, Jamie. Now."

Like I've flipped a switch, Jamie yanks both of us up so that I'm on all fours and he's draped over me. The hem of his t-shirt brushes up against the top of my ass, teasing my skin slightly. "Fuck, Briar," he whispers. His voice is gentle, but urgent. "You have to tell me if I'm hurting you, okay? I never want to hurt you."

He couldn't. Nothing about this moment could ever hurt me. I feel untouchable and light with adrenaline as Jamie thrusts completely into me, burying himself so deep in my body that it's hard to imagine we'll ever be separate again. Sure, there's some light pain and discomfort as my body adjusts to his—but that's not hurt. Not real hurt. Whatever pain there is feels wildly good, and my own cock only gets harder and harder as Jamie's moves back and forth inside of me.

"Briar," he says into my ear, "I know you think I'm a sex aficionado or whatever, but I'm not sure how long I'm going to last." I can feel his dick twitching with excitement as he pumps into me. He hits my prostate once, then twice, then again, and I know I'm not going to last long either. I think of the next part of this scene in the book, and I know how I want to come: up on my knees, with Jamie holding me upright and using my hips as leverage as he pumps himself inside of me. "Pull me up," I tell him urgently.

Luckily Jamie knows *Lost Key* as well as I do, and he knows exactly what I mean. He somehow manages to keep pumping his dick in and out of me as he eases me up and into his arms, so that we're locked together, his body pressed tightly into mine, both our knees on the bed. The springs creak below us as he thrusts back and forth, and his cock truly does feel like it was made for my body. Like it was made to be inside of me.

"Jamie," I warn him. "I'm going to . . . ."

He flicks a finger against the head of my cock just as his pushes against my prostate again, and then my entire body is exploding while I shake and shudder in Jamie's arms. Jamie's shaking with the same energy, and I can feel him pulsing deep inside of me.

We collapse together on the bed. Somehow we end up cleaning up. I manage to find a washcloth, and Jamie ties off the condom and gets it into my trashcan.

We fall asleep together with him wrapped around me again, just the way he was when I woke up in the middle of the night.

I have two thoughts before I fall asleep.

One: *Holy fuck, that's the best sex I've ever had.*

Two: *I can never have sex with Jamie Morin ever again.*

9

WHERE JAMIE MAKES AN AGREEMENT WITH BRIAR

I have two thoughts when I wake up the morning after Briar invites me over to his apartment.

One: *Holy fuck, that's the best sex I've ever had.*

Two: *I can never have sex with Briar Nord ever again.*

Despite what Briar seems to think, I am not a sex aficionado. I've only had sex with three different people in my life, and I've only fucked one other guy at all—my high school boyfriend, Sean. And it usually wasn't all that great. It was messy and awkward and most of the time we just stuck to handjobs and blow jobs, because those always worked out better for us.

But last night, with Briar, it was like my body just knew what to do. Briar obviously wanted me to be the Lance to his Porter, and I know that scene where Lance fucks Porter for the first time like it's written on my arm. There was never any question or thought about what I needed to do next to make Briar—or myself —feel good. I just kept moving, following the rhythm of that scene from the book, following Briar's sounds and reactions, and everything just kept working. I've never had sex like that in my life. Honestly, I didn't know that sex could even feel like that.

Too bad I can never, ever have sex with Briar again.

It's not that I think our next round in the sheets wouldn't live up to the first one or something. I have a feeling that Briar and I could pull off plenty more successful iterations of last night's endeavor. The problem is that the sex would almost definitely stay good, and that good sex would probably lead to Briar or me or both of us wanting a relationship, and that . . . can't happen.

I'm a dairy farming librarian with a full load of courses on my schedule and an exceptionally needy family. There's no time for boyfriends in that mix. There's never going to be any time for a boyfriend in that mix. I tried it right after Aaron left, for about a month. I met a girl in the library named Shana, and she and I really hit it off. We tried dating. But she got sick of me after I canceled on her for the eighth or ninth time, and I couldn't blame her. I'm not good boyfriend material right now, and I know it.

Briar stirs lightly in the bed next to me as he flips onto his side. His eyes are still closed, his hair sticking up in tufts around his ears. I was going to ask him if he wanted to go to the maple festival with me today. I was going to hand him his first tastes of maple cream and maple cotton candy. I was going to see if I could make it through an entire afternoon of fun with this guy I really like without getting called to the farm for another Morin emergency.

Now I'm wondering if spending the afternoon with a broken gutter cleaner would be better than spending it with Briar. Because he's moving around again, which means he's probably going to wake up at any second . . . and I have zero idea how to tell a guy I just had universe-exploding sex with that I'd make a terrible boyfriend.

Briar stretches his arms up above his head as he cracks an eyelid open. "Jamie," he mutters. His voice is soft and gentle with sleep, and the way he says my name almost sounds like a prayer. Then his eyes go a little wider. "*Jamie.*" He says my name again, but this time the word is laced with a little bit of horror.

Maybe I'm not the only one who woke up with some regrets about last night. That realization shouldn't sting as much as it does, though.

"Uh, hey," I say weakly, tugging the sheets up a little tighter around my hips. We're both still naked from the waist down and wearing our t-shirts. I'm kind of surprised that fucking with a t-shirt on turned out to be so incredibly hot.

"Hey." Briar pulls up his section of the sheet, and for a moment we both just stare at each other. Silence echoes through the apartment. I've never been more tempted to pick up my phone and start scrolling through something—anything. I'm not normally someone who spends a lot of time on their phone (mostly because I have no time), but right now I'd happily stare at any mindless ten-second dance video over staring awkwardly at Briar.

This is a guy I definitely like talking to, and a guy who runs the book club that I don't want to leave, and a guy who I would really like to keep as a friend.

Those thoughts are what drive me to speak first. "Last night was hot as hell," I blurt out. "But we should probably never do it again." Then I wince. Because those words don't sound great in my own ears.

Briar's face relaxes into complete relief, though. "That's a really good idea," he says. "I mean, it's a really good idea that we never do that again. Yeah."

I should be happy he agrees, but instead I want to ask him why he thinks so. My reasons have nothing to do with him and everything to do with a bunch of large animals that never seem to stop needing me. What are his reasons, though? Is there something wrong with me? I so want to ask him that, but I can't figure out how to make those words come out of my mouth. So instead we both sit there, the silence hanging between us like a noose that no one can figure out how to tighten or take down.

I should get up and put my pants back on. I should leave right now and end the awkward silence. That's the only way I'm going to get out of here without regretting my choices and without second-guessing myself. Never mind that I have no idea how I'm ever going to have sex with anyone else again now that I know what sex with Briar is like.

I should leave. It is one hundred percent the most logical and reasonable thing to do. But I don't. I blurt out, "Do you want to go to the maple festival with me today?"

Briar tilts his head slightly in surprise, and then a slow smile spreads across his face. "Is that the place with the maple cream?"

"Yeah. And probably the best blueberry pancakes you'll ever have in your life."

Briar shrugs, smile still in place. "Sure. Why the fuck not."

I can think of plenty of reasons. But I'm planning to ignore them, and it looks like Briar is too.

The maple festival is in Fairlington, the town where I went to high school. It's about a fifteen-minute or twenty-minute drive from our farm in Morse's Line, and about a forty-five-minute drive from Burlington. Briar and I take turns showering before we take the bus to where I parked my truck downtown, and then we start the drive.

In silence.

I'm pretty good at silence. Sometimes I even love silence. There's nothing like a morning milking in the barn when the only sounds are the buzzing of the milking system and the occasional cow mooing. Silence is where all my thinking and dreaming happen. It's where all my favorite books have been read.

But this isn't one of those kinds of silences. This silence is filled with a whole lot of questions and very few answers. Briar stares out the window while I drive, but we both know he's not really paying attention to the scenery. This stretch of I-89 is basically just trees lining both sides of the highway. It's not all *that* interesting.

"It's not that I don't want to have sex with you again," I blurt out. Next to me, Briar's entire body stiffens. "I mean, I don't want to. But that's not because I *really* don't want to. It's because I shouldn't, and I know I shouldn't, so that's why I don't want to."

The words are spilling out of me like I have zero control over my own mouth. Great. I've forgotten how to people again.

Briar's turned away from the window, and now he's just looking at me, a neutral expression on his face. "I'm not sure if that was English," he says. "But somehow I know what you mean. It's the same for me."

"Yeah?" I concentrate on passing a tractor trailer so that I don't have to look at Briar.

"I'm not a relationship guy. You seem like a relationship guy, Jamie. If we keep doing what we did last night, it's probably not going to end well."

I burst out laughing. "Man, I'd love to be a relationship guy." And it's true. I've been told before that I'm an excellent boyfriend, and I suspect that's because I really like being a boyfriend. I like falling for people. I like spending time with them. I like happy endings.

I like romance novels. I like love.

It surprises me to hear Briar say he's not a relationship guy. He likes romance novels for all the same reasons I do. "Why aren't you a relationship guy?" I ask.

Briar's back to looking out the window. He frowns at the glass. For a few moments he says nothing, and when he does speak, the words are harsh and almost angry. "Because people," he says. "People always end up being disappointing."

I want to ask more about what he means, but I can tell from his expression that he's not going to want to expand on that answer. And it's not really my place to ask, anyway.

"That's exactly why I can't be anyone's boyfriend," I tell him. "Because right now, I'd just end up disappointing anyone I date. I'd never be around or be the boyfriend they deserve. That's what happens when cows always come first. Anyone I date right now is just going to end up resenting me for not being there when they need me, and I don't want that."

Briar looks back across the truck at me as I do my best not to ride the ass of a tiny Toyota. "It's too bad, isn't it? Because I won't lie, Jamie. Last night was some of the best sex I've ever had." The words come out of his mouth all matter-of-factly, like he just said *those were the best donuts I've ever had.*

"Right?" I make a move to pass the Toyota. "For me too. I swear, Briar, I'm not actually a sex aficionado. Last night was like . . . ."

"Like something out of a really good Alyssa Samuel novel," Briar says with a smirk.

"Yeah."

And then we're back to silence. What's left to say now? It's clear that we both had an amazing time last night, and now we've somehow got to make sure we never do it again.

Unless.

"You know," I say slowly. "If you don't want a boyfriend, and I can't have one, then it's not like there's any reason we couldn't screw around again. If we both know what we're getting into, then what's the harm?"

"I guess." Briar shrugs. "Except friends with benefits stuff like that never works out, you know?"

I do know. I've watched Jeremy have more than one messy FWB situation in the past two years. But Jeremy and I are very different people. "It only gets messy when the people don't talk to each other. When they're not on the same page, you know? One person wants one thing and the other person wants something else and it gets all weird and awkward or whatever. But I know you'd only be into having sex and being friends. You'd know the same thing about me. So maybe it could work."

"I mean . . . ." Briar trails off as he looks out the window again. "I mean, yeah, maybe it could work. You sure you'd be cool if all I ever want to be is friends?"

"Briar, I don't even have time to sleep. You think I have time to go on dates?"

It stings a little to say that out loud. The honest truth is that I'd like nothing more than to date-date Briar. I'd love to take him out to my favorite restaurant on Church Street, the one that makes meatloaf with the maple syrup crust. I'd love to bring him with me on Jeremy's dad's sailboat on Lake Champlain this summer and show him what the mountains of Vermont look like when they've got miles of perfect blue water in front of them. I'd love to spend hours on a couch reading with his head in my lap, the corner of his book bumping into the corner of mine.

Too bad you need time to do all those things. Or maybe it's not, in this case. I can't have a relationship with Briar anyway, I remind myself. He doesn't want one. What he does want is some fucking phenomenal sex, and I sure as hell could use some of that too.

"Okay." Briar says the word slowly, almost carefully, like he wants to make sure I'm hearing every syllable. "So we're fuck buddies now. Lucky for you I've got most of *Lost Key* memorized. Remember that scene where Porter rims Lance in the shower and then sucks him off?"

I spend the rest of the ride to Fairlington shifting around next to the steering wheel of the truck, trying to rearrange the massive hard-on in my jeans.

10

WHERE BRIAR DISCOVERS YOU REALLY CAN PUT MAPLE INTO ANYTHING

I'm not much of a Jane Austin fan. I've tried, I swear. I know she's kind of the mother of the romance novel, and I've given *Pride and Prejudice* more than a few chances. But I always end up feeling like maybe I'm missing the part of my brain that understands Austin, because I just don't have the obsession with her that so much of the human population does.

She could write a killer line, though, and I do like the phrase that launches *Pride and Prejudice* probably more than I like the rest of the book: "It is a truth universally acknowledged, that . . . ."

Sometimes I play a game in my head where I try to finish that phrase to fit whatever place or situation I find myself in. My first thought when Jamie parks the truck in downtown Fairlington, Vermont and we step into the noise of the 38th Annual Fairlington Annual Maple Festival is this: *"It is a truth universally acknowledged, that if something exists, Vermonters will find a way to put maple syrup into it."*

"This is wild," I tell Jamie after we walk by a table covered in maple jelly beans and then watch people sniff the table of maple soap right next to it. We're in the park in the center of Fairlington, and there's a beer tent set up off to our right where people are sipping on pints of—what else?—maple-flavored beer. A towheaded little kid walks by carrying a large swath of brown cotton candy that's got to be maple flavored. "Geez, I'm surprised you weirdos haven't figured out a way to put maple on pizza."

"Maple bacon pizza is the best," Jamie tells me seriously. "We can get some for lunch later if you want. We haven't had breakfast yet, though. Want to find the pancake tent?"

Because of course there's a pancake tent. Since I was promised the best pancakes I'll ever have in my life, I follow Jamie as he makes his way through the park.

Fairlington's not nearly as big as Burlington, but it is a lot larger than I thought it would be. A quick Google search earlier, when Jamie was in the shower, told me that about 7,000 people live here—nothing compared to Burlington's 40-ish thousand. Still, the small park that's sitting right in the center of their downtown seems packed with people. Jamie mentioned on the drive up here that the maple festival is really a county-wide thing, and people come from all the towns nearby to eat themselves sick and listen to music and do whatever else it takes to make themselves forget that it's been gray for five fucking months straight.

He didn't say the last part. I added that.

I study Fairlington and its county-famous maple festival as I follow Jamie across the park. The buildings around the town have an older, regal look. There's a line of churches on one side of the park, and several of them look like they've seen a few different centuries. On the opposite side of the park from them are stores and business fronts, and the streets all around the park have been blocked off so that people can walk back and forth between the festival and the businesses easily. People are sitting on benches at picnic tables eating every kind of food imaginable, and there's a band playing a cover of a Beatles song in a gazebo in the center of everything. It's the kind of scene you expect to see in a movie that's set in a small town. I've always figured that places like this really existed in Vermont, but I haven't gotten out of Burlington enough to see them for myself.

"Pancakes." Jamie stops triumphantly at the front of an

enclosed tent with outdoor heaters on either side of the entrance. Inside I see lines of plastic tables scattered with people, and at the back of the tent is one long table where a few people are cooking on griddles. "The Barnsby Sugarhouse sets up a tent here every year and the owners make their great-grandmother's famous blueberry pancake recipe. It's the only time of the year they sell them. I swear, I dream about these pancakes sometimes."

"You had me at 'blueberry.' Let's go."

There are more space heaters inside the tent keeping the whole thing about ten or twenty degrees warmer than the outside. I unzip my jacket, grateful that people who decide to hold a food festival in March in Vermont like outdoor heaters. It's only about fifty-five degrees out and—as usual—cloudy. Though the forecast does claim we're going to have more sun later in the afternoon.

"Jamie!" A voice calls from across the tent. I look up to see a short, redheaded girl flipping pancakes on a griddle. She's waving madly with one hand and holding a spatula with the other.

"Lexy!" Jamie's smile widens and he waves back. I follow him through the scents of flour, blueberries, and pure sweetness wafting in the air.

Jamie's grinning as he introduces me to the redhead. "Lexy, this is Briar. He founded that book club I joined. Briar, Lexy and I went to high school together, and now she goes to Moo U with me. She's a pre-med major, though, so she spends most of her time trapped in science labs."

Lexy laughs and uses her arm to push some strands of hair out of her face. She's wearing a quilted vest over a red shirt that says BARNSBY SUGARHOUSE in wide letters across it, and there's a smear of blueberry across the N. "I told this asshole to pick a major that meant we'd get to see each other once in a while. But noooo, he has to spend every hour of his life training to be a monk."

"You have a very dull view of librarians," Jamie points out. "Two orders of pancakes, obviously. It's the least you can do since you've made me wait an entire year for them," he adds grumpily. Then he tells me, "Lexy is a Barnsby, so she has the recipe. But she refuses to ever make it except at the maple festival."

"You know it's a family secret," Lexy replies seriously as she finishes flipping a stack of pancakes onto a paper plate. She hands them to the person standing next to her, and I almost do a double-take when I realize that person is a mirror image of Lexy. She's got the exact same face, hair and build—the only difference is that Lexy Number Two is wearing a large flannel jacket and a hat that says FAIRLINGTON COOPERATIVE CREAMERY in huge letters. It doesn't take a genius to figure out that the two of them are twins. "Jamie, you know how this works. You either marry into the family or you get these pancakes once a year. Just like everyone else in Vermont."

"See?" says the girl next to Lexy. "Jamie, I told ya you should've hooked up with Lexy back in the ninth grade."

Jamie and Lexy both burst out laughing. I try to ignore how much my stomach twists at the idea of Jamie hooking up with Lexy. "I think we tried that," Lexy says. "Didn't we, Jamie?"

Jamie shudders. "Hot mess. It was like kissing my sister. I thought I was gay for two months after that."

"Then he kissed Portia Sherman and landed back at bi again, though, so all's well that ends well," Lexy adds cheerfully. "Briar, this is my sister, Mindy. She runs the sugarhouse with my dad. She's the heir to the Barnsby maple syrup throne." Mindy blushes. There are worse things to be than a maple syrup heir, I think as I watch Mindy ladle a pile of blueberries onto the stack of pancakes and then pour a small fortune's worth of maple syrup over the top. She hands the stack to me. "Are you Jamie's new boyfriend?" she asks.

"What?" Jamie asks at the exact same time that I say "no!" at a volume that is *way* louder than necessary. Half the tent turns to look at us. Lexy starts laughing, and Mindy's eyes widen.

"Sorry!" she says, blushing again. "It's just that Jamie never goes to the maple festival with anyone but his family, so I thought maybe . . . ."

"Briar just moved to Vermont," Jamie interrupts. "I'm showing him around. He's from Massachusetts."

Lexy and Mindy make identical faces, their noses scrunched and their eyes drawn in. "Ugh, Massachusetts. I'm so sorry," Mindy says seriously. "That's terrible." It's like Jamie just announced that my dog died.

"Yeah," Lexy agrees. "But you're in Vermont now, so that's what matters." She passes another plate of pancakes to Mindy, who douses it in syrup before handing it over to Jamie. "Are you two here all day?" Lexy asks. "I have a break in a few hours."

"I think so," Jamie says. "I've gotta make sure Briar tries maple cream for the first time."

"Ooh, he's never had it? Take him to Skyler's tent. His is the best."

"You think I'm the one who just moved here?" Jamie says jokingly. "I'm definitely taking him to Skyler's. And we're going to find him some cotton candy. And then I thought I might show him the high school library."

"You're taking me to a library?" I ask Jamie. "Really?" I get that Jamie wants to be a librarian, and that books are the only reason we even know each other, but it still seems like a weird place to show off to someone.

"Of course he's taking you to the library," Lexy says seriously. "Everyone who comes to Fairlington visits the high school library. Hey, guys, we've got customers behind you. Can I catch up with you both later on?" Sure enough, a crowd of older women with white hair and t-shirts that proclaim they are members of the Vermont Maple Strong Society have assembled in a long line behind us.

"Text me," Jamie tells Lexy.

"Yup. Pancakes are on the house," she adds in a lower voice, waving away me and Jamie as we both try to hand her cash at the same time. Jamie rolls his eyes and thanks her, and I feel a small wave of relief wash through me. Nothing at the festival seems very expensive—these pancakes are about half the cost of what they'd go for in a restaurant—but I watch every penny that goes in and out of my wallet.

"So what's up with the library?" I ask Jamie as we find a place by ourselves at a table near the side of the tent.

"Oh," says Jamie, like he's already forgotten the subject even came up. "It's kind of famous. Because it's haunted."

And then he takes a giant bite of pancake, like he's just said the most normal sentence in the history of the world.

"Okay," I mutter to myself as I go in for my first bite of pancake.

"What do you think?" Jamie asks eagerly.

I let the soft dough settle into my mouth, where it merges with the sweetness of the maple syrup to create possibly the most brilliant fucking sensation I have ever experienced in my life. I don't answer him for a long moment because I'm too busy chewing and swallowing. No way I am going to rush through eating any bite of food that tastes this good.

"Well," I tell him, "I can see why a ghost would want to hang out in this town. Holy hell, what is in these things?"

Jamie sighs. "I ask Lexy that at least once a month. But she's not telling."

We make the pancakes last as long as we can, but eventually we're both full. Jamie promises that we can always come back for more later on if we decide we want pancakes again instead of pizza. "One festival I ate these for six meals straight," he informs me seriously. "Just to make sure I was prepared for another year without them."

Makes sense to me.

We wander around the booths of the festival, with Jamie running into someone he knows every ten minutes or so. Sometimes he just gives a quick wave or a "hey, how you doing," and sometimes he takes the time to introduce me to the other person.

Everyone's incredibly polite. Mrs. D will be happy to know that I don't feel like a flatlander for a second.

We buy the famous maple cream Jamie keeps talking about, which turns out to be what would probably happen if butter and maple syrup had a baby. I have a feeling my toaster's going to get a lot of work for the foreseeable future because the stuff is *delicious.* Jamie insists on buying a large cotton candy from a booth surrounded by energetic children, even though it's not even noon and we've just eaten breakfast. "This festival is a dentist's worst nightmare," I say as we make another lap around the park, eating the cotton candy. It's hyper sweet, the way cotton candy always is, but somehow the maple smooths out the sweetness slightly. Makes it a lot more bearable. I can't seem to stop eating it, even though I can basically feel cavities developing with every bite.

"I used to date this guy named Sean," Jamie says as he finishes chewing on a ball of cotton candy. "He hated sweet stuff. This festival was his least favorite part of the year. Hey, it's the donut booth! Their donuts are almost as good as the ones at The Maple Factory. Want to go? They have crullers too, of course."

We're still eating the cotton candy, but somehow my stomach growls.

"Jamie Morin!"

The loud voice from behind us has Jamie's entire body going stiff. "Uh," he mutters, "so did I mention that my mom and sister might be here today?"

Honestly, I can't remember. I spent too much of the morning trying to figure out whether or not Jamie or I would ever have sex again to think very much about his family. "Maybe?"

"Oh, good. Because it sounds like they're here." Jamie turns around and I follow his gaze to the woman standing behind us. "Hey, Mom."

"Hi, honey!" It's a good thing Jamie told me this was his mother, because I definitely wouldn't have guessed she was. She's about a foot shorter than Jamie, and she's wide where he's long.

Her hair's a dark blond color, and her eyes are a light blue. Jamie couldn't look less like her if he tried.

"I didn't know you'd be here today!" she rushes up to him for a hug that Jamie has to bend over for. She squeezes him tightly. "You said you weren't coming to the farm until later. Who's this?" She looks over at me as she lets go of Jamie, and there's a questioning spark in her eye.

"Jamie!" Another blur of blond hair comes streaking into the picture, and then a girl is hugging Jamie around the stomach in full force. She's a little taller than her mom, but not much. I'm not very good at guessing kids' ages, but she doesn't look like she'd be in high school yet. "You should have messaged me to say you were coming."

Jamie hugs her back hard. "Hi, Lissie. Mom and Lissie, this is Briar. He runs that book club I joined. I wanted to show him the maple festival."

"Oh!" Jamie's mother claps her hands together. "I wish I could come to a meeting sometime. Do you read any Alyssa Samuel? I just love her. Jamie used to read the books I left all over the house, you know. That's where his love of romance novels came from."

Now my brain has nowhere to go but last night—when Jamie and I acted out one of Alyssa's scenes. Suddenly my cheeks are on fire, and I can't seem to speak anymore. "Uh . . . ."

"Briar's a big Alyssa Samuel fan, Mom," Jamie interrupts. I can see him trying not to smirk. Jerk.

"We'd love to have you at a meeting anytime, ma'am," I say once I've gotten myself back together.

"Maybe one of these days," Mrs. Morin says, but I can see the dark circles underneath her eyes. They match the ones her son's usually wearing. I have a feeling I won't be seeing her at any book club meetings anytime soon.

"I'm so mad you didn't text me that you were coming!" Lissie smacks Jamie in the arm. "You and Briar could have had pancakes with me and Mom."

"Sorry," Jamie says. "It was kind of last minute. Let me make it up to you. Want to get crullers with us?"

"I was promised donuts," I remind him.

Jamie sighs. "Briar refuses to acknowledge that the cruller is superior to the donut."

"Well why should he, when it's not?" Mrs. Morin winks at me as she hooks her elbow into mine. "C'mon, Briar. Let's go stuff ourselves with even more food and you can tell me all about whatever trouble my son's been getting up to down in Burlington."

"He's a perfect gentleman, ma'am."

"I doubt that. And please, call me Ellie!"

We end up eating together out of a ridiculously sized box of donuts and crullers at a picnic table near one of the churches. "We'll bring the leftovers home to your father," Ellie tells Jamie.

"He couldn't come?" I ask, even though the answer to that is kind of obvious.

"He did the morning chores so Mom and I could come see some of my friends march in the parade," Lissie says as she goes into the box for another donut. "Then we'll do chores tomorrow because there's a local farming meet-up thing he goes to every year."

"It must be weird to always have to plan your schedules around cows," I say. "Do you ever get to do things together?" They're the kind of family I used to dream of having as a kid. They laugh and hug each other and genuinely seem to like spending time together. It's hard to imagine them as ships passing in the night, always on separate shifts.

"We do," Ellie answers. "Whenever the cows' schedule allows for it. And we spend so much time working together on the farm that it's not like we're deprived of each other's company. Once Jamie tried to move into the haymow because he said he'd had enough of the rest of us. Needed some space," she teases. Jamie rolls his eyes, but she keeps going. "He took a sleeping bag, two bags of beef jerky, and a can of baked beans. No can opener, though."

"Stop telling that story. I was seven." Jamie passes the cardboard cup of coffee they've been sharing back over to her. "Plus, Briar probably doesn't even know what a haymow is. It's the place above the barn where we store the hay we feed the cows," he adds for my benefit. "And Mom, in my defense, I was just trying to read that new book series I liked about pirates. None of you would leave me alone."

"All Jamie ever wants to do is read," Lissie says. "It used to drive Aaron crazy. He said—"

She stops mid-sentence. Jamie's eyes are on the table now, and Ellie's wearing a frown for the first time since I met her.

"Whoops," Lissie mumbles. Now her face has gone overcast too. "Didn't mean to bring up the jerkwad's name."

Ellie smooths back Lissie's hair with one hand. "It's okay, honey. You can talk about him."

"But why would I want to?" Lissie stands up from the table. "I'm going to go get a soda. Anyone want one?" We shake our heads, and she takes off over the patchy brown grass.

Ellie sighs. "Sorry to lay our family drama at your feet, Briar."

They haven't laid anything at my feet, though. I still don't really have any idea who Aaron is, or why he's gone, or why just saying his name is like casting a dark spell on the Morin family.

But Jamie's expression right now makes me think that Aaron has a lot to do with why his life is such a mess.

11

WHERE JAMIE BARES HIS SOUL AND SHARES HIS GHOSTS

Running into my mom and sister at the maple festival wasn't exactly planned, but we end up having a good time with them. For someone who thinks he doesn't belong anywhere, Briar seems to get along okay with everyone he meets, and that includes my mom and sister. It doesn't take much for my mom to like someone anyway. She's always been the type of person who adopts everyone who walks into her life as her own, whether they need to be adopted or not.

Briar seems like he could use some adopting, so that's probably not the worst thing in the world.

"He seems nice, hon," she whispers to me when Briar and I walk her and Lissie over to our old Subaru. "Bring him over for dinner sometime."

Lissie's not quite as subtle as Mom, because that kid couldn't do subtle if her life depended on it. "Bye, Briar!" she calls out as she gets into the car. "It was nice meeting you. I hope you and Jamie end up dating. All my friends will think you're hot!" Mom tries not to laugh, and they both wave at us as they drive away.

"So," I tell Briar. "That was my family. Some of them, anyway. You'll meet my dad if you ever want to come to the farm for dinner."

Briar's eyebrows go up as he nods, and I try not to think too hard about what I just said. Am I planning to bring Briar to the farm? Am I really going to bring him home for dinner?

I could. We're friends, right? Friends do stuff like that.

"Anyway," I tell him, because I don't like the weird silence that's starting to fall between us again, "you ready to see the haunted library?"

"Sure, why not. Might not even be the weirdest thing I see today. Maple soap is a trip." I laugh as Briar falls in step next to me, and we start walking north of the park, up the one main street of downtown Fairlington. The remnants of the festival are all around us as we move away from it—children who are high on sugar and shouting at their parents, lollipops leftover from this morning's parade littering the sidewalk—but the noise quiets the further we get from the square. Briar's not saying much, so I fill up the walk by pointing out random places from my childhood.

"That's the pizza parlor where Lissie once threw up all over me after she ate too many breadsticks. That's the used bookstore where I used to hide from my mom between shelves so that I could stay there after she said it was time to leave. That's a coffee shop that opened up when I was in high school. Some friend of mine convinced me to read some of my poetry at an open mic night there. I was so embarrassed, and I wasn't going to do it, but then Aaron made me and—"

My mouth stops around the forming words. I forgot where this story was going.

"You write poetry?" Briar asks. "That's cool. So who's Aaron? You don't have to tell me if you don't want to," he adds quickly.

I'm tempted to take him up on that. It would be so easy to just change the subject and pretend I never said anything. But I'm also tired of never, ever talking about Aaron. Most of my friends don't know what happened because I never told them. Lexy knows, of course, since her family lives in the area and the gossip mill in our county is strong. But she's never asked for details, and I've never offered them.

I've never wanted to before. Talking about what happened just makes the pain too real—the hole too gaping. But right now, in the middle of this street with Briar, words start to spill out of me for the first time since everything happened.

"Lissie and I have a brother," I blurt out. "An older one."

"Oh," says Briar. He keeps walking next to me, our steps slow and relaxed. His left hand brushes up against mine, and a quick burst of energy crosses the air between us. "Do you want to tell me about him?"

A few blocks ahead, I can see the school. It's an older brick building, built in the 1920s. It stretches across an entire block of its own, and at the front of it is a large clock tower that sits above most of Fairlington.

The clock tower isn't far away now, but this story also isn't very long. It turns out you can tell the story of how a family fell apart in less than five minutes—I know, because I've told myself this story over and over again. On nights when I couldn't sleep; and in the middle of morning milking, when the barn is soft and quiet; and standing in the middle of silent libraries, where the only thing to do is stack books and think too hard.

"My whole family, we've always been really close," I tell Briar. "Probably because of the farm. We've never had the money to hire full-time help, so it's always just been us. Milking the cows together, fixing fences together, whatever. Mom, Dad, me, Lissie, and my older brother. Aaron."

I don't say his name out loud very often anymore, and the syllables feel kind of strange on my tongue. But Briar just nods, so I keep going.

"Aaron's a few years older than me. I used to worship him. Followed him everywhere we went when we were kids. He said it drove him crazy, but I think he loved it, at least a little bit. I refused to wear any clothes that weren't his hand-me-downs. I think even my security blanket was his before it was mine."

"Isn't that kind of the opposite of how kids are supposed to be? Aren't they supposed to hate hand-me-downs and stuff? I never had any brothers or sisters, so I don't know," Briar says softly. Mentally, I stack that onto my very short list of things I know about Briar: *no siblings.*

"Maybe. But I wanted to be just like Aaron, and that meant looking just like he did. He was my best friend. Our farm is kind of isolated. We don't have a lot of close neighbors, so Aaron and I always spent a lot of time together. He's the first person I told when I realized I had a crush on a guy. I was freaking out a little, but Aaron just smiled and asked me when I was going to make a move."

"Nice," says Briar. "That's some A-plus brothering right there."

"It was." This is the part where the story gets really hard to tell, but I'm determined to do it. And the school's clock tower is still two blocks away anyway. "Aaron went to Moo U like me, and he came home to help all the time, just like I'm doing now. That was always the plan for both of us. Aaron was pre-law, and he was gunning to get into some really good law schools. We all knew he'd leave eventually. But we didn't know that Aaron is even more of a genius than any of us thought, and he took extra courses every semester and tested out of a bunch of classes and ended up graduating a whole year ahead of time. One day last spring he came home and told us that he'd gotten into Harvard Law, and he was leaving in the fall."

"Holy shit." Briar shakes his head in amazement. "Harvard? Your parents must have been so fucking excited."

"Mom was. But Dad was more panicked than excited. He always knew that Aaron and Lissie and I didn't want to take over the farm, but he also wasn't ready to retire yet. He still isn't. But his body just can't do what it used to. He and Mom both have some problems with arthritis, and Mom needs one of her hips replaced. He thought he had a few more years of both of us working with him, and then Lissie's help once she gets a little older, and he was counting on at least another year from Aaron."

"Oh." Briar's voice goes softer.

"Yeah. It was a mess. I offered to cut back my schedule at Moo U, but I have a scholarship there and I would've lost it if I did that. For weeks we all talked and argued and tried to figure things out. And Dad ended up asking Aaron to defer his place at Harvard so he could stay another year at the farm."

"Shit."

"Yeah. Aaron was so angry that Dad was asking him to give up Harvard after he'd worked so hard, even if it was only for another year. I remember him telling me that it wouldn't just be another year because our dad is never going to be ready to retire —not for a long time, anyway. They got into a screaming match during the evening milking one day, with Aaron yelling that Dad was the one who wanted to be a farmer, not him, so why was he trapped to a bunch of cows and giving up everything he wanted? And Dad was yelling back about how Aaron only even had a college education because of the cows and the money they bring in and . . . yeah. It got really ugly."

"What did you do?" Briar asks.

"I didn't know what to do. So I didn't do anything." The truth is that I still don't know what I should have done. I knew that Aaron was right, and that giving up Harvard was something Dad shouldn't be asking of him. I also knew that running the farm without Aaron was going to be a nightmare, and that retirement might kill my father. The guy hasn't done anything but work twenty hours a day his entire adult life.

"Most farm families around here," I explain to Briar, "are bigger than ours. There are cousins and brothers and uncles and aunts and you can usually find someone to help. But our family's not like that. My mom's from southern Vermont, and her parents were teachers like she is. My dad inherited the farm from his father, but he's an only child and both of his parents died years ago. There's never been anyone else but the five of us. Not really."

We hit the marble steps leading into the school. I could use our arrival as an excuse to stop telling the story, I guess. I could just tell Briar I'll finish telling him later and lead him into the library. Maybe I really would finish the story later, and maybe I wouldn't.

But instead I sink down onto the steps and keep talking.

"By late last summer we still didn't know what we were going to do. Aaron and Dad were fighting all the time. Mom was trying to keep the peace, but Aaron kept accusing her of taking Dad's side. Every time I did say something I ended up making it all worse. Then one day Dad had to go pick up a cow he'd bought from another farmer and Aaron went with him. When they came back, they weren't speaking. At all. Aaron wouldn't talk to me or Mom or Lissie. He packed up his stuff, got into his truck, and left."

Briar just nods, like he's not surprised at all. Maybe he always expected the story to end up there. Maybe he saw that end coming.

I wish I'd seen it coming. Then maybe that day wouldn't have crushed me the way it did.

"Did he at least say goodbye?" Briar asks as he sits down next to me on the wide brick steps.

"Kind of, I guess. He hugged me and Lissie and Mom really fast, like he was running away from us. He told us not to worry about him. Then he drove away. Now he doesn't answer our texts or Mom's calls."

"And you started your sophomore year of college trying to be two people at once," Briar murmurs.

"Yeah, pretty much." That's exactly what happened. I poke at a piece of brown grass sticking out between two of the bricks in the steps. A plant growing in concrete. Sights like that never stop impressing me.

"And that's why you don't want to tell your dad about the library job offer," Briar goes on. It's a statement, not a question, but I nod anyway.

"I know my dad," I explain. "Me leaving too would break his heart. I might end up wrecking the entire farm or losing my family the way Aaron did. I can't do that. I can't be the one who destroys our family for good, no matter how much I want that job. So instead we all just keep going along, milking cows and eating donuts and pretending like Aaron never fucking existed, even though the ghost of him is everywhere." I gesture up at the building behind me. "Our house is more haunted than this place."

"Ghosts are the worst," Briar mutters, and the way he says the words makes me think he knows what he's talking about. "Especially the ones who are still alive. What's the story with this place, anyway? With this haunted library?"

"Oh, yeah. The library." I've gotten so lost in thinking about Aaron that I've almost forgotten why I dragged Briar all the way down Main Street. "The story goes that in the 1940s, during the war, some kid who had enlisted freaked out and changed his mind about going overseas. But he didn't want to tell his family because he was too ashamed. He spent a lot of time in the library, I guess, and the night before he was supposed to ship out he came here instead. The next morning the librarians found his body on the floor of the library with a note on it that just said *I'm sorry.*"

"What the hell, seriously? Did he poison himself or something?"

"That's the weird part. No one could find the cause of death. It was the 40s, so maybe they just didn't have the medical knowledge yet to figure it out, but the coroner swore there *was* no direct cause of death. His heart had just stopped. People swear all the time that they see him in the library. Even if they've never seen a picture of him, whatever they see matches his description perfectly."

"That's creepy as fuck." Briar stares at the building towering above us. "Have you ever seen him?"

I shake my head. "No. And I've spent a lot of time in that library. You want to go in? Go ghost hunting?"

"Nah." Briar stands up from the steps and puts his hand out. "That was a nice walk, though. Let's go back to the festival," he adds quietly. "We can let the ghost stay hidden."

Let the ghost stay hidden.

I put my hand in his, and he pulls me up from the steps. Our walk back to the festival is slow and meandering and quiet. Aaron is a ghost in my life—one I almost never acknowledge. And yet I just spilled that entire ghost story to Briar as if I tell it to people all the time. As if it's just another Alyssa Samuel plotline.

It's amazing how comfortable I already feel with Briar. It's amazing how right it felt to tell him all of that.

"Hey, thanks for listening to that story," I tell him as we walk back toward the festival. "Really. I don't talk about what happened with Aaron very much. It's not a secret or anything. I just . . . ."

"Don't like talking about it." Briar finishes my sentence for me. "I get that," he adds. "No problem."

It's pretty clear by now that Briar's got ghosts of his own, and I keep half-expecting him to say something about them. To spill a little of himself in front of me, the way I just spilled a little of myself in front of him.

But all he does is ask me if we can get more pancakes.

12

WHERE BRIAR GETS VERY LUCKY AND THEN VERY UNLUCKY

You should've told him about Gina.

And Luke. Definitely should have told him about Luke.

And Paul.

I shudder as their names go through my head. The last thing that I want to do is tell innocent, sweet Jamie Morin about shitheads like Luke and Paul. Jamie probably doesn't even realize assholes like that exist in the real world. He's probably only ever read about them in books.

"Like *Lost Soul*," I whisper to myself. That's an Alyssa Samuel novel that has one of the worst villains ever created by an author. She somehow managed to combine Darth Vader with Mr. Hyde and the shark from *Jaws*.

"Huh?" Jamie's busy trying to get his truck into a tight parking space near my apartment. We didn't stay at the festival long after our trip to the library. We picked up some more maple cream and Jamie said goodbye to Lexy, and then we left. I wouldn't have minded some more of those pancakes, to be honest, but I could tell that Jamie was wearing down. Telling that story about his brother seemed to take a lot out of him.

It surprised me to hear that he doesn't talk much to anyone about what happened with him and Aaron. Jamie Morin seems like the sunshine that other planets revolve around. Everywhere we went today he saw someone he knew, someone who wanted to say hi and talk to him. The guy's got to have friends for days. How come nobody seems to know that he's kind of a hot mess right now?

Except you know! He told you everything! And you still haven't told him anything about yourself. The obnoxious voice in my head won't stop reminding me of everything I'm doing wrong right now.

"Did you just say *Lost Soul?*" Jamie asks. He's somehow managed to wedge the truck between a silver Prius and a Dodge that's bigger than my apartment, and he's putting it into park. "Isn't that the Alyssa Samuel book where the main character has this crazy-ass backstory no one knows about, and they all just think he's this barista with this really normal and calm life?"

"Uh, yeah." I concentrate on trying to get out of the truck without scratching the Prius. "I was thinking I might re-read that one."

"I liked the storyline in that one, but I couldn't get into it as much as some of her other books. Felt kind of unrealistic, you know? I mean, are there really ex-boyfriends out there who are that evil?"

Yup, it's just like I thought. For Jamie Morin, true assholes—epically terrible assholes—have only ever been characters in between the pages of books. Books that he thinks are unrealistic.

I just shrug in response. There's no way I'm telling Jamie about Paul.

It might make you feel better. No one else here knows about Paul and Luke, says the voice.

No one else here knows that I have a record. And I'd like to keep it that way, thanks, I remind it.

The voice goes quiet as Jamie walks me up to my apartment. "Thanks," I tell him as I step inside. "For taking me today. I had a really good time."

Jamie beams. It's like actual light is shining out of his face, I swear. "Thanks for coming with me. I'm really glad you liked it.

The festival is special to me, you know? It's nice to see it through a flatlander's eyes." He grins and elbows me lightly in the ribs.

"I'm definitely telling Mrs. D you said that word. You are going to be in so much trouble, Jamie Morin."

"Yeah? What's my punishment going to be, Briar Nord?"

"Remember that scene in *Lost Key* when Lance screws up and makes it up to Porter by going down on him?"

Jamie grins. "Oh, yes I do. I definitely do."

The words sound like rushing waves in my ear, and the next thing I know I'm pulling Jamie into my apartment by his shirt and slamming the door behind us.

It turns out this friends-with-benefits thing might just work.

That's my first thought after thirty minutes and a few *highly* successful blow jobs.

Jamie groans. "I have to go," he props himself up on one elbow and leans toward me. We're both lying in bed together, and for a moment I think he's going to kiss me. It occurs to me that Jamie and I have never kissed. But that's normal, right? Friends with benefits don't kiss. Do they?

"Got cows to get back to?" I'm trying to tease him, but that kind of friendly teasing isn't really my strong suit. I just end up making Jamie grimace.

"Yeah, unfortunately. You know my roommate Jeremy's leaving for fucking Cabo tomorrow? That's where he's spending most of his spring break." Jamie stands up and starts pulling on jeans. "While I spend mine fixing a gutter cleaner that needs to be put out of its misery and making up about five assignments I'm late on. I've seriously got no idea why my professors are so nice to me."

"Probably because when you shake out your curls and frown you look like a sad puppy," I tell him seriously. Jamie smirks.

"Are you going to talk to your dad this week?" I ask him. I'm a little worried I might be crossing some lines here, but that seems like a friend-type of question. Friends are supposed to care about whether or not their friends are happy. And Jamie's clearly pretty miserable right now. He's tying on his boots like they've done him some kind of personal harm.

"I need to." Jamie stays focused on the poor boots. It's amazing he hasn't snapped a lace yet, he's pulling on those fuckers so hard. "It's not like I even want to go to Cabo," he mutters. "Fuck Cabo. Who cares about Cabo? All I want is to spend the summer doing a job I really love. Cows are great, but I don't want to be around them all day. I want to be around books."

He's talking more to himself than me, and I don't know what to say in response to that anyway, so I don't answer. What is there to say? I've got a lifetime of experience proving that some people get to go to Cabo and some people just have to get through the day. It's the way the world works.

But then again, even I've gotten lucky a few times. I got incredibly lucky when DeShawn set me up with a job at V and V. I got so very, very lucky the day Mr. Fletcher decided to take a chance on me, and I don't ever want to forget that.

"Talk to him," I tell Jamie. "Just try it. You don't know exactly what went down with your dad and Aaron, and you keep telling me how close your family is. You have to tell them about this offer. Just tell them."

Jamie picks up the copy of *Lost Key* that's sitting on my couch. "Lance never would have had a problem talking to his father," he mutters to himself.

He probably wouldn't. Lance is sunshine like Jamie, but he's also louder. A little more confident and self-assured. A little too confident and self-assured for me, actually. "Nah, probably not. But he also kind of sucked at blowjobs, remember? Porter had to teach him." I reach down and jack myself slightly through my underwear. My dick comes back to life as it remembers the treatment Jamie just gave it. "You can definitely do plenty of other things better than Lance."

Jamie laughs out loud, and the sound is better than any piece of music that's ever been played in this apartment.

—

My apartment's been chronically empty except for me since I moved in, but somehow it feels even emptier after Jamie leaves for Morse's Line. I put some music on my cheap Bluetooth speaker just because everything's *too* quiet. Then I do some dishes and toast some bread to put my new maple cream on.

I swear, that stuff is crack. It really is like butter and maple syrup had a baby together.

I'm pulling together a bag of laundry, because the laundromat is somehow starting to sound like a great place to spend the afternoon, when there's a short rap on my door.

The only two people in Burlington who know where I live are Jamie and Louie, and I know Louie's working today. My heart speeds up slightly in my chest. Did Jamie come back?

"Did you forget something?" I ask as I open up the door, only to find Luke standing there.

Because of course he is. Because fuck my life.

"What do you want?" I ask. There's no way I can keep the resignation and frustration out of my voice. But Luke's used to people talking to him like that anyway. He doesn't even flinch.

"Aren't you going to invite me in?" He asks. He smiles around the piece of gum he's smacking loudly in his mouth. He can chew a piece of gum like it's a jackhammer. The noise used to drive me insane when we shared a room.

The last thing I want to do is let him in. What the hell is he doing back here? He said he was staying in Rutland. But I've never figured out how to get rid of Luke. Not when we were kids at Hope House, and not in the years since.

I just can't seem to quit him.

"Whatever." I move away from the door so he can step inside. "Just lose the gum, okay? Trash can's by the sink."

Luke shrugs and walks the twenty steps over to the trash can. "You always were a pussy about gum."

Luke thinks everyone is a pussy about everything, so I don't bother to answer that. "What are you doing here?" I stay standing, crossing my arms over my chest. Maybe if I don't invite him to sit down he'll get out of here faster. "Aren't you supposed to be in Rutland?"

Luke's looking around, studying my apartment like he didn't just see it a few weeks ago. "You still haven't told me what you're paying for this place."

This fucker. When we were kids, this shit worked on me sometimes. He'd change the subject or keep moving the goalposts of whatever conversation we were having until he'd somehow talked me into whatever it was he wanted me to do. Most of the time it happened when I wasn't even paying attention.

I wanted friends so badly back then. What Gina had done to me had really messed me up. One day I'd come home from school to find her *gone.* All Gina's note said was that she'd decided to move to Florida, and I should take care of myself.

What kind of mother tells an eleven-year-old kid to take care of himself?

So yeah, I'd been lonely and screwed up in the head and desperate to belong anywhere by the time I ended up in Hope House. Luke always knew how to play on that. He always knew how to make me feel like we were some kind of team, working together against the world, even when it was obvious to anyone with eyes that Luke was never going to care about anyone but himself.

"What are you doing here, Luke?" I ask again, and I don't try to hide any of the resignation or frustration in my voice.

Luke pulls out a chair at my tiny table and sits down in it. I clench my hands into fists inside my armpits.

"Rutland didn't work out." Luke shrugs. "Turns out the girl I was seeing had another guy who didn't want me around. She was a terrible lay anyway. I figured I'd try out Burlington for a while. Maybe stay with my old friend Briar."

My blood pressure is spiking so high it's amazing I'm still standing up. I try to keep my voice as calm as possible—Luke's the kind of guy who thrives on making other people uncomfortable, so I can't let him see that he's getting to me. "You can't stay here, Luke," I tell him, my voice even and low. "This is a studio. And you know I like my space."

Luke chuckles. The sound feels hard and ominous as it moves through the apartment. "Yeah. You always got so weird about me being in your bunk or whatever, looking at all those dumbass books you were always reading." He tils his head to the right slightly. "Working in a bookstore must be your fucking dream job, huh? You ever read that book we were talking about the other day? You know, the one I told you about? Must be a damn good read to be worth that much money." His smile stretches into something wide and dangerous.

It takes every ounce of energy I have to keep my voice even as I answer him. "I've never even seen that book, Luke. I already told you that I can't help you."

"You know what's fucked up?" Luke stands up again and starts circling the table. He ends up in front of me and crosses his arms so that we're standing a few inches apart in identical positions. Two sides of a mirror image gone horribly wrong. "You should be a lot more excited to see me, Briar. I'm your oldest friend, right? No one knows you like I do. I know shit about you that no one else *will* ever know. Right, Briar?" He steps an inch closer to me, and an involuntary shiver runs through me.

"I know about the stuff you helped me do when we were kids. I know what you got arrested for. I know what's in your sealed record. I know what you and Paul did together." I flinch slightly at the sound of his name, and Luke laughs. Now he knows for sure he's hit a nerve. "I never told the police what I knew about you and Paul. I could have, Briar. But I didn't. Because I'm your friend, right?" He takes another step forward, and I will myself not to back away from him. "You told these new friends of yours at the bookstore about yourself, Briar? What do they know about you?"

A shot of panic rolls through me, and I very nearly throw up all over Luke and his thinly veiled threats. I suck down the bile that's gathering in my throat. "Stay away from where I work, Luke."

Luke laughs again, that same dangerous laugh that's making me feel like a lost child in my own apartment. I've spent far too many years listening to that laugh already. "Of course I'll stay away, Briar. Just as long as you're taking care of the scouting work I need you to do for me."

"Luke, I already told you that I'm not—"

He cuts me off before I can finish speaking. "You've gotta stop worrying so much about shit, Briar. It's just a fucking book. Get me a little information and I'll take care of the rest. You get a cut of the money, I get to leave Burlington happy, and your coworkers never find out what I know about you. That book's insured anyway—you know it is. Who the fuck loses?"

Me. Me. I lose. Just like I always end up losing when you're around.

But I don't say those words aloud. I just stand there, arms wrapped up around myself, body clenched and tight like I'm standing in front of a poisonous snake.

I may as well be.

"Yeah, you're right. This place is too small for me to stay here." Luke backs off and takes a step toward the door. "I'll find something better. But it turns out I like Burlington. Think I'll hang around for a while. Wait for you to get your head out of your ass." He yanks the door open. "Just don't make me wait too long. I might get bored and end up visiting you at that fancy bookstore." He pauses again, his handle on the doorknob. "Don't forget that this is gonna be good for you too, Briar. You'll have plenty of cash in your pocket after this. You won't have to worry about ending up like you did after Paul fucked off on you. Or Gina."

"Don't say their names." I growl the words so low it feels like they're coming from the back of my throat.

Luke shrugs and tugs the door open. "I'm just sayin' that you need this as much as I do. And you know it."

The door slams hard behind him.

For a long time I stand there in one spot, barely moving. I let out all the shaking I was holding in when Luke was there. I rack with those shakes as they move through me. At first they're filled with anger, and then some fear, and then some guilt.

I end up lying on top of my bed. Just thirty minutes ago Jamie was lying in this bed with me, his eyes full of light and his moppy curls dragging across my skin. That moment feels like a hundred years ago. It's been drowned out completely by the dirty memories Luke brought into this apartment.

I should have known he'd get tired of waiting for me to say yes. I should have known he wouldn't take no for an answer. I should have known he'd come back with threats, dangerous and determined to convince me to go along with him no matter what.

That's the problem with me: I'm pretty good at guessing what's coming next when I'm reading a book. But in real life, I'm never a step ahead of anybody. Not Gina. Not Luke. Not Paul.

Other people just keep writing my story for me.

13

WHERE JAMIE STEPS IN SHIT, BOTH REAL AND METAPHORICAL

"I'm finally ready to do it," I tell Briar. I'm standing in the middle of a cow pasture next to a giant pile of cow manure while we talk on the phone. Cow piles are an occupational hazard of farming. It's impossible to stay away from all of them—you just do your best to avoid them, knowing that it's only a matter of time before your boots are covered in shit again. God bless hoses.

"Really?" Briar's voice perks up. He's sounded distracted and a little out of it up until now, and I haven't really been sure why. I was worried maybe he was rethinking our FWB arrangement or regretting the blow jobs we gave each other before I took off for Morse's Line a few days ago. But now he's back to sounding like himself, so maybe that was all in my head. Or he's just having a bad week.

Sometimes I forget that other people's feelings aren't *always* about me. Maybe it's because I'm so bad at peopling.

"How are you going to do it? When?" Briar asks. I can hear the sounds of talking and laughter in the background behind him. He's on a break from his shift at V and V. I wish I was spending the day there, curled up on a couch reading our newest book club pick, rather than planning how to break my father's heart and probably destroy my family once and for all.

"We've got more fences to repair. There are always a lot of fences to fix after all the snow melts, and the stretch we need to do today is a long one, over by the field where we keep the dry cows. Dad and I are going down there after we finish the morning feeding. Should be just the two of us for a while, so I think it might be the right time."

Briar's quiet for a minute. Then he asks, "What's a dry cow?"

I know he's trying to distract me from how nervous I am, so I happily dive into the explanation of how cows go "dry" or stop giving milk for a few months before they have a baby and start producing milk again. Briar asks a question here and there, and by the time I've finished giving him a lesson worthy of any kid who spent ten years in 4-H, Dad is walking out of the barn to find me.

"I gotta go," I tell Briar. "Dad's looking for me. Thanks for . . . ."

I don't even know what to say. Listening? Making me talk about dry cows instead of how terrified I am right now? Being the one person I wanted to call today?

But Briar answers before I can figure out the ending to that sentence. "No problem, Jamie. Hey, you can do this, okay? Ghosts aren't real. Maple donuts are."

It's such a lame thing to say that we both start laughing. Dad hears me and turns around, then waves and starts making his way across the pasture.

"Gotta go," I tell Briar.

"Do it. Don't back down."

We both hang up.

"You ready to head down to the fence?" Dad arrives next to me wearing an old sweatshirt with the Burlington University logo across it. Something catches in my chest when I realize it's Aaron's old sweatshirt. I wonder if Dad even knew that when he put it on. Mom went to Burlington University too, so between her and Aaron and me our house is covered in Moo U merchandise. We even have coasters.

"Nice sweatshirt," I tell him. My voice sounds more strangled than I thought it would.

Dad looks down and shrugs. "Found it in a box in the guest room. Is it one of yours?"

My heart sinks. If that shirt was a sign that I'm about to do the right thing, the sign may as well have just been buried under a metric ton of cow manure. Just like everything else in my life.

"I'm ready," I mumble.

Dad nods. We hop in his truck, ready to make the short drive down the dirt road that weaves in between some of our pastures to the one at the far back of the property. The pasture butts up against the edge of the forest. When we were kids, Aaron used to tell me stories about how the forest was haunted and dead cows would come after me if I ever went in there. He was just trying to keep me from ducking the fence and going into the woods by myself, but Mom wasn't happy when I started climbing into her and Dad's bed every night because I was having nightmares of cow skeletons following me around the house, mooing incessantly and trying to eat me.

"Hey, Dad," I say as we start to unload posts and wire from the back of the truck. "I need to talk to you about this summer."

"Yeah?" Dad starts examining an area where heavy snows have broken down an old section of the fence. "I've been meaning to talk to you about that as well. You know how your sister wants to go to that fancy guitar camp in June? Your mom and I were going to say no, because we're short on cash right now, but then I was thinking that when you're home this summer we can add a few more head to the herd. Between the two of us we should be able to take care of a few more, right? That should give us a little more cash for Lissie's camp and also help us pay down some of the debts from that extra hay we had to buy last November. Now, mind you that if the milk prices keep dropping . . . ."

He keeps talking, but my brain tuned out somewhere around "add a few more head."

I clench a rubber mallet in one hand and try to take a deep

breath. I want to scream. I want to throw the mallet into the woods behind me, the woods that are supposedly filled with dead cows. Only it's not dead cows I'm being haunted by now. It's these new live ones Dad wants to buy, who will need to be milked and fed and have their crap cleaned up all day every day, just like the ones we already own.

"Dad," I say through slightly clenched teeth, "how are we going to increase the herd size? I have to go back to school in the fall. You can't take care of that many by yourself."

Dad shrugs and stays focused on a fence post. "We'll figure something out. I keep telling you you're doing too much anyway. Maybe you can quit that work-study job at the library? I know it doesn't pay much, and we'd probably make more here if we were working together with a bigger herd. Just something to think about. Don't tell your sister I said anything, though. I don't want to get her hopes up about that camp. She's all excited. Pass me that rubber mallet?"

I pass him the mallet. And then I think about another summer here. Another summer neck-deep in shit with more cows to milk and more fences to fix and more hay bales to throw.

I want to shout at my father that we need to talk about what happened with Aaron and I need to know exactly why he left. Because I can't keep doing this. I can't keep pretending that everything is fine while I try to balance all the different worlds I've been living in.

But I just stand there. I don't shout. I don't say anything.

It's strange, growing up in a world where life is so tethered with work. People at Moo U always talk about "work-life balance," and the first time I heard that term I had no idea what it could mean. I couldn't even imagine a world where people worked for periods of time and then completely stepped away from it. That's not how life on our small farm has ever worked.

All of it—work, play, family, life as I know it—is woven together into a giant piece of cloth I can't pull strands from. The pond where Aaron and I went frog catching as kids is the same pond our cows drink from on hot summer days. The haymow that Lissie and Aaron and I played hide-and-seek in for hours and hours on end when we were little is the same haymow where I spend hours and hours every summer, stacking and restacking bales of hay on top of each other. The twice-daily milkings that are taking me away from my college papers right now are the ones that have given me hours of time with both my parents and my siblings.

I told my father about Sean for the first time when I was cleaning the gutter. I cried about my first failing grade to my mother while we were washing milk equipment together.

Aaron first told me he wanted to be a lawyer in the pasture next to the one I'm standing in. We were moving the herd. "I love this place," he told me. "But I won't be here forever."

How do you build separation between yourself and a place when that place is a part of your soul? How do you choose between a job you want and a job that has defined your entire life?

How do you choose between what you want and what your twelve-year-old sister deserves to have?

So I don't yell. I don't say anything or start screaming or even say Aaron's name. I just nod at Dad, shrug, and let the conversation fall away.

I don't mention libraries or summer jobs.

I don't mention anything that I want. At all.

I take a step toward Dad, planning to hand him a wrench, and there's a loud squishing sound. The sensation of my boot being pulled toward the ground by something soft and wet runs up my leg. "Fuck," I mutter.

Dad glances over. "Step in some crap, huh?" he says. "Gotta watch where you're going there, son."

"Yup." I pop the *p* on the end of the word loudly and don't say much for the rest of the job. When we get back to the barn, I turn the hose on my boots so hard that I end up soaking my entire leg.

Mom begs me to stay at the house that night, but I make up a story about needing to get in some hours at the library and start the drive back to campus as soon as we're done with the fences. The truth is that I need to get as far the fuck away from Tiny Acres as possible. I need to get back to Burlington, I tell myself. Back to my dorm room and those assignments I'm behind on.

Briar, a voice in the back of my head whispers. *You want to go back to Briar.*

Okay, so maybe I do. So maybe there's nothing I'd like to do more right now than drive to V and V and sit on a couch with Briar and whine all about how messed up my family is and how much I just want to quit working on our farm and spend the rest of my life in libraries.

But Briar's not my boyfriend. I'm very aware that I'm already pushing the boundaries of what a person can reasonably expect from a friend they just met a few weeks ago—even a friend they're having mind-blowing sex with. Briar's not my therapist or my life coach. I need to figure out how to stop stepping in shit all the time, both figurative and literal, and it's not his job to get me there.

I park my truck in the lot closest to my dorm and make my way past blasting music from doorways and a group of people crowded around a video game on the large screen TV in our floor's common room. "Jamie, bro!" someone calls out. "Want in?"

I shake my head and keep walking, and they don't push it. They're used to me telling them no. It happens all the time.

Because cows. Because cows and shit.

I hit the door of my room and want to throw something again. There's *another fucking sock* on it. "Jeremy!" I take a fist to the door, pounding loudly. "What the hell, man? You're supposed to be in Cabo!"

Suddenly the door swings open a few inches. Jeremy's there, out of breath and looking flushed, despite a new tan. He seems a little panicked. "Hey, Jamie! I, uh, came back early. Can you give me a minute here?"

Is he serious right now? "No, I can't. I've got books to read and a paper that's way overdue to write. I don't care who's in there with you. Please just cut me a break and send them home so I can come in, okay?" I'm being an asshole. I know it, and I don't even care. Every ounce of my patience has been used up and spit out by my talk with Dad near the woods.

"No!" Jeremy's voice is abrupt and high and now he *definitely* sounds panicked. "I'll send them home, okay? I promise. Just go away and come back. In like twenty minutes or something?"

"Can't I just come in? Please? I really don't care who's in there with you." I realize Jeremy is pushing against the door heavily with one hand, like he's terrified I'm going to try to open it wider. "Who's in there, anyway? Why are you being weird?"

"No one!" Jeremy's voice goes up another octave, and my eyebrows go up with it. "Listen," he says, and there's some definite begging in his voice. "Please just go away for a little bit, okay? If you do, I promise I won't put a sock on the door for the whole rest of the week. The whole week!"

He sounds desperate, and I'm not above using that to my benefit. "You're going to go the whole rest of spring break without sex?" I don't even bother to ask why he came back early instead of finding people to have sex with in Cabo. Jeremy does whatever Jeremy wants, and his decisions only make sense about fifty percent of the time.

"Hell no. I'm just going to go the whole rest of the break without having sex in our room." He says that sentence so seriously that I almost laugh.

"Fine, whatever." I step back from the door and Jeremy breathes out a small sigh of relief. "But later on you're telling me who you've got in there that you don't want me to see."

"Never going to happen," Jeremy says cheerfully. "See you in a little bit." Then he slams the door in my face.

Fuck. Now what do I do?

I could go join the game down the hall. Or maybe see if Lexy is on campus. But video games were something Aaron and I used to play a lot together, and I haven't touched my Xbox since he left. I text Lexy as I'm walking back down the hallway, and she doesn't answer.

So I let my feet carry me back to my truck. And the next thing I know, I'm parking the car on a side street about a block from Church Street.

"This probably isn't a good idea," I mutter to myself as I walk past The Maple Factory and into the door of the bookstore side of V and V.

"Hi, can I help you?" A man with hair even curlier than mine, only blond, greets me as I come in. "Oh!" he adds a second later. "You're part of The Booklover Club, aren't you?"

Talk about a place where everybody knows your name. "Yeah. Jamie." I hold out my hand and we quickly shake.

"I'm Louie. Are you looking for anything in particular today?"

Briar. I need Briar.

"No, not really. Just browsing. I already have the next book the club is discussing." I'm itching to step away from this guy so I can start walking around, looking for Briar. Then it occurs to me that Briar could be done with work for the day. What if he's not here? "Uh, is Briar working, by any chance?"

Louie's smile slowly widens. "He is. He absolutely is. He's in the stockroom unpacking a new shipment. Why don't I take you back there?"

"Oh, you don't have to do that. I mean, I don't work here, and—"

"Nobody will mind," Louie interrupts. "Not if you're with Briar. It's a big job, so he's going to be back there for most of the rest of his shift. C'mon. You can say hi. He's probably about to take his break, anyway."

I follow Louie past the New Arrivals shelf and the circle of couches where the club meets. We come to a door with a code lock on it. Louie punches in some numbers, and the door swings open.

I swear I've entered Valhalla.

I work in a library. I spend a good portion of each week surrounded by books. I unpack book shipments all the time. I've been surrounded by piles of books as high as my head. I've stood in mountains of them.

But there's something about seeing Briar knee-high in stacks of paperbacks and hardcovers, staring intently at the inside cover of a new biography that makes me instantly hard.

I strategically adjust my jeans and hope Louie doesn't notice.

"Briar," says Louie. "Jamie here stopped by to see you."

"Huh?" Briar looks up from the book he's holding, and something in his face changes. It goes softer, a little lighter. The wrinkles near his eyes ease slightly, and the corners of his mouth lift. "Jamie," he says softly. "You're here," he adds. "I, uh, I . . . ."

Next to me, Louie raises an eyebrow.

"I didn't mean to bug you at work," I interrupt. "I can leave. I came back from Morse's Line and Jeremy's got our dorm room *occupied* again, so I figured I'd stop by while I was waiting."

"Ah, the days of sharing dorm space with oversexed twenty-somethings," Louie says smoothly. "I do not miss college at all. Briar, it's about time for your break if you want to take it." He steps out of the door of the stockroom, closing it gently behind him.

"Seriously, I can leave," I repeat. Just in case Briar didn't hear me the first time. It's probably messed up, me bothering him at work like this. We're not even dating.

But Briar says, "Don't leave," a little quickly, and I just nod. And then I say what I'm thinking, because fuck peopling correctly.

"You look hot like that," I tell him. "Surrounded by books. You're like a scene out of my dream porno."

Briar laughs out loud. "Yeah? Is that why you've got a giant boner in the middle of a bookstore?" His smile falls away. "Shit, you came back to Burlington. Does that mean the talk with your dad . . . ?" his words trail off.

"He didn't kick me out or anything. I chickened out. Couldn't tell him." Suddenly the world feels very, very exhausting. I sit down on the carpeted floor in between a stack of board books and a pile of paperback thrillers. "He started talking about needing money for this camp Lissie wants to go to, and I just chickened out. I chickened the fuck out, Briar."

Briar sets down the book he's been holding and makes a careful mark on a piece of paper. Then he steps over another pile of books and sits down on the floor next to me. "That sucks," he says.

I shrug. "There's no way I can take that job this summer. I have to tell him, soon. I can't keep stringing him along like this. I can't keep—"

Briar tugs me toward him, and the next thing I know I'm leaning into his chest, nearly sitting in his lap, and my face is buried in his flannel shirt. My lungs are heaving a little and I'm pretty sure I'm crying. I can't remember the last time I cried.

Logically I know that I am crying on top of my not-boyfriend in the middle of the storeroom where he works. Logically I know that probably anyone could walk in the door of this storeroom at any moment. Logically I know that there are a whole bunch of book shoppers and wine drinkers just a few feet away from us. But the entire world right now feels like it belongs to me and Briar —like it's just the two of us and these giant stacks of books against everything else. I sob quietly into his chest and he strokes my hair, as if that's a perfectly normal thing to do in the middle of a bookstore stockroom.

I stay where I am even after the tears fade away. "Thanks," I whisper. I think about sitting up, but it's just so comfortable where I am. "I'm sorry I lost it like that."

"Don't be sorry." That's all Briar says.

"But I—"

"You don't have anything to be sorry for."

"I like how simple you keep things sometimes." I roll out of his arms slightly and almost knock over a sci-fi novel. "You know," I tell him, "I once had a wet dream about fooling around with a guy in between the bookstacks in the library where I work."

"Yeah?" Briar's eyes are fixed on me and a little bit hazy. He sets a hand on top of my crotch. My cock, which had gone soft during my little crying jag, immediately starts to come back to life. "You want to see if we can make that one a reality?"

I put my hand on his crotch. He's hard too. "What if someone comes in?"

"Louie and I are the only ones working right now. And I'm pretty sure he's going to leave us alone."

I'm pretty sure of that too.

Suddenly Briar's rolling me over on my back so that I'm laid out on a long stretch of carpet in between piles and piles of books. He's on top of me, and for a moment I think he's going to kiss me. *We've never done that,* I realize. How do you not notice that you haven't kissed someone? Especially someone you've had amazingly intense orgasms with? Briar's face comes in close to mine, and for a moment I'm sure he's going to do it. But then he backs up slightly, just as he's working open the button of my jeans. I return the favor, and a moment later both of our cocks are out and he's holding them together in one thick hand.

He never takes his eyes off of mine. I can't seem to look away from him as he begins to gently jack our dicks together, his facial expression intense and focused.

I place my own hand over his, strategically maneuvering two fingers so that they bump against the top of Briar's cockhead. He gasps slightly.

"I like feeling our dicks together," I murmur to him. That's an understatement. This is definitely the hottest handjob I've ever had in my life. Maybe it's the books surrounding us, or the way Briar's hand moves so gently and quickly at the same time, or the way my own hand is moving with his. My peripheral vision strays to one of the stacks of books next to me, and I can't help but think of my dream. "This is even hotter than what dream me did in the library," I mutter.

"Yeah?" Briar says the word so softly I almost miss it. I brush my hand against the tip of his cock again. He collapses his face into my neck, and for a moment I just breathe in the scent of his shampoo. Apples and melons.

The pressure builds back and forth in between us, and I clutch his head into my neck. Every movement of his skin against mine has me ready to explode. Every second that his dick rubs against mine has me wondering how I've gone so many years without having sex with Briar Nord inside a bookstore storeroom. I pull one hand away from his head and reach for his free hand. I grasp it in mine and pull it up the floor towards my mouth until it's close enough for me to suck on his first finger.

"Fuck, Jamie," he whispers into my neck. He jacks our dicks together faster, until the friction is almost a little bit painful. We're both dripping pre-cum, and soon the friction is something fast and smooth and wonderful and—

"Briar," I say in a strangled voice.

Briar's face lifts away from my neck, so that he's staring into my eyes again. "Me too," he whispers. "Are you ready?"

I nod, and he does something with the hand on our cocks— moves it so that he's suddenly pressing a finger up against my balls. The pressure is so quick and intense that it sets me off right away. He's exploding too. I can feel him shuddering in my arms and I want to kiss him so badly, but he's got his face in my neck again. I settle for sniffing his hair like a weirdo and imagining what it would be like to make out all day in a bed with him, naked, our mouths pressed together and our dicks in his hand.

We both shake and shudder together for a long moment, and then the storm's over. We lay still, the piles of books watching us silently. Briar's hot breath feels right against my skin.

I wish I could have something like this every day, all the time.

Actually, I realize, I wish I could have *this* every day, all the time.

But that isn't how the world works. That's something I'm reminded of fast when Briar sits up, winks at me, and grabs some tissues to clean us up without saying another word.

14

WHERE BRIAR ALMOST TAKES A PICTURE

It's arguably not the best idea to get off with your fuck buddy in the storeroom where you work.

Arguably. I say arguably because I'm pretty sure I am not the first person at V and V to do this. The way Louie was looking at me, all eyebrows and winks, when he closed the storeroom door behind him suggests that I am almost definitely not the first person to do this.

Plus I've seen the way Mr. Fletcher looks at that chicken farmer he's shacked up with. How do you date someone that hot and not bone them in your own storeroom at least once?

I also say *arguably* because getting off with Jamie continues to feel like winning an Olympic medal, eating a maple donut, and starting the first page of the best book you'll ever read in your life all at the same time. Not that I've done the first one, and I sort of hope I haven't done the last one yet. I like to think I've got the best book of my life still ahead of me.

Sex with Jamie continues to prove that my relationship with Paul really was just a waste of sixteen months of my life, as I've always known it probably was. Sex with Paul was like running a cash register: quick, perfunctory, and everyone got what they needed out of the exchange.

Sex with Jamie is very definitely a whole lot more than that.

"Uh, wow." Jamie sits up, brushing strands of hair out of his eyes. "Fuck, I'll never be able to come in here again." Then he blushes. "Pun not intended. I mean, if you even noticed it. Maybe you didn't, because—"

He's so fucking cute when he starts talking himself in circles like that. I hope I look half as cute when I start rambling, but I have a pretty solid feeling I don't. "It was a good pun," I tell him. I stand and offer him a hand, then pull him up from the floor. "My break's probably over."

Jamie's face falls. Shit. Did I say something wrong? But my break probably is over soon, and the truth is that I sort of need Jamie to leave right now or I'm going to jump him again. Odds are eighty percent in favor of a blow job if he's still in this room in five minutes.

"But," I add, "maybe you want to come over again some night this week? Like tomorrow night? Just to get away from your roommate or whatever," I quickly throw in. So far I think we're both doing a solid job of holding down the friends-with-benefits expectations here, but it's good to re-draw lines sometimes.

Jamie smiles. "Yeah. I think I'd like that. And we've got book club this Saturday. You maybe want to hang out after that?"

"Oh. Yeah. I've got to finish that book." It's a historical romance this time, a pretty classic Regency about a valet who falls in love with a duke who's way above him in social class. "I like the grandmother."

"She's the villain!" Jamie laughs. "I know what you mean, though. She's fun."

You're fun, I want to tell him. Not like the quasi-villainess in the book, who's really just a snob. Jamie's fun in a much realer, truer sense of the word. Since I've started hanging out with Jamie, I've felt more a part of this place than I did in the five months before I met him. And so far all he's done is take me to a maple festival and get off with me a few times.

It's a little scary to imagine how much fun I could have with him if we spent even more time together. I grab one of the books I'm supposed to be stocking off of a pile. "I'll see you later, okay?" I say quickly. Jamie's face falls again, but only for a quick second. Then he pulls his smile back into place and nods. "Yeah, of course. Later." He's out the door before I can make things any weirder.

"Fuck," I mutter to myself. Sucks that I'm going to be spending the day unpacking and tracking books. This is the kind of job that can get you stuck inside of your head for a while, doing nothing but thinking. And that's honestly the last thing I want to be doing right now.

I pick up a pile of YA fantasy novels, and something appears behind them: the corner of a large, black, metal safe.

Fuck again.

This room was covered in books when I first stepped into it a few hours ago. Logically I knew the safe was still in here; no one would move something that's a few hundred pounds just because a shipment of books came in. But it was so buried under boxes that I haven't thought much about it while I've been working. I definitely wasn't thinking about it when Jamie stopped by.

Most of the time he was here I was thinking with my dick anyway, if I'm being honest.

But now the stupid fucking safe is staring directly at me. It's about four feet tall, all sharp corners and dark finishes, and the giant lock on the front lets you know right away that there's probably more in there than some little kid's baseball card collection.

It's been a few days since Luke appeared in my apartment to harass me. Every day when I get home I half-expect him to be there, sitting on the steps, waiting with a threat to out me to my coworkers. Or maybe he'll go back to sweetly begging the next time he visits, and he'll just remind me how much money is in it for me if I help him out. It's hard to tell what Luke will ever do next. He's always operated in a funnel and swirl of chaos.

I could take a picture of the safe. Right now, I could snap a picture on my phone. No one would ever notice or know, and that's probably all Luke would need at first to get started with his plan. I know some of the work he and Paul used to do back in Springfield. I know they both worked with plenty of safes.

My hand drifts toward my back pocket, where my phone sits. One quick picture. Then maybe I could stop worrying about my bank account. I could stop worrying about what Louie and Mr. and Mrs. Fletcher and Rainn and everyone else here would say if they knew the things I did, back when I was running with Luke and Paul.

Just one quick picture. My hand comes to rest on my phone, and I begin to tug it out of my pocket. My heart speeds up slightly, and for a moment I second-guess myself.

And then the door clicks and swings open.

I drop my phone away from my hand like it's burning, and Mr. Fletcher steps into the room.

Guess I was wrong about me and Louie being the only ones here right now. I'm lucky he didn't open that door a few minutes earlier.

"Briar! I'm glad I caught you." Mr. Fletcher always reminds me of one of the guys I used to see walking in downtown Springfield, moving between high-rise office buildings and high-rise apartment buildings. He could have stepped right out of the Italian restaurant where I used to work, the one that was between two major financial corporations. Tons of stockbrokers and accountants ate lunch there every day. I'm not sure exactly why Mr. Fletcher reminds me so much of those guys, since I've never seen him in a suit or a tie once. He tends to wear button-up shirts and dress pants or jeans when he's on the job here, but I know he used to be some kind of businessman, and it's not hard to make the leap to what he would have looked like in a suit. The guy is mid-height and fit and wears dark-rimmed glasses that match his dark hair and eyes, and he almost definitely would have been the duke and not the valet in any Regency story about two people of different classes who fall in love.

Only he fell in love with a chicken farmer. An incredibly hot chicken farmer who's got more muscles than I ever thought someone who works with chickens would need to have. That thought I had earlier about whether or not Mr. Fletcher and his partner have ever gotten off in this storeroom pops back into my head, and I have to look away from him for a second. I pretend to be intensely focused on a fantasy novel.

"Hey, Mr. Fletcher," I say, as casually as I can. Like I wasn't just about to set a plan in motion to rob him *and then* thinking about him and Finn having sex all in the space of three minutes. "What's up?"

"Briar, I keep telling you to call me Harrison. I wanted to tell you that Mom and I were just going over numbers together, and we were noticing how much business both the wine bar and the bookstore are getting because of The Booklover Club." My neck goes up immediately at the sound of the club's name. "It sounds like your members have been spreading the word about the store to their friends, and their compliments are getting around. The members must be very happy with what you've set up. I know you put a lot of thought and time into getting that off the ground, so I just wanted to make sure I said thank you. Wonderful work, Briar."

For a moment my mouth gets stuck around the obvious words I need to say. I'm really not used to people thanking me or telling me I've done a good job. "Thanks," I finally manage to stammer out. "I mean, Mrs. D helped a lot. And we've been lucky to have really dedicated readers join the group."

"Briar!" Mrs. Fletcher, Mr. Fletcher's mother, pops her head around the corner of the doorway, a stack of picture books in her hands. "You marvel, you! This book club was such a wonderful idea." She beams across the room, and for a moment I'm worried she's going to rush me for a hug. Mrs. Fletcher has been known to make comments about how she can't wait to have me over for a good meal, and that's why I tend to avoid her in the shop. Louie jokes that she likes to adopt people who need rescuing.

I wonder sometimes if she convinced Mr. Fletcher to hire me. But the idea of being rescued by anyone always makes my stomach churn, so I do a lot of smiling and nodding and running away to deliver coffee when she's around. What would I have to talk about with someone like her if she did get me over to her house? She used to work in New York City, and she always looks so put-together and regal. I start stammering when she gets within three feet of me. I'd probably pass out at the table from nerves if I tried to have dinner with her.

Mr. Fletcher smiles. "Briar and I were just talking about that," he says. "He seems to think he's been lucky with the club. But I think you've made some of that luck," he tells me. "If we're seeing a bounce in business after you've only had a few meetings, that means you've been giving our customers something they want and making them happy." He reaches over to pat me gently on the shoulder, and I carefully work to make sure I don't flinch.

"Like I said, you're a marvel," Mrs. Fletcher agrees. "Well done, Briar!" she waves wildly at me as she leaves, and I try not to breathe a sigh of relief when she closes the door behind her.

"So, how's the new shipment look?" Mr. Fletcher asks.

That's a topic I know how to talk about. Mr. Fletcher and I don't really talk very much—probably because I don't talk very much to anybody, especially the boss who I still can't believe hired my ass in the first place—but when we do talk it's always about books and the store and shelving and displays. We go through some boxes together as we get into a conversation about whether to center the next window display on the new middle grade release that's coming out this week or a popular mystery series that just hit the NYT list again.

"I'll trust you and Louie to make the call," Mr. Fletcher decides. Since Louie's an artist, he's usually the one who ends up designing the window displays. "The two of you always seem to know what the customers want." He pushes up the sleeves of the button-up he's wearing and starts pulling more books out of boxes.

We work together for the next hour or so, mostly in silence, but with Mr. Fletcher occasionally asking me a question or mentioning something about a book he likes. Somehow he ends up telling me about how he met Finn when a bunch of Finn's chickens were delivered to the store by accident, and he has me laughing my ass off when Louie calls him away for something to do with the wine bar. I end up standing in the storeroom, surrounded by much more organized stacks of books and a large, black safe.

My phone burns in my pocket.

It's going to crush Mr. Fletcher if this store is robbed. Crush him.

And it's not just Mr. Fletcher and his mom who are going to get hurt if I help Luke do this. Stores like V and V don't operate on massive profit margins. Anything could happen if Luke gets his hands on that book.

I can't take a picture of that safe. I can't do something like that to everyone at V and V who's been so good to me.

I wonder what Luke's going to tell them when he realizes I won't help him. Will he tell them about the shit I did when we lived at Hope House? Probably. I bet he'd love to make sure everyone at V and V knows I spent some time in juvie. Will he tell them about the things I let Paul talk me into doing?

There's no way I'm going to keep my job here once Luke starts talking to my coworkers. No way.

But maybe I'll get lucky. Luke's never had a very good attention span, and he gets bored easily. Maybe he'll find something else more interesting to distract him, or another girl who lives in another town he can go live in. Maybe I won't have to make a choice between myself and the people who gave me a chance at a real life.

Maybe, just once, I'll get one of those happy endings that Alyssa Samuel's characters always get.

Sure, that voice in the back of my head sings out. *You just keep telling yourself that.*

15

WHERE JAMIE'S MOST EMBARRASSING STORIES ARE REVEALED

The rest of spring break disappears way too quickly, because that's what always happens to spring breaks and summer breaks and winter breaks. As the great Calvin of the *Calvin and Hobbes* cartoons once said, "There's never enough time to do all the nothing you want."

I love that kid and his tiger. Right now I'd give a lot to have half of his sage wisdom and his reckless disregard for others. It's the last Saturday of spring break and I haven't seen Briar once since we got off together in the stockroom of V and V.

I had late papers to make up, and Briar ended up covering some extra shifts at the bookstore when his coworker Oz got the flu, and Dad decided that since I had time off from school this would be a great time to knock out about twenty hours of repairs in the barn in less than two days. I'm more exhausted than ever, and classes are starting up again in less than forty-eight hours.

At least I get to see Briar today. There's only an hour before our next club meeting, which means I've got forty-five minutes to finish the last twenty pages of this Regency romance and see if the duke and the valet figure out a way to be together.

Obviously they're going to. That's why I read this genre. But I still can't figure out exactly how the author is going to make this happen in nineteenth century London.

"Hey!" Jeremy appears at the side of the couch in our room where I'm reading. "What are you doing tonight?"

"Sleeping, I hope, if I don't end up back in Morse's Line again." Actually, I'm sort of hoping I'll end up sleeping at Briar's place. And doing a lot more than sleeping.

The last few days have proven that a friends with benefits arrangement is the right one for me and Briar. If we can't even manage to spend much time together when I don't have classes, there's no way we'd ever have a chance as a couple. I can't get the image of the two of us in the stockroom out of my head, though, so I'm not planning on letting go of the "with benefits" part of this friendship anytime soon.

We've been messaging back and forth over the last few days, so I know it's not like he's forgotten me or anything. Mostly we just talk about maple donuts and book quotes. Sometimes I find myself reading our text exchanges when I can't seem to concentrate on anything else.

Me: *so it turns out that a calf CAN break a whole water pipe themselves with just their hoof. Who knew.*
Briar Donut: *"I can't tell if you want me to laugh or soothe your troubles right now, so I'm going to choose to do neither."*
Me: *Did you just quote Alyssa Samuel to me? In a text?*
Briar Donut: *Fuck yeah I did. If I were a better friend I'd cheer you up by bringing you a cruller. I'm about to go on a bakery run for Rainn and Tanner and me.*
Me: *Yeah you would do that. If you were a better friend.*
Briar Donut: *And also if I had a car.*
Me: *Hahahaha that would help. Tell the crullers I said hi.*
Briar Donut: *I'll tell them they're sub-par but you refuse to realize the truth.*

"Fuck sleep." Jeremy pulls me back out of my thoughts about Briar as he lays down on the couch and puts his head in my lap. "Lexy and I have decided that we don't see you enough. We're taking you out for pizza."

"I never should have introduced the two of you," I mutter. "All you do is gang up on me and refuse to give me recipes." It's a sore spot for me that *Jeremy,* of all people, has the famous Barnsby pancake recipe. He and Mindy had a quick thing during our freshman year, after I stupidly decided that it would be a great idea to introduce my new roommate Jeremy to my good friend Lexy and her sister. Mindy got drunk one night, declared Jeremy the love of her life, and passed over the recipe. Two weeks later they were broken up and Jeremy had sworn on his life to keep the recipe secret. And somehow he and Lexy and Mindy are all still close friends. Lexy and Mindy even went to visit Jeremy at his family's beach house in Connecticut last summer.

I have to spend a lot of time reminding myself that I don't hate Jeremy just because he always seems to get everything he wants.

"You know I can't pass along the recipe. Mindy would never forgive me."

"Mindy's known me for years longer than she's known you," I grumble.

"The world is an unfair place," Jeremy agrees. "So! Pizza? I told Lexy we'd meet her at seven. And then maybe . . . ."

I see where this is going now. "You want to do more than just grab pizza tonight, don't you?"

Jeremy sits up and stares at me eagerly. "You know how the bars and clubs here rotate doing LGBTQ nights?" Of course I know that. It's how Burlington makes up for not having any kind of real gay bar other than V and V, which isn't the kind of place that hosts club dancing. I've only gone to one or two LGBTQ club nights since I've lived in Burlington. They give me a headache, and I usually need sleep more than I need to go out partying.

"Tonight that bar Lexy really likes is hosting it and her entire pride club is going and she wants us to come. Please come with us? Please? I promised Lexy I'd get you to say yes." Jeremy bats some serious puppy dog eyes at me. "You can even bring that guy you've been messing around with. Lexy said he's hot as fuck."

I guess I could invite Briar. I have a feeling he won't want to come, though. He doesn't exactly strike me as the party type either, and the dude definitely likes to keep to himself. But if I could get him to come, maybe that would mean I'd get to go home with him . . . .

My entire body likes that thought. A lot. Particularly one very exact spot on my body directly under my hip area.

"Maybe I'll come. And I'll ask Briar after book club if he wants to go too."

"Yes." Jeremy pumps his fist like some old movie character. "This'll be lit. It's been forever since you went out with us, Jamie."

I just shrug and start packing up my stuff for The Booklover Club. I still have a few pages of the book left, but I figure I can finish them off at the store.

It's kind of crazy, I think, how I'm never really going to be able to explain to Jeremy that my life just doesn't look like his.

"I just felt the duke's choices were incredibly unkind," Betty tells us all as she sips at a cup of coffee and shakes her head. "Imagine, finding the love of your life and then choosing the family fortune over him! I was utterly disgusted with his behavior." She sounds like she's talking about one of her students, and I notice Cherry trying not to laugh out of the corner of my eye.

"Yes, it was very disappointing," Cherry agrees. "But let's not forget the historical context of the story."

"Context, schmontext. Love is love! I know the two of them couldn't be together, but that doesn't give the duke the right to break poor Thomas's heart!"

Bart gently pats her hand. "It was a difficult scene. I cried a little."

"Me too," murmurs Emily. "How could he be so selfish? All he was thinking about was money! Who cares about money?"

"It's easy to say that if you have it," Briar says from the other side of the couches, and all of our eyes swing his way. He's been quieter than usual during this meeting, letting Mrs. D and Betty sort of run the show. I've been a little worried about him, to be honest, so it's good to see him jumping into the conversation here. "Don't forget that the duke had those years before his family found him when he had nothing. He was basically living on the streets. He knows what it's like not to have a place to live or people who care about him. He knows what it's like to be miserably poor. He doesn't want to live like that again. He doesn't see what he does as selfish. He just sees it as doing what he has to do to survive."

Emily looks personally wounded by this idea. "But love is more important than anything!"

"Technically, it's not, according to Maslow's hierarchy of needs," Cherry interjects. "Eating, sleeping, and security come first. I'm with Briar. I wasn't mad at the duke for doing what he did."

"Let's not turn this into a psychology class," says Lucia. "Jamie, what do you think?"

I guess I've been a little quiet too, at least on this point. The truth is that I'm not sure what I think. "I think that what the duke does is selfish, but that doesn't make it wrong," I say finally.

"But being selfish is always wrong!" Emily crows at the same time Briar quietly asks, "What do you mean?"

I keep my eyes on him as I try to explain. "I mean . . . yeah, it's selfish. He broke Thomas's heart. He caused pain. But he didn't do it out of malice or hate or ill-intent. He did it out of self-preservation. Yeah," I say as I finally realize what I first meant when I started speaking. This is another problem that happens when I try to people: sometimes I can't figure out my thoughts until I'm saying them out loud. It doesn't always go over well in my lit classes. "I think that's what I mean. What he did wasn't about selfishness. It was about self-preservation. That makes the choice a little more relatable, you know? A little more understandable. Even if it was the wrong one."

Briar's face takes on some strange looks, one after the other, as I'm speaking: first surprise, then relief, then something that's very close to sadness.

Betty sighs. "I suppose I can understand self-preservation. But I still think he was a bit of an ass."

"Betty, language!" admonishes Lilah, and Bart lets out a loud snort.

Briar's eyes stay on me the whole time.

The meeting ends on a stalemate regarding the duke's choices, and then Bart suggests a sci-fi title for the next week. "Hey, what are you doing after your shift's over?" I ask Briar as everyone else drifts away from our circle of couches and he starts cleaning up leftover crumbs and coffee cups.

He looks up at me. "We're a few days late on hanging out, aren't we?"

"Yeah. Lexy and my roommate Jeremy want me to go out for pizza with them, and then they want me to hit a bar with them that's hosting an LGBTQ club night tonight. Do you want to come?"

He hesitates, and for a minute I'm sure he's going to say no. I quickly remind myself that we're not dating, and it shouldn't bother me at all if he says no.

"Is that the roommate who keeps putting socks on your door?" he finally asks.

"That's the one."

"So . . . ." Briar gathers up a napkin, looking thoughtful. "Chances are good he'll find someone he wants to bring back to his room tonight, right? Which means you'll need a place to stay?"

I can't help but smile. I definitely like where he's going with this. "Odds on that are pretty solid, I'd say."

"Then I think I'm in." Briar takes off with the coffee cups, and I do my best not to internally cheer.

I mean, it's just sex. I've never even kissed the guy.

Right?

"So then," Jeremy says, "I start talking to this girl, and I turn around and Jamie's gone. I can't find him anywhere."

"Please stop telling this story," I beg as I let my head flop down onto the table. I moan as if I'm in great pain, because I am. Great emotional pain.

You do a few drunkenly stupid things during your freshman year and your roommate will never, ever let you live them down.

"I will never stop telling this story," Jeremy says. "It's my favorite Jamie-Morin-fucks-up story! Mostly because there are so few of them and this one is excellent. So anyway," he goes on. "I head to the bathroom, because what better place to look for someone who's just lost four games of beer pong than in the bathroom? And there I find Jamie, trying to go to sleep across a row of sinks."

Lexy is laughing so hard I'm worried beer is going to come out of her nose. Briar's cracking up too. "A row of sinks?" he asks me. "How did they support your weight?"

"Apparently Moo U bathrooms are designed to accommodate large, drunk eighteen-year-olds," Jeremy replies for me. "Those things held strong. Took me forever to get him off of them, though. He kept swearing he just needed a ten-minute nap and then he was finally going to kick Erin Flaherty's ass at the pong."

"She's stupid good," I inform Briar. "Really, it's freaky."

Briar takes another bite of his pizza and grins at me. "Who knew Jamie Morin had a bad boy side? Here I thought you were

Mr. Perfect all the time, helping out your family and working in libraries and spending your evenings reading fine literature."

"Oh, most of the time he is," Lexy interjects. "That's why it's fun to roast Jamie's ass for the two or three times he's let loose. We've got about ten million douchebag stories about Jeremy, so they're just boring."

"It's true." Jeremy nods. "I once tried to kidnap a pig from a farm on a dare and ended up almost getting myself arrested."

Briar stares at him in astonishment. "That didn't happen," he says.

"No, that's true," I tell Briar. "I was the one who had to talk the deputy into letting him go."

"I'm so glad my sister got her head out of her ass and broke up with you," Lexy says. "No offense, of course."

"None taken, obvs," says Jeremy cheerfully, as Briar says, "Wait, you dated Mindy?"

"It is a tale of mischief and woe," Jeremy tells Briar somberly. "I fell for a sugarmaker whose heart I could never have. Mostly because I don't have a heart. And also because she plans to spend the rest of her life attached to a forest of trees. Boring. No offense, Lexy."

"None taken, obvs," she replies with a wry grin.

"I still can't believe the two of you thought that dating was a good idea," I grumble. "Or that she gave you that stupid pancake recipe."

Briar's eyes widen. "You have the famous pancake recipe?"

"It's a definite sore spot with my parents," Lexy says. "And it would be with the entire rest of the family too if they knew. But Jeremy's sworn himself to secrecy, so we all just pretend it never happened."

Briar shakes his head. "I mean, I don't know Mindy or anything, but I can't really picture the two of you dating."

"It was cringe," Lexy informs him. I nod in agreement because it definitely was. Jeremy had never been in a real relationship before and decided to put everything he had into that one attempt. It ended up being a combination of every romance novel I've ever read mixed with the worst season of *The Bachelor* that's ever been produced. Jeremy doesn't know how to do anything at normal volume or pacing, and when he decided to try and have an actual girlfriend—for the first and last time in his life—he went at it hard. An actual helicopter was involved. Since then he's recommitted to non-commitment.

Jeremy points at Lexy. "You're just jealous because I picked the other Barnsby twin instead of you," he says with a jab of his finger.

Lexy laughs and pushes another slice of pizza toward him. "Yes, that's the problem, J-Bear. I'm jealous."

They start bantering back and forth about Lexy's weird nicknames for Jeremy. I catch Briar watching them with a sort of wonder that I'm surprised to see. It's like he's never seen two friends have this kind of easygoing and fun, teasing relationship with each other.

"You okay?" I ask, nudging him gently in the side while I grab another slice of pizza from the tray on the table. "They can be kind of a lot, I know."

"Nah, they're not a lot at all. They're . . . ." Briar studies them again as Lexy starts throwing pepperoni in Jeremy's direction while he ducks. "They really like each other," he finally says. "You all really like each other."

"Well, yeah," I reply. "We're friends. I mean, they both drive me nuts sometimes—especially when Jeremy's hitting on every person on campus and locking me out of my own room every five minutes. But I love 'em. They love me."

Briar looks like he's got no idea how to respond to that statement. It's pretty clear that he's never really seen or had this type of friendship before. And that makes me suddenly, immeasurably sad. Because someone as good and sweet as Briar deserves to have friends who drive him crazy with socks on doors and throw pepperoni at him and tell terrible stories about his worst moments just to embarrass him.

Everyone deserves those kinds of friendships. But Briar especially deserves them.

Across the table, Jeremy finally surrenders to Lexy and she stops pummeling him with pizza toppings. "You are ruthless," Jeremy tells her as he takes a sip of soda. "I don't know why you insist on behaving so rudely toward me. And there are guests at the table, no less!"

Lexy laughs. "Briar's not a guest. You're here to stay, right, Briar?"

Briar's eyes widen in surprise. "I guess? I mean, I really like Burlington and my job and everything."

"Then we're keeping you," Lexy tells him bluntly. "Jamie seems to like you, and you work at a kickass place where you can hopefully get me free wine, and Jeremy is Jeremy. I need someone new to entertain me. Someone who has actual problems and interests in life besides whether or not his daddy's boat is going to be cleaned properly so he can use it to get laid on Lake Champlain summer outings."

In a small, almost imperceptible motion, Jeremy winces at the words *actual problems.* Then, just a second later, his face is set back into the smooth, carefree smile that he's worn since I met him on the first day of our freshman year.

"You okay, man?" I ask him.

"Of course. Why wouldn't I be?"

But for the first time ever, I find myself wondering how real Jeremy's smile is. Can you be friends with someone for two years and not know whether their smile is real or not?

I don't get very long to think about that, though, because Jeremy's gone off on a treatise about the boat his dad keeps on Lake Champlain and all his summer plans for it. "Lexy is just jealous," he tells Briar. "She knows that having access to a boat on Lake Champlain means I have infinite game here in Burlington." Lexy rolls her eyes. "Luckily for her, I'm not bothered by her disrespect, and I plan to make sure she and Mindy spend plenty of time on the boat with me this summer. And Jamie, too, of course, if he ever finds the balls to tell his father he wants to work in Burlington."

"I know exactly where my balls are, thank you," I inform Jeremy.

"Have you tried talking to your dad yet?" Lexy asks.

Then, it happens: Briar reaches a hand across the bench seat in between us and grabs mine. Underneath the table, of course, so Jeremy and Lexy can't see us holding hands. But I can feel his, calloused and warm and comfortable, and it gives me the strength to say "nope" in a voice that doesn't even wobble the way it might have otherwise.

Lexy sighs. "J, you need to talk to him," she says softly. "I can't imagine how I would feel if I couldn't do my volunteership at the hospital in Fairlington this summer because my family wanted me to work for them. You *have* to talk to him. Soon."

That's easy for her to say. She has a twin sister who's been dreaming of taking over the family business since she was in the third grade. But that doesn't mean she isn't right. "I know," I tell her. "I know. I just—"

"Well, look who's here!" I'm interrupted by some stranger who's appeared at the side of our table. He's wearing jeans, a baseball cap, a stained winter jacket, and an expression that suggests he's just hit some kind of lottery jackpot. "If it isn't Briar Nord."

Jeremy, Lexy and I all glance over at Briar at the same time, and then back at each other when we quickly notice the same thing.

Briar looks ready to murder someone.

16

WHERE BRIAR SUCCESSFULLY AVOIDS KILLING ANOTHER HUMAN BEING

I should have known.

I should have known I should have known I should have known I should have known.

Those are the only words that roll through my head as Luke makes himself comfortable at our table, pulling up a chair from somewhere else and then introducing himself to Jamie and Lexy and Jeremy like I'm not even there.

"Briar and I've known each other since we were kids," he tells them. "Isn't that right, Briar? In Springfield."

"Oh, you're from Massachusetts too," Lexy says sadly. "I'm really sorry to hear that."

The look on Luke's face when she says it like that, all serious and mournful, would be hilarious. Except for the fact that *fucking Luke* is sitting at a table with me and Jamie and Jamie's staring at him with an expression that could definitely be described as suspicious.

"You're . . . a friend of Briar's?" he finally asks. I realize I'm still holding his hand below the table, and I make a move to let go, but Jamie holds on. I relax my grip into his and let the feeling of his warm fingers wrapped around mine settle into me. A little bit of the tension bleeds out of my body, just for a minute. "Briar's never mentioned you," Jamie adds.

"Yeah? What's the fucking deal, Briar? You never told your new fancy college friends about me?" Luke flashes me an old mischievous grin that I've seen too many times, sharing at least one browning tooth with everyone at the table. "You three are all students at the university here, right? That's probably why he never told you about me. Because he's embarrassed. Briar and me barely got our GEDs."

"I'm not embarrassed," I say clearly, even as a small twinge of shame burns in my belly. I've never told Jamie I didn't graduate high school, and this wasn't how I was planning on telling him. But there's no way I'm letting Luke get the upper hand in this conversation that quickly.

"Good," says Lex. "Because there's nothing wrong with a GED. That's what Mindy has. My sister," she adds for Luke's benefit.

"Okay, okay." Luke holds up his hands like he's surrendering to us all or something. "Didn't mean to get everyone all upset. I'm just surprised Briar never mentioned me before. Should I tell 'em some stories about the shit we used to get into, Briar?" He flashes me that grin again, but it's easy to hear his words for what they really are: a threat, through and through.

Before I can answer, though, Jamie's interjecting himself into the conversation. "What are you doing here in Burlington?" he asks casually, but there's a hint of something under his voice that I've never heard from Jamie before. A kind of defensiveness.

"Yeah," Jeremy adds, and he doesn't sound nearly as carefree or amused as he did a few minutes ago. "And how'd you find us here at good ol' Tito's Wood Fired Pizza, man?"

"That would be a good story to hear," Lexy adds as she wipes tomato sauce off her fingers.

I'm slow when it comes to reading people, so it takes me a few minutes to figure out what's going on: they're, like, circling wagons around me or something. They've all figured out that I don't want Luke here, and they're making sure I know that and he knows that. All without saying the words out loud.

Luke glances over at me again, surprise written onto his face, but it can't be greater than the surprise that must be all over mine right now. I barely know two of these people. And just because Jamie and I are holding hands under the table doesn't mean I expected him to notice how fucking pissed off I am that Luke's appeared here.

But he did. They all did. And for some weird, unexplainable reason, they all just assumed that I'm the one who deserves defending.

Wild shit.

"Well," Luke says slowly. "I ended up in Burlington because I was looking for my friend Briar, and then I decided to stay. It's a nice little city, you know?" I notice he doesn't mention how he found me at the pizza place. I probably don't want to know that detail. "Briar," Luke adds, "like I was saying, we should tell these three all about the trouble you and I used to get into at Hope House. You told them about Hope House yet, Briar? About the things you and I used to do together?"

A new pool of shame and anger burns bright in the pit of my stomach as his threat grows less and less hidden. *I'm going to tell them, Briar. I'm going to tell them and everyone else here who you really were. Who you really are.*

I don't know what to say. I don't know what to do. I don't know how to get rid of him. I don't know how to save V and V from him or keep my coworkers from finding out exactly what I've done and been. My heart feels like it's going to beat out of my chest and my breathing's starting to get a little shallow and strange, and I'm trying to figure out what the hell I'm supposed to say next when—

Jamie squeezes my hand.

It's just a tight, quick squeeze, but it sends a jolt of calm all the way through me. And then Jamie's talking again.

"Sorry, man, we got places to go," he tells Luke as he stands up from the table, pulling me along with him. Luke, Lexy, and Jeremy's eyes all flash to the spot where our hands are still joined together, now easily visible to all three of them. Jeremy's face widens into a grin, and Lexy makes a pleased *O* shape with her mouth. "Lexy, Jeremy, you coming?" he asks. "We can pay at the front."

"Aww, that's too bad." Luke shrugs and stands up too. "Sorry this isn't a good time. But we'll catch up later, won't we, Briar? I'm gonna tell you now that I'm really looking forward to it." He zips up his jacket and heads toward the door of the pizza parlor.

The message is clear: I don't have much longer to either go along with Luke or figure out how to get rid of him.

"What an asshole," Lexy says. "I mean, he is an asshole, right? Is it okay that we basically kicked him to the pizza parlor curb like that? The look on your face when he walked up to us was just so awful—it was worse than the way Mary Ella LeGrande looks at Jeremy when she sees him."

Jeremy sighs. "Ah, Mary Ella. She really did not understand the phrase 'no strings attached.'"

He and Lexy are calmly pulling paper bills out of their wallets to pay for dinner, like they didn't just rescue me from one of my greatest nightmares. "He's a complete asshole," I confirm for them. "An asshole who's followed me to Burlington, unfortunately. Thanks for getting rid of him for me like that. You really didn't have to do that, not at all. Here, let me get dinner for us . . . ." I move to pull out my wallet. I owe them big time, and I'm going to pay for this meal even if it means I end up eating noodle cups for the rest of the week. But Jeremy just snorts and pushes my hand back.

"No way," Jeremy informs me. "We're splitting it, just like we were going to. Asshole-repelling is just part of the friendship contract."

"Exactly," Lexy says, beaming at me. "And Jeremy would know, given that he's the asshole in the room approximately eighty percent of the time."

"Stop underestimating me. It's at least eighty-five percent," Jeremy grumbles as Lexy pulls him toward the counter at the front of the restaurant.

"You okay?" Jamie asks me softly as we fall into step behind them. "The murder eyes you had when that guy walked up were pretty intense."

"Murder eyes?"

"Murder eyes, man. Like, I thought actual lasers were going to come out of them." He hesitates, but only for a second. "Listen. You don't ever have to tell me anything about your past, not if you don't want to. I don't give a shit about that guy or what you did when you were kids together. But if you ever want to tell me, I'm here to listen. You listened to me when I needed to spill some stuff. The least I can do is return the favor."

Part of me wants to take him up on that so badly. I want to put so many words out in the world: the words about Gina and Luke and Hope House and Paul, just to get them a little farther away from me. And then I'd know, I guess, if I get to keep Jamie as a friend no matter what. If he knew all that and still chose to stick around and talk to me and stay in my book club . . . that would mean a lot. That would go a long way toward making me feel like maybe Vermont could be home—like maybe I do belong here after all.

But I'm not ready for that yet. I'm not ready to test that hope out. What if he walks away the second he knows more? I can't take that chance. Not on the same night that Luke showed up at the table where I was having a good time with Jamie and his friends.

"Thanks," I tell him. "Really, I mean that. And maybe I'll take you up on that someday."

Or maybe not, the voice in my head interjects.

17

WHERE JAMIE GETS A REMINDER

We all pile into Lexy's giant truck, and she drives us to the bar. You can tell from the outside that the place is bumping. People are standing around everywhere, talking and laughing and smoking cigarettes and weed, and the music from the bar spills out every time someone opens the door. Two people wearing parkas are making out next to the entrance.

Jeremy rubs his hands together. "I have a very good feeling about this evening," he tells us. I look over at Lexy, expecting the simultaneous eye roll we usually do together when Jeremy goes into full-on player mode, but she's got her eyes laser-focused on the building in front of us. "So do I," she says eagerly.

Okay. It looks like Jeremy isn't the only one in full-on player mode tonight.

We make our way inside and straight into a club mix of a Taylor Swift song. Briar's face brightens immediately. "You're a Swiftie?" I ask him over the music, and he shrugs.

"Kind of. I don't go to concerts or anything. I just really like her music."

"Yeah, me too," I tell him. Taylor Swift writes a great sound-track for an early morning milking alone in a barn surrounded by cows. I wonder if Briar would understand that if I tried to explain it to him.

I have this weird feeling he would. Or at least he'd try.

"Hey, that's Emory!" Jeremy spots one of his buddies from the club soccer team he plays on and disappears into a sea of bodies. I'm not surprised by that—it's pretty rare for me to keep track of Jeremy longer than five minutes at a time when we go out. I *am* surprised when Lexy disappears into the crowd in a different direction a few seconds later with the words "Don't wait up for me, okay?"

"Guess we're getting our own ride home," Briar says, but he's smiling. "Want to get a drink?"

We end up crowding next to each other at a corner of the bar that's standing room only, the entire right side of his body pressing directly into mine. I don't mind at all. Briar gets a beer, and I ask for a soda. "Still got a little time before I can legally order," I remind him.

"What are you going to do for your first legal drink?" he asks me as he takes a sip of his beer.

"Go to V and V, of course. But technically I already had my first legal drink. After we turned eighteen, Lexy and I would sometimes cross the border with friends of ours and check out the bars up in Quebec. One time I had to hold Lexy upright in the backseat so we could make it back through border patrol."

"You should tell that story the next time the bathroom sink comes up."

That stupid story. I laugh. "Yeah, I really should. Sometimes your friends just insist on following you around with your past trailing behind them, right?" I mean it as a joke, but Briar winces. Shit. I wasn't even thinking about that asshole who just showed up at the pizza parlor. "Briar, I didn't mean—"

"No, you're fucking right." He shakes his head. "I know I said it before, but you and Lexy and Jeremy really didn't have to do that, you know? You didn't have to get rid of him for me like that."

His voice is laced with the same surprise it was when he first thanked us. He's that shocked that we all kicked Luke to the curb when he clearly didn't want the guy there. It's moments like these that make me wish I knew just a little more about Briar's past. I'd never push him, of course. He obviously keeps his stories close to his chest, and I respect that. But I wish I understood why Briar's so convinced that he doesn't belong here.

In the meantime, maybe I'll just keep reminding him that he does. I grab one of the belt loops of his jeans and pull his body in a little closer to mine. "Who told you that you don't deserve to have people who care about you?" I ask him softly, and his eyes go wide. "Because I'd like to throw them straight into our manure pit."

"What the fuck's a manure pit?" Briar murmurs.

I burst out laughing. "Exactly what it sounds like, dude." The opening notes of "Freedom" by George Michael come blasting over the bar speakers just then, and I let out a whoop. "I love this song!" I yell over the notes to Briar. "It's one of my mom's favorites. She used to play it all the time."

Briar smiles wickedly and grabs my hand, and the next thing I know he's got me out on the dance floor with him, our bodies moving back and forth together in time to George's words about giving what you take. I'm not the best dancer, but Briar definitely has some moves, and we spend most of the song with him leading me as he pulls me closer and closer into his body. We're only halfway into the second verse when my dick starts standing at attention, and by the time we hit the bridge of the song it's hard as a rock. I let my hand fall away from my body so that it brushes against Briar's groin, and he shudders. He's hard as hell too.

"Briar," I ask. "Do you want to go back to your place?"

"Fuck yeah," he says.

We get a Lyft back to his apartment and hold hands in the backseat the entire ride. The driver's a nice older guy with long gray hair who's wearing a quilted fishing vest. Classical music plays softly through the car's speakers. "You kids have fun tonight," he tells us as he drops us off in front of the giant pink building Briar lives in. "Don't forget to wrap it up!" he adds as he drives away.

Briar laughs. "Guess we're not that hard to read," he says. We're still holding hands, and he tugs at mine ever so slightly, until our bodies are wrapped together on the sidewalk in front of his apartment building. No one's there except us, and the world is quiet. There's just black sky and stars and streetlights and the sharp Vermont air all around us.

I remember what I was thinking that day we were together in the storeroom. "We've never kissed before," I tell him.

Briar studies me intently, his expression serious and thoughtful. Kissing doesn't seem like something Briar does with just anyone, and for a minute I'm not sure how he's going to respond.

But. "Let's give that a shot tonight," Briar whispers into my neck, and then he leads me up the stairs and through the hallways to his small studio.

This is only the third time I've ever been here, but it already feels comfortable. The place is just so Briar—it's filled with books and furniture that's all function over fashion, and it's so softly quiet. It's at the top of the house, away from anyone else who lives here, and the moment Briar closes the door it feels like we've stepped into our own world. Our own space. Neither of us turn on the lights. There's enough streetlight coming in through the front window to light up the area where the couch sits, and we both end up standing next to it, back in each other's arms the way we were in the bar and again downstairs.

I want to do something for this guy, this friend of mine who feels like more than a friend every second that we spend together. I tug my phone out of my back pocket and mess around with it until the sound of Taylor Swift's voice fills the room. It's a song about making rules in a new relationship filled with hope and promise. It's a romance novel in verse, and I watch Briar's face carefully, wondering if I've gone too far by clicking *play* on this song. You're probably not supposed to play romance novels in verse for someone you're just friends with, even if you did meet them at a book club for people who love romance novels.

Briar's face lights up when he hears the first notes of the song, though. "Good choice," he says.

"Yeah, I like this one. You know what the ending is going to be right from the beginning. There's never any mystery that this song ends happily."

"Exactly," Briar agrees. We start dancing together, alone in Briar's tiny studio, our feet bumping as we shuffle around the room. His torso fits perfectly up against mine, and he lays his head down on my neck like it's always belonged there, and I can't seem to imagine being anywhere else in the world except with him. No one in their right mind would call what we're doing *good* dancing, but that doesn't matter to me, and I'm guessing it doesn't matter to Briar either. What matters is the softness. The music. The feel of his cheek against my neck. The way his hair is brushing into my skin every few seconds. It's beautiful and slow and peaceful.

It's a scene right out of a romance novel.

I want to feel his skin against mine more than I've ever wanted to feel anything else. I tug at the hem of the hoodie he's wearing until he takes the hint and lifts his arms, allowing me to pull the sweatshirt, along with the shirt underneath it, up over his head. He follows by slowly pushing my sweatshirt up over my torso and over the top of my body. It hits the floor with a soft thud, and then we're both standing there, shirtless, the skin of our chests together.

The music hits a crescendo as I unzip Briar's jeans and he unzips mine. Our circles around the room have gotten smaller and tighter, and now we're basically just moving around each other's feet as we shove each other's pants and underwear to the ground and take turns stepping out of them. Taylor sings words about forever and ever as Briar takes my dick in his hand and I take his in mine.

And then he presses his mouth into mine, and it's nothing and everything all at once.

This is nothing like Sean and I trying to figure out how to kiss in high school. It's nothing like kissing any other girl or guy I've ever been with before. This is spark and pleasure and all the best crullers I'll ever eat and all the best books I'll ever read. It doesn't seem possible that a kiss could feel this intense, this important. This hot. It's like Briar's holding my dick and sucking me off and pressing his cock into my prostate all at the same time, and all he did was put his lips on mine.

I need him to be inside of me.

"Briar," I whisper into his mouth, and my voice sounds almost pained in my ears. We somehow make it to the bed, with me on my back and him kneeling over me. I can't get enough of his mouth. I can't get enough of his tongue up against mine, of our lips moving back and forth in new patterns together.

Briar whips a bottle of lube and some condoms out from under the pillow. "Figured I should keep these nearby after last time," he says.

"Good thinking." The words come out more like a groan because I've having trouble speaking in complete sentences right now. "You like kissing me," I manage to get out. "I like kissing you. Let's make out while you fuck me."

Briar doesn't answer. He just attacks my mouth with his, and I attack right back. He covers two fingers in lube and gently eases one of them into my hole while I grab our cocks and rub them together. Every inch of my skin feels like it's burning up as we fuck our tongues into each other's mouths. He adds another finger, and then another, until pain and pleasure are woven so tightly together that they're almost indistinguishable. I've been fucked before, but I can already tell this time isn't going to feel like any of those other times. He thrusts his tongue in and out of my mouth like he's letting me know what's coming, and all I want is for every inch of him to be as deeply inside of me as he can possibly be.

I tilt my hips up just a little farther off the bed, letting him know I'm ready.

He sits up to roll on a condom. Then he pushes my legs up and eases the tip of his dick inside of me.

I almost go off right then and there.

"More," I call out as I grab him around the waist and try to pull him deeper in.

"Okay," he whispers. He attacks my mouth with his again as he lets me have all of him in one tight, fast thrust.

I scream. Just a little bit, but I definitely scream.

He jackhammers his dick into my body while he jackhammers his tongue into my mouth, and I grab at his hair, gasping and begging for more, and there's so much sweat between us that he's almost slipping as he fucks me harder than I've ever been fucked in my life. But as much as this is fucking—and it absolutely is, this is fucking in the very most intense sense of the word—this is so much more than that. This is the closest connection I've ever had with another human being, and I absolutely don't want it to end.

But I also know I'm not going to last much longer. Every time he crashes his dick into my prostate he takes me one step closer to the edge. "So close," I say into his mouth.

"Come with me," he says as he wraps a hand around my cock. My body takes his words like an order, and I go off in his hand like a spigot, my body clenching around his, and then it's his turn to yell as he shakes hard inside of me.

Eventually we both go still. He slowly pulls his dick out of my body, each movement a jarring and complicated sensation against my nerves, and then collapses on top of me like he's just run a marathon. I definitely feel like I have. Our muscles relax into each other as he pulls his head up to press a slow, sweet kiss against my cheek. "So the kissing thing worked out," he says.

I laugh. "Yeah, I think so."

And that's not the only thing that's working out.

It's impossible to deny that this is the best sex I've ever had. Or that I crave seeing Briar in weird moments when I really shouldn't. Or that I wanted to mess that Luke guy up tonight when he was bothering Briar.

"Maybe . . . ," I start to say. Then I stop, because what I'm about to say has huge ramifications. What if I suggest a relationship and Briar says he's still not into it? What if he says that's still not what he wants? What if I can't figure out how to step away from the farm?

"Maybe what?" Briar asks sleepily.

Maybe we could do this. For real. I want to say the words so badly. Maybe Briar would say yes. Maybe I wouldn't be such a shitty boyfriend after all.

Just then Taylor, who's been playing on repeat, stops singing. The sound of my phone ringing echoes through the room. Briar rolls off of me. "You need to get that, right?" he asks.

We both know who's probably calling me in the middle of the night. I can't look at him as I force myself off the bed and over to the coffee table. The phone's lit up with a picture of the caller. My mother. My shoulders sag. I'm going to have to leave Briar right after he's just given me the best sex of my life. I'm going to have to abandon this sweet guy, who already doesn't seem to think he deserves nice things, and drive a whole bunch of miles in the cold night air to take care of some cows.

Briar does deserve nice things. And as I move my finger across the phone's screen to answer the call, I remember that I'm never going to be one of those nice things.

Because the cows will always come first.

18

WHERE BRIAR OVERHEARS SOMETHING HE SHOULDN'T

I'm not going to lie: It would have been pretty sweet to have Jamie spend the night with me after the mind-blowing sex we had last Saturday. But I wasn't surprised when he had to ride off to Morse's Line like a white knight. I guess his whole family came down with bad colds, and everyone was coughing too hard to do the milking the next morning. Jamie left, and I read myself to sleep, trying not to relive the amazing sex we had over and over again in my mind.

Eventually I gave in and got myself off again thinking about it. Because the sex was *that* good.

Honestly, there was a moment right after we both came together that I started to wonder if maybe I had this all wrong. Maybe I was being an asshole by keeping Jamie at arm's length. Jamie's clearly nothing like Paul or anyone else I've ever known. He's good and kind and he makes me feel like I deserve things. It's a heady feeling, and I seem to want it all the time lately. I basically crave Jamie when he's not around.

I never craved Paul. Not once. I realize now that should have been a red flag.

So I was about two seconds away from telling Jamie that we should try to be more than just friends. The words were right there in my mouth, and Jamie said the word "maybe" and I thought he might have been about to say the same thing . . . and then his mother called.

It was a good thing she did. It definitely jolted me back to reality. I'm still a fucked-up guy with a bad history and a full-on criminal darkening his doorstep. Jamie's still got obligations bigger than I can even imagine. I'm going to have to find a way to make sure we stay just friends with benefits. This whole *craving* thing has got to stop.

"You good out here, Briar?" Mr. Fletcher says from the other end of the sales counter at V and V. "Mom and I are going to go over the accounts together quickly in the office. We'll be done before your book club meeting starts."

"Sure, of course. No problem." I shake myself out of the Jamie-dreams I've been stuck in. Work's been slow today, but I still need to have my customer service face ready for the next person who comes up to the counter or wants help finding a book or whatever. It's just Mr. Fletcher and me on the floor today. Louie landed a show at some fancy gallery down in Brattleboro later this spring, so he's been working fewer and fewer hours at V and V while he gets ready. I have a feeling he might not be here much longer, especially if the show does well.

I don't like thinking about that, so I try not to.

Mr. Fletcher makes his way to the office, and I take advantage of the empty store by dusting some of the books on display in the front window. April has come into Vermont with a wet flourish, and a steady drizzle of rain is falling outside the window. At least the weather has started to warm up, and the snow is almost entirely gone now. But Jamie warned me that Vermont Aprils can feel just as gray as Vermont winters when they decide to stay rainy.

I don't mind the rain so much, though. I even walked home in it last night, my hood up, the water falling at a steady pace around me like it was trying to wash the earth of all its sins. I tilted my head up into the sky and let it fall in slow droplets across my face, cleansing me.

Of course, it's not really the rain that's cleansed me of any of my sins. It's this place. Far away from Springfield, I've been able to shake off almost every vestige of the life I had there. People like Gina and Paul are distant memories. The things I once did that I've felt so ashamed of feel farther away every day that I'm here, in this quiet city working in this quiet bookshop with some of the nicest people I've ever known.

Except. Except. Except. Except.

Except Luke.

It's been a week since he showed up at the pizza parlor, and since then he's been making his presence more and more known. Text messages have started appearing on my phone, even though I know I never gave him my number, and there was a note on my door the other night. I'm honesty surprised he hasn't showed up at the bookstore yet, but Luke's always been good at pushing and pulling me like a dog on a leash. He always knows just how hard to pull before I'll decide it's too much and stop following him.

He always pulls just enough to keep me in line.

I put a new number in my phone the morning after Luke found me at the pizza parlor. It's the number for the Burlington City Police. There was a time when I never would have even considered calling the cops on Luke, no matter how much he pissed me off or what he asked me to do. But that was before I found Burlington and V and V and . . . people. People who want to stand up for me in pizza parlors. The people in The Booklover Club, which is meeting here in less than an hour.

That was before I met Jamie.

Every morning for the last four days I've opened up that number for the police department and stared at it, trying to decide if it's time to call. Logically, I know it probably is. Luke seems even more unhinged than he was back in Springfield, and that's saying something. It's become clear that he's not going to leave me alone, and he's not going to leave V and V alone.

But if I call the police, there's no way I'm going to be able to keep my past a secret from Mr. Fletcher and everyone else here at V and V. The police will ask questions and it will all come out eventually. They'll find out what Luke wanted me to do, and they'll find out that I didn't tell anyone right away.

I'll probably lose my job. I'll probably lose my apartment. I'll lose this entire life I've built here—the best life I've ever had.

I'll probably lose Louie and Rainn and everyone else I've met here at V and V.

And I'll almost definitely lose Jamie.

Some days it feels like my life is just the same terrible choices over and over again on repeat, and no matter what I choose, I never get to win. It's been that way since before Gina left. Just once I'd like to be faced with a choice where I know I get to be the winner if I make the right decision.

"Damn," I tell the empty room as I realize one of the chapter books at the end of the window display has juice stains on it. It's not the first time we've found out a book has been compromised by a shopper, and it's not a big deal. But now I need to go find another copy of *Mollie Rabbit's Big Day Out* in the storeroom, and I can't remember if we have any more of them.

I grab the stained book, which will no doubt find a good home from its new place on the discount rack, and I head toward the storeroom. Mr. Fletcher and Mrs. Fletcher have left the door to the office open, and their voices drift across the space as I put in the code on the storeroom door.

"It needs to be sold," Mrs. Fletcher is saying. "It's time we found a buyer for that diary. It's too much money just sitting there in that safe."

My spine immediately goes stiff. They have to be talking about the diary Luke wants. As far as I know, it's the only diary worth a ton of money that's sitting in the storeroom safe right now.

Mr. Fletcher sighs. "I know you're right. It will be a huge cash influx. And we need that if . . . ." He must be moving around because his voice suddenly goes muffled, and I can't hear the rest of what he says.

If what? My heart speeds up as I start finishing that sentence in my head. If the store's going to stay open? If V and V is going to keep their employees? Why would they need to sell that book so badly all of the sudden? Are the Fletchers in financial trouble?

Oh no.

I push my way into the storeroom and close the door behind me. Then I grab a rolling chair that's sitting there and sort of fall into it. Nobody's out on the bookstore floor right now, and that's bad. I need to get back out there.

Except. Except. Except. Except.

Except it may not matter whether I call the police or not. Maybe I'm about to lose my job no matter what I do. What if there isn't going to be a V and V for me to work in much longer?

My mind travels back to the last time I was jobless and homeless, to those terrible days after Paul kicked me out, back to the begging I had to do just to find couches to sleep on. The nights I spent in alleyways. They were cold and lonely and so hopeless, and I swore if I got out of that mess I'd never end up back there again. I swore to myself that I'd do anything to keep a roof over my head.

The safe's sitting right in front of me. All it would take is one picture. Just one quick press of a button and then a quick text message to Luke.

It's a whole lot of money in that safe, the voice in my head says. *And you need to take care of yourself.*

"Briar?" I stand up with a jolt as Mr. Fletcher pushes open the door to the storeroom. "Everything okay? People are starting to arrive for The Booklover Club. Why'd you leave the floor?" He's frowning.

Crap. I hold up the copy of *Mollie Rabbit.* "Oh, sorry. Damaged book in the window that had to be replaced." I completely forgot that the club meeting was starting soon. Right now it feels like a personal victory that I can even talk to Mr. Fletcher without my voice shaking.

If he knew what I've been sitting here thinking about, he'd hate me so much.

"Ah, poor Mollie." Mr. Fletcher grins and holds his hand out for the stained book. I pass it over to him. "I'll get her a replacement. You go get set up for your meeting."

I can barely look at him as I walk back out into the store. I wonder if he notices.

"Briar, my favorite bookish darling!" Mrs. D crows. She and Betty are standing next to the couches where we usually meet, and she takes my cheeks in her hands and squeezes. "You've look pale, love. Betty, doesn't he look pale?"

"He does," Betty agrees. She grins wickedly. "I would have thought he'd have more color in his cheeks, given the way he's been dancing with some other members of our book club lately."

"Excuse me?" I choke out.

"We have eyes everywhere, dear Briar." Mrs. D beams. "And our sources tell us that you've been out dancing at LGBTQ night with one Jamie Morin."

"The source is Emily," Betty adds cheerfully. "She was there too."

I feel like I have information whiplash. One moment I'm learning that I may be losing my job, the next minute I'm hearing that the entire club thinks Jamie and I are an item.

Which we're not. Right?

"It was just dancing," I assure Mrs. D. This seems important, since I'm pretty sure Emily has a huge crush on Jamie. "We're not . . . I don't want Emily to think . . . ." I can't seem to figure out how to finish my sentence.

Mrs. D finally lets go of my face and winks at me. "Not what, hon? Never mind, don't worry about it. And don't worry about Emily. Maybe she'll finally stop making a fool of herself in our meetings now."

"That's a bit harsh, Lilah," Betty says as they both sit down.

"Tough love," Mrs. D responds.

Bart and Lucia and Cherry arrive, and everyone starts making small talk about rain and flower beds and vegetable patches and planting season. April is already starting to make me feel like the only person in all of Vermont who doesn't garden. There's no sign of Emily. Jamie appears just as we're about to start, breathless and shaking water out of his hair.

"Sorry. I was in the middle of writing a big paper." He sits down between Cherry and Lucia. "Where's Emily?"

Mrs. D clears her throat loudly. "I don't know if she'll be joining us today. Hopefully next week. Let's just get started, shall we?"

This week we read a contemporary romance about two gay hockey players. Mrs. D picked it. She says she's trying to learn more about the game for "her grandbaby." I really liked it, despite the fact that I know next to nothing about hockey, but I can't focus on the conversation at all. My eyes keep tracking over to Mr. Fletcher, who's working at the register, or to Mrs. Fletcher, who's shelving books and talking to customers as they come in and out of the store.

Are they in trouble? Is the store in trouble? Am I going to lose my job? And how much of an asshole am I because that's the only thing I'm really worried about right now? Shouldn't I be worrying about Taylor and Rainn and—

"Briar!"

"Huh?" I whip my head up at the sound of Jamie calling my name. Everyone in the group is staring at me. "I just said your name like five times. Are you okay?"

"Oh. You did? I'm really sorry. I uh . . . ."

I can't figure out how to answer. I don't feel like making up some excuse about a headache—Betty will just make me rub oil all over my face. And I'm tired of being stuck alone in my head with so many different scenarios for how this amazing world I get to live in is probably going to disappear at any moment. "Do you ever feel like you don't deserve anything you have?" I blurt out.

"Huh? Oh, you mean like Gary, when he didn't think he deserved both hockey and Devontae," Lucia says.

"Uh, yeah, sure." Actually, that makes a lot of sense. *Thanks, Lucia.* "Just like that."

Jamie's sitting back against the couch, his arms crossed, looking thoughtful. He doesn't say anything.

"Personally," says Bart, "I think Gary needed to get his head out of his ass and get some therapy for his PTSD. But what do I know?"

"PTSD?" I ask. "Isn't that something you get if you were, like, in a war?"

"No, no, no." Cherry shakes her head. She's studying psychology, I remember. "PTSD just means post-traumatic stress disorder. It can be caused by any traumatic or highly stressful incident or situation. Or, in Gary's case, multiple traumas."

"But no one ever beat him up or anything," I point out.

"That's physical trauma. Mental trauma, like the bullying Gary experienced, can be just as damaging—if not more so. Bart's absolutely right. I kept waiting for the author to get him into therapy. He was crying for it."

Mental trauma? That can be a thing?

"Damn mental health stigmas!" Betty cries loudly, and everyone in the store looks over at us. "Sorry!" she calls out. "I get excited."

The meeting ends soon after that, with Jamie still sitting back against the couch with his arms crossed. He seems to be studying me, but I can't tell.

We choose the book for the next week, but I refuse to join the debate. What's the point? The store probably won't exist by then anyway. Either Luke will have robbed Mr. Fletcher—with or without my help—or Mr. Fletcher will have announced that we're closing down and everyone's getting fired or whatever. It sucks that this could be my last meeting with The Booklover Club. I spent the whole meeting stuck inside of my head.

I realize I'm spiraling. I know I am. But I can't seem to make myself stop.

Jamie stays on the couch as everyone else packs up and leaves. "Go get 'em, Tiger," Betty whispers in my ear when she notices him still sitting there. Mrs. D rolls her eyes, but she pats both my cheek and Jamie's cheek excitedly before she leaves.

Jamie raises an eyebrow. "Something going on with them?"

"Emily saw us dancing," I tell him as I start sweeping cheddar cheese crumbs onto a plate with a napkin. "Think that's why she didn't come today."

Jamie winces. "Damn. I hope she's not too upset. Hey, Briar, you're off tomorrow, right?"

I am, actually. "Yeah," I say, not sure how I'm going to respond to whatever his next question is. All I want to do is spend time with Jamie. All I want to do is say yes to whatever he's about to ask.

But that's a terrible idea. For so many reasons.

He stands up. "I really have to go finish that paper. But can I pick you up tomorrow at your apartment? Around eleven?"

It's a terrible idea, I remind myself. But my mouth doesn't seem to care about that, because the answer that comes out of it is "Yeah, sure."

I spend the rest of the day and night thinking about what Cherry said about PTSD. I wonder if I have that. I do some quick Googling, and it turns out sometimes PTSD can cause irrational decision making.

But I can't tell anymore if the decisions I make are irrational.

19

WHERE JAMIE INTRODUCES BRIAR TO HIS DEAD DOG

"So where are you taking me?"

Briar's question as he hops into the cab of my truck is a mini minefield. Do I tell the truth? He's going to think I'm nuts.

I go for it anyway. "I'm taking you to meet my dead dog," I tell him as I put the truck into gear and guide it out into the street.

Briar stares at me. "Say the fuck what?"

"Yeah, I know it's weird. But I think it will make sense soon. Maybe." And if it doesn't, then Briar and I are definitely never meant to be anything more than fuck buddies. I could never date someone who doesn't immediately love the place I'm about to take him.

"Okay," Briar says slowly. "I brought food, anyway." He sets a white paper bag in between us. "Donut holes from a place near my apartment. They don't make crullers. Sorry." He grins.

I grin back. "I guess I'll just have to make do." I grab one of the donut holes out of the bag with one hand while I steer with the other. "Thanks."

It's a perfect day outside—sunny and warmer than it's been in months. It feels like spring for the first time, and Briar and I both roll our windows down a little bit. This is one of the reasons I asked Briar to come with me today. I knew what the forecast was going to be, and I knew exactly where I wanted to take Briar on this day when it feels like all of Vermont is waking up for the first time after months in hibernation.

We make the trip up I-89 with the radio playing in the background. "Are we going to Morse's Line?" Briar asks me once, and I just nod. He doesn't ask any more questions.

To get to Morse's Line, you have to drive through Fairlington's main street. Briar stares out the window at the square where he and I ate blueberry pancakes and cotton candy and I spilled the biggest secrets of my life to him. "You must have had the most kickass childhood," he says, more to the window than to me. "I know it wasn't perfect or anything," he adds hastily. "With all the work and stuff going wrong on the farm and all that. But still . . . ."

"Nah, it was pretty great," I agree. "And you still haven't seen some of the best parts of it." That's okay, though, because I'm taking him to one now.

I hope I'm not making a mistake. Briar's clearly not in the best headspace right now, and there's a chance this all could backfire on me. But I don't think it's going to. I'm starting to trust my instincts when it comes to Briar, and I think this place I'm about to take him is exactly where he needs to go.

We drive down long two-lane roads, stopping for a cow crossing and navigating around a large tractor. Briar's eyes get wider as the scenery becomes almost all dairy farms next to each other, the houses just stopping points in between barns and silos and fields.

"That's Tiny Acres," I tell him as we crest over the top of a small hill. Briar sits up in his seat.

Our farm is one of the smallest on this road and in this county, but that's never mattered much to me. I've always liked this view of it. From here you can see the back acres of the farm where some of our dry cows are munching on hay in the grass that's just greening up. You can see the cow pond where Aaron and Lissie and I spent summers chasing frogs and where I still like to read and study on the shore. You can see the red side panels of the barn that stand out like beacons and the large wraparound porch of the farmhouse that's held so many hours of my life.

It was a kickass childhood. And I want to share some more of it with Briar.

I pull the truck into the driveway and park next to Dad's pickup. Briar steps out of the cab and I hold out my hand.

He takes it without saying a word, and I lead him into the house.

No one's in there, which isn't very surprising. Everyone's probably out in the barn doing chores. I only brought Briar in here for one reason, anyway: boots. He stares into the house's huge kitchen while I take us to the long line of rubber boots that always stand at attention in my parents' mudroom. You never know when you're going to need extra boots, so we never throw any of them away.

"What size are you?" I ask Briar.

"Ten."

"That's easy enough." I'm a nine and a half and Aaron wears a ten and a half. I find a pair that should fit Briar. "Put these on," I tell him, and I try not to think about the fact that these were Aaron's. Briar slides them on while I go into the kitchen long enough to fill up two large travel mugs with the coffee from the pot that's still hot on the countertop. You can always count on my parents to have fresh coffee in the house. I hand one cup to Briar and slide my own boots on. "Let's grab those donuts out of the truck and then we can start walking," I say as I open the front door.

"Where are we walking, again?" Briar asks.

"I told you," I call over my shoulder. "We're going to see my dead dog."

I take Briar up the driveway and into the barnyard. The long doors at the end of the barn have been pushed open, a sign that spring really is here. I used to love when we opened the barn doors all the way for the first time after a long winter. "Jamie!"

Mom appears around the corner of the door holding a pitchfork. "Baby, I didn't know you were coming home today. Briar, it's good to see you." She wraps me up in a hug and then gives Briar one too. He does a pretty good job of hiding how nervous he looks. "What are you doing here?"

"Hey, son." Dad comes around the corner. "You're here to do the next feeding, right?" He grins and Mom elbows him gently in the side. "I'm kidding. Oh, hi there. You must be Briar. I keep hearing about that book club of yours. Sounds like Jamie's really enjoying it." He grabs Briar's hand and shakes it heartily. "I've never been into those books like Ellie and Jamie. I'm glad Jamie's found other people down there in Burlington to talk with about 'em. So, son, about that east pasture—"

"No!" Mom cuts Dad off, but they both look like they're trying not to laugh. "Honey, are you bringing Briar down to your spot?"

As long as I live, my mother's ability to read my mind will never stop amazing me. She always just seems to *know* what I'm thinking or about to do. "Yeah," I say. "For a little while anyway. Maybe we can help you with the east pasture when we get back. Right, Briar?"

"I mean, I don't know much about cows," Briar stammers nervously. "But I'm a hard worker, and—"

My dad waves his hand. "Won't be the first time Jamie brought a city boy home. You can't be worse than the one who was afraid of the baby calves."

Briar's face softens. "There are baby calves?"

I laugh out loud. Looks like Briar might be another farm boy in the making. "You can see them later. C'mon, let's get out of here before these two find ten other chores for us to do."

"I've got at least twelve," Dad calls out as we walk away, and Mom adds, "You kids have fun! Watch out for cow pies, Briar!"

"What's a cow pie?" Briar asks, right as he's about to step into one. I grab his arm to hold him still.

"Cow shit." I point to the giant pile of it in front of him.

"Taking a walk on a farm is like stepping into an obstacle course. Watch the ground."

Briar follows me through a grassy meadow where Darla and a bunch of the other younger stock are munching on a large, round bale of hay Dad's dropped into a feeder for them. I stop to pet her head because she's one of my favorites in our herd, even if she does like to knock books out of my hand while I'm trying to read. She nuzzles happily into my arm and Daisy, a Guernsey with a coat that's spotted in bright orange and white, comes up to join her. Briar stops abruptly as I pet them and let them push at me in the hopes that I've brought them grain or some other treat.

"They're huge," Briar says nervously. "Isn't it dangerous to be that close to them?"

"No way. I mean, yeah, you have to be careful not to get your foot stepped on, but these girls are some of the friendliest we have. C'mon. Try petting one of them. Daisy loves it when you rub between her ears."

Briar takes a tentative step forward. *Very* tentative. I guide his hand out and hold it while he gently strokes the top of Daisy's head. She tilts her head upward happily, just like one of the barn cats would when you pet them in the same place.

"See? They're really friendly animals. And they're super serene and calm most of the time. They care about food and water and they like being with each other, and if you give them that, they're happy."

Briar pets Daisy as she pushes into his hand. "Sounds like a life I can get behind," he says softly.

"Me too. I don't want to work with cows the rest of my life the way Dad does, but I really do like them. It's like . . . they see the world on a level I can't even imagine."

Briar nods, and we each pat Darla and Daisy on the head one more time before we start walking again. "You and your dad seem to get along pretty well," Briar says.

"Yeah, we do. I mean, that's what makes talking to him so hard." Briar nods again as I do my best to explain. "It's not just leaving the farm. It's leaving him. He's not getting any younger, and I worry about him working too hard or hurting himself or whatever. Here, follow me." I pull open an old, barbed wire fence gate, and Briar follows me into my favorite place in the entire world.

"Wow," he breathes.

Yup. I knew this was the place to bring him.

We're standing in the middle of a half-circle of four young cherry blossom trees planted at the edge of the forest that runs all around our property. The gate separates the trees from the pasture, so the grass in the middle of the circle is free of cow pies and green with the beginning of spring. The trees themselves are just beginning to blossom, edges of color popping out of their branches, and the air is soft and still and quiet. Only the sound of the occasional chirping bird or a cow's deep bellow in the distance pierces the air.

I sit down on the grass and take a sip of coffee. "Aaron planted these trees," I explain. "I had this dog when I was little. A border collie named Sid. That dog was my life—I loved him so fucking much. He used to wait for me to get off the bus every day. He just stood there, at the end of the driveway, every day at three-thirty."

Briar settles into the grass next to me, only inches from my body. He leans back on his elbows, and soon his left elbow is up against my right hip. Our bodies feel like they fit perfectly in this space and time. Just like I thought they might.

"I joined Boy Scouts," I go on. Briar stays quiet next to me. "And one day I didn't get off the bus. Sid was confused and he tried to chase it, and . . . ."

"Oh," Briar says softly. Sadly.

"Yeah. He got hit by a truck that was driving too fast. Dad said this was the most beautiful spot on the farm, so we buried Sid here. Aaron planted the trees a few years later—he's always been great with making stuff grow. Since then this has always been, like, my place. When I'm stressed out or happy or sad or whatever, this is where I come. Kind of weird, huh? Sometimes I come to a grave to cheer up."

Briar pushes his left hand over farther so that it's resting up against my thigh. "Not weird at all," he says. "This place . . . it's perfect. Why'd you bring me here?"

I hope I haven't miscalculated. I hope I'm right that he's ready to tell me.

"Because," I explain. "I wanted you to know that if you want to tell me all of it—all your shit, the way I told you mine—you can. You don't have to. But you can."

Briar closes his eyes as a quick breeze moves through our little protected space. "I don't tell people stuff," he finally says, and my heart falls just a little bit in my chest. *It's okay*, I remind myself. *He doesn't have to tell you. It's not like you're dating.*

"But I think maybe I want to tell you. I think I'm ready to do that."

I resist the urge to stand up and shout excitedly and pump my fist. Because isn't it weird enough already that we're sitting in the middle of a pet cemetery?

Still, it's hard not to feel like I've won the lottery. Here, in one of my favorite places in the world, Briar Nord has just announced to a cow pasture that he trusts me.

20

WHERE BRIAR SHARES THINGS

"You don't have to tell me," Jamie says again. His voice is quiet against the sound of the wind moving through the trees. He makes a few movements, and soon he's got the fingers of his right hand laced into the fingers of my left, and he's staring up at the sky. The cloud he's watching bears an almost creepy resemblance to a handlebar mustache.

"Weird cloud," we both say at the exact same time. Then we both start laughing.

"I want to tell you," I answer when I can breathe again. "I do. Really. And it's not like . . . I mean, I never murdered anyone or anything like that, okay? I don't want you to get the wrong idea. It's just not a story I tell a lot of people."

Jamie turns his body slightly so that he's lying on his side, looking right at me. "Yeah. Mine was like that too."

I know that telling me about Aaron had to cost him a lot. And he did it anyway. He trusted me with that story, and maybe it helped him to say it out loud.

I wonder if it did. I wonder if saying my shit out loud will change anything for me.

"I'm kind of worried I have PTSD, like that guy in the book

we've been reading for the club," I blurt out. I'm not sure how I expect Jamie to react to that, but he just nods understandingly.

"I guess you could," he says. "Have you ever tried talking to someone?"

"A therapist? Nah. I wouldn't even know how to find one or how to deal with health insurance stuff or what to say once I got there." My entire body tenses up just thinking about the idea. Jamie must get that because he nods again.

"Okay, no pressure. I just wondered. All I'm saying is that if it's something you're worried about, there are people who can help you. A lot of us here want to help you, Briar," he adds. "We like you."

"That's what's so weird." I shake my head. "That's the part I don't get. People don't worry about me like that, you know? Not before I came here, anyway. Well, I guess DeShawn did, but he was kind of the only one . . . ." I expect Jamie to ask who DeShawn is, but he doesn't say anything. "I mean, hardly anyone's cared about me since Gina. I'm not even sure she cared all that much. That was sort of the problem, I guess."

"Who's Gina?"

"She was my mother. She was a waitress. We lived in this apartment in Springfield that was gross and falling apart. She cried a lot. Especially when I tried to ask her questions about my dad."

Jamie doesn't say anything. He just sits there, listening. Like what I'm saying matters.

"But I didn't mind that much, because we were a team. For a long time it was just the two of us. I guess we weren't a very strong team or anything—we definitely lost more games than we won." Jamie responds to my dumb joke with a small smile. "But we were a team."

Jamie squeezes my hand.

"So yeah, it was just the two of us. But then Rick came." My lower lip curls up into a sneer, the way it does whenever that asshole's name crosses it. "He worked at a car dealership, and he made Gina a lot of promises. He said he'd move us to Florida, get us a better house, better food. All that. He bought her cheap jewelry at the pawnshop, and she loved it. She started cutting pictures out of magazines of all the beaches in Florida he was going to take us to."

"Was he nice to you?"

"He didn't like that I was around. He never said it, but I could just tell. Gina didn't tell him about me when they first met, and I'm not sure he would have gotten involved with her if he'd known she had a kid. So I wasn't too surprised when it happened, I guess."

Jamie's eyes narrow. "When what happened?"

"I came home from school one day and they were both gone. All their stuff was gone too. Just . . . gone. They went to Florida without me."

Jamie sits up on one elbow. "Holy shit. How old were you? What did you do?"

"I was eleven. I didn't know what to do, so I didn't do anything. I didn't tell anyone for twenty-two days. I just sat alone in the apartment, went to school, and waited for them to come back. I ate all the food that was left and waited. Then the landlord showed up."

"Briar . . . ." Jamie leans in my direction, like he wants to give me a hug, but I shake my head. If I let him hug me right now, I'll break down in tears or something. I definitely won't finish this story. And there is, it turns out, something weirdly cathartic about saying these words out loud. I've never said all the words of this story out loud to anyone before, but here, in this space, it feels safe. It feels like I can maybe keep going if I just don't stop.

"Things were okay at first. I lived with a family that was pretty good for a while, then one that wasn't as great. Then I ended up in Hope House, which was a kind of group home for older kids they couldn't find placements for. That's when I met Luke."

Jamie scowls, but he doesn't say anything.

"Yeah. He was my first bunkmate there. He was fifteen, and I was fourteen. He drank a lot. He stole even more. He asked me to be his lookout all the time. Gave me beers. I said yes a whole lot more than I should have. I just wanted to be on a team again. I wanted a teammate so, so badly."

Jamie's scowl deepens.

"Sometimes we got caught. By the time I was about to age out of the system, I'd done some time in juvie and I had a record. I wanted to be better than all that, though. I was tired of Luke and his games. I had a new social worker by then—DeShawn—and he was great. He helped me land this job at a restaurant. He tried to tell me that finding a team was a good thing, but I had to make sure it was the right team. He said some teams weren't worth playing on." I shake my head, remembering all the talks DeShawn tried to give me right before I aged out. "I said I'd listen. I didn't, though. I'm such an asshole sometimes."

"No, you're not." Jamie's voice is quiet, but certain.

"Well, I should have paid more attention to him. I was doing okay for a while, on my own. I liked the restaurant job. But then I saw Luke again and he introduced me to this guy Paul, and I forgot everything DeShawn told me. Paul was older, and he was running a crew Luke belonged to, and I was like my dumbass mom when she fell for Rick. I listened to everything he said, and it was all lies. He promised to be my team, and I said yes before I even knew who that fucker was. The next thing I knew I was playing lookout again and doing worse shit than that. He even convinced me to quit my job at the restaurant, and I ended up, like, dependent on him." I can hear the anger in my own voice. "And then one day he disappeared too. Just like Gina and Rick."

"Motherfucker," Jamie whispers.

"I got lucky," I tell Jamie. "I was wrapped up in some bad shit with him, and I probably would have ended up in jail if he'd stuck around. But the whole thing still sucked. I was living with him, so I was homeless for a little while, and I couldn't get my old job back. I was living on couches and in alleys and garages and on any corner I could find. I couldn't get another job and I was starting to feel so fucking hopeless." I pull in a deep, dark breath. "I think I was ready to give up at one point. I know I was. But then this guy Almont, who I also knew at Hope House, found me sleeping in the garage of someone we both knew. He basically yelled at me to get my shit together, and he got me into his guest room, and he got DeShawn back in my life."

"How did you end up here?"

"That's kind of a weird story. DeShawn went to college with Mr. Fletcher, and he heard Mr. Fletcher had started a bookstore up here. He knew that I loved to read and that I'd demolish any book I could get my hands on, and he thought I needed a fresh start. He called Mr. Fletcher and found me some money for a bus ticket and a security deposit, and here I am."

"Sitting in the middle of a pet cemetery," Jamie says quietly.

"Sitting in the middle of a pet cemetery." *With you,* I add in my head.

"Shit, Briar. I definitely get why you like books that you know are going to have happy endings." Jamie sighs heavily. "Briar, you deserve better than all that. You deserve better than the people who treated you like you were worthless. You know that, right?"

I roll over on my back and watch the mustache cloud merge into one that looks something like a mushroom. They float across my field of vision together, forming and reforming through space.

"Sometimes I think I still believe in happy endings," I tell him. "This place sort of looks like one, I guess? With all the fields and the cows, and your parents still love each other. But even this isn't perfect."

"No," says Jamie. "But who ever said happy was perfect?"

I smirk at him. "Said the guy who's killing himself because he can't even tell his dad he wants to be a full-time librarian this summer.

Jamie grins. "Fair enough. I grew up believing happy endings had to be real, and not just because of all the romance novels my mom read. It was my family that made me believe that. My parents didn't have a perfect marriage or anything, but they were happy. And my brother and sister and I were happy. Everything was always a lot of hard work, but that wasn't so bad. We all did it together, you know? It sounds weird to say it, but every day was our happy ending. Even if it wasn't happy."

It doesn't sound weird at all. In fact, it's what I've been looking for my entire life.

"So I believe that you deserve better," Jamie tells me. "In fact, I know you do."

I wish I believed that. But I still can't even bring myself to tell Jamie the rest of the story—why Luke's here in Burlington and what he really wants.

Jamie rolls a few inches, until he's lying up against me. And then, like we're in some fucking Alyssa Samuel novel, he leans over to kiss me.

In the middle of a field, under some cherry blossom trees.

It's not a sharp, intense kiss like the ones we shared the night we went dancing. This one is soft and sweet and slow, and it turns into more soft and slow kisses, where Jamie's tongue and mine are exploring one another and finding a rhythm together. My dick starts to harden in my pants. Jamie does some maneuvering and soon he's kneeling above me, pushing some stray hairs out of my face, and whispering, "Let me take care of you."

And then he does. With his hands and his mouth and every other part of him.

And in those perfect, beautiful moments, lying somewhere between pure ecstasy and a young cherry blossom tree, I start to wonder if maybe I really could deserve Jamie Morin.

21

WHERE JAMIE TAKES BRIAR ON AN UNLIKELY DOUBLE DATE

I'm not sure exactly what just happened in that field. But I have this weird feeling that Briar might be my boyfriend now.

Except I'm not sure he thinks the same thing.

I realize we should probably talk about that, and maybe examine the details of whatever we are a little more closely. But right now Briar looks sort of shell-shocked, and I don't blame him. He just spilled twenty years of pain all over my dead dog's grave, and now doesn't seem like the time to bring up conversations about putting labels on whatever this "it's complicated" situation really is.

I'm not sure I'm ready to do that anyway. If Briar and I are starting something here, then that means I have to *really* commit to having some hard conversations with my father. And I'm not sure I'm ready to do that either.

Briar and I arrive back in the barn hand-in-hand. "Hey, son," Dad calls across the barnyard. "Your mom and I were just about to take a break and go over the border together to that bakery we all like. You want to come?"

This is a somewhat rare moment in Morin life: my parents taking time off together. One of their favorite things to do is drive across the border and go to this bakery that makes the best croissants. That actually sounds like the kind of thing Briar and I need right now: a few moments in another country, where maybe we could pretend that none of the hardest parts of our lives are real. But you need either a passport or an enhanced driver's license to cross the border, and I doubt Briar has either on him. And there's no way I'm going anywhere without Briar right now. "I don't think Briar has the right kind of license," I say.

"I think I do," Briar says quietly. "The special one? The one that lets you cross into Canada? They asked me if I wanted it when I got my new license. It didn't cost much more, so I figured, why not?"

"Right answer!" Dad says. "You're goin' to live this close to another country, you better be able to visit it. Mom's already in the house showering. I'll finish up here and then we'll be ready to go."

"Is Lissie coming?"

"She's over at her friend Erin's practicing for their next recital."

This will be a first for me, then: a double-date with my parents. I wonder just how strange this is going to feel.

It ends up feeling surprisingly *normal.* Almost too normal.

Mom and Dad and Briar and I all pile into the Subaru, with Mom and Dad in the front and me and Briar in the back. Briar seems tired, but he manages to answer the questions Mom peppers him with about where he's from and how he likes V and V. The three of us end up talking about the new Alyssa Samuel novel that's about to come out, and Dad focuses on the road and listens to us. Occasionally I see him glance up in the rearview mirror at me and raise his eyebrows. Like he's trying to say *I like this guy.*

Just what I need. More pressure.

Morse's Line has such a small border crossing that there's only ever one person on duty there, and she asks us a few questions in a deep French accent about weapons and drugs. Then she waves us through.

"I thought that would be a bigger deal," Briar says. "She didn't even check to see if we were lying about the guns."

"We cross here a lot," Dad tells him. "They know what red flags to look for, and we don't raise them. Although one time when Ellie did her grocery shopping over here she brought some grapes back that weren't allowed in the US, and the border agents sure did have a temper tantrum over that."

"They threw them away," Mom says grumpily. "I was excited to try those grapes."

"The bigger border crossings get more traffic and have longer waits and all that," I tell Briar. "But this one's always been small. People here go back and forth all the time." I point out a house that's behind us now. "That property's actually on both sides of the border. It happens here. Borders cross people and all that, you know?"

Briar stares at the house, wide-eyed. "That's so weird," he says softly. He looks back at Mom and Dad. "So you do your grocery shopping in Canada sometimes?"

"They have ketchup potato chips," Dad replies easily.

"Which are disgusting," I add. "But Dad loves them." Aaron did too.

The first few miles over the Morse's Line border don't look all that different from the American side: just miles of farmland with barns and silos and houses scattered in between. You can only really tell you're in another country because the signage is all in French and the speed limits are in kilometers. But Briar stares out the window like he's never seen a road or a tractor before. I guess he's never seen French-Canadian ones.

Dad turns down a long, narrow road, and we start passing the signs for the Wine Route that winds through this part of Quebec. "Are there wineries here?" Briar asks.

"It's becoming a big industry in this part of Quebec," Dad tells him. "The bakery we're going to is connected to one of the wineries. Owned by the same people. Too bad I can't hold my ice wine."

"He really can't," I tell Briar. "Last time he and Mom brought some home he had some with dinner and got smashed. Lissie and I had to finish chores."

"Ice wine?" Everything Briar says is a question right now.

"You make it from frozen grapes. They're known for it up here," Mom explains. "We can get you some at the bakery. But we'll make sure Frank just sips." She winks over at Dad, and then stretches her hand out across the front seat. He takes one of his off the steering wheel and places it into hers, and the other hand stays firmly in place as it guides the car forward.

Briar's eyes come completely away from the window, and he stares at where their fingers are intertwined together.

Dad turns the van off the main road and steers it down a side road covered in signs for the LeChambeau Vignoble et Boulangerie. I've been here with my parents before, but not very often, and usually it was with Aaron and Lissie. Everything about this day feels different, and the winery even looks different somehow. It's too early in the season for the grape vines to be bright green and covered in fruit, but you can see the long rows of plants stretched out over fields, and I feel like I'm seeing them through Briar's eyes. He's got one eyebrow raised as he studies how far back they go. "I didn't even know you could get grapes here."

"You can. And luckily for my carb addiction, you can also get pain au chocolat," Mom informs him solemnly.

Briar smirks at me. "Why do I always end up eating baked goods when I'm with you?" he asks.

"Because carbs are delicious," Mom answers while I'm trying to come up with something super witty to say in response.

From the outside, the buildings that make up the winery and the bakery don't look all that special. There's just a large barn and a house standing next to each other, remnants of an old farm that's been converted into the business. But whenever I walk into the house where they serve baked goods and do wine tastings, I always feel like I've stepped into part of old-world Europe or something. The floors are stone and the counters are all wood, and everything's decorated to look like something out of the past century. There are pictures everywhere showing the history of the property, and Briar stops to look at each one of them as we make our way over to a table.

My French vocabulary isn't great despite the fact that I studied it for four years in high school, and Dad's accent is terrible even though his vocabulary is decent, so Mom does the ordering for us. "Dad and I are going to share a glass of the ice wine," she tells us. "But I got you two boys a tasting."

"Oh, yeah. You can drink here, can't you?" Briar asks me. I know he's thinking about our night out together at the bar.

"Yeah. And I can handle my ice wine better than Dad."

Dad nods, not remotely ashamed.

The server arrives with flights of wine for me and Briar, a small glass for Mom and Dad, and plates of chocolate, plain, and almond croissants for all of us. Briar looks like he's about to have an orgasm when he takes his first bite of croissant—and I would know. "Holy shit, that's the best thing I've ever put in my mouth," he says.

"Thanks a lot," I mutter under my breath. He kicks me under the table.

"Seriously, I thought The Maple Factory was good. But these things . . . ." Briar devours the rest of his croissant and then basically chugs two tasters of wine as a follow-up while Mom and Dad smile at him. This part of Quebec has always been a place they love to visit. I know the fact that Briar's enjoying it so much is making them really happy.

The four of us devour an embarrassing number of croissants and Briar drinks a lot of wine. He's definitely buzzed by the time the two of us end up wandering around the vineyard while Mom and Dad place orders for croissants to take back to the farm. They like to store them in the giant freezer in our garage.

"I wonder if Tanner and Mr. and Mrs. Fletcher know about this place," Briar asks as we sit down on a bench next to a row of grapevines. "I don't think they carry ice wine at V and V. But maybe they do? I don't spend much time in the wine bar. I should ask them. Or maybe I should bring some wine back for them to try. I should do that, shouldn't I?"

I kind of like seeing this side of him. He's all loose and open and talking like he's not worried that he's going to say the wrong thing and make me disappear. It's refreshing.

"Yeah, that's a good idea," I tell him. "They may already carry some of the Quebec wines. But if they don't, I bet they'd like that you thought to tell them about this place."

Briar buries his face in his hands. "They're such good people," he says into his palms. "Jamie, I'm fucking it all up. I'm going to ruin everything for them."

Where the hell did that come from? "What are you talking about?" I ask him, stunned.

And then Briar tells me another story, his second one of the weekend. It's short and quick and to the point. It's all about that asshole Luke, and a safe, and a diary, and my eyes stay wide with shock the whole time he's telling it.

I open my mouth to respond just as Mom appears.

"Boys?" she calls. "Are you ready to go?"

Shit.

22

WHERE BRIAR TAKES A CHANCE

Shit. Shit. Shit. Shit. Shit. Shit.

Shit.

That's all I can think the entire drive back to the farm. Jamie's mom—who keeps insisting I call her Ellie—wants to talk about the last book she read, a historical romance she really liked, so I do my best to sober up and listen and nod and respond in sentences that make some kind of sense. But the entire time I've got the corner of one eye on Jamie.

He's nodding at his mom too, his expression completely normal. Like I didn't just tell him I'm thinking about ruining his favorite business of all time—not to mention the one I work for—because I can't seem to stop being a criminal who associates with criminals.

What the actual fuck is wrong with me? Why did I tell him? He could turn me over to the cops. He could tell Mr. Fletcher. He could never speak to me again.

And *that,* I realize, is the one thing I'm most worried about. I'd rather get fired or spend the rest of my life in jail than never hear Jamie Morin's voice again. That thought is weird, and more than a little unsettling.

But it is what it is.

I somehow make the drive back without having to ask Jamie's dad—Frank to me, apparently—to pull over so I can throw up all over the side of the road, even though the wine and the croissants are churning around in my stomach in a very uncomfortable way. I can't figure out if I'm relieved or terrified when we pull into the Morins' driveway and pile out of the van together.

"Do you two have to head back to Burlington?" Ellie asks us cheerfully.

Jamie glances over at me. "Yeah," he says. "I think we do."

She stuffs our arms with bags of croissants that I very definitely do not deserve, and she kisses my cheek and hugs Jamie goodbye. Frank shakes my hand. "Hope to see you around again, son," he tells me. "We gotta get you on the milking schedule."

"You're hilarious, Dad," Jamie calls out to him as he gets into the truck. I follow him, even though I'm sort of surprised to find that he's willing to be in a vehicle alone with a common criminal like me.

"So," Jamie asks cheerfully as he pulls out of the driveway, "What did you think of Canada?"

I turn to him, stunned. "That's what you want to ask me right now?"

"Well, yeah. You've never been to another country before, right? So it's kind of a big deal."

I just stare at him.

"Okay," Jamie says. "We need to talk." He steers the truck off the road and onto some dirt drive I didn't even notice, and the next thing I know we're parked in a pull-off next to a cornfield. "This is Morin land," Jamie informs me. "No one's going to think it's weird if we sit here in the truck for a minute. I can tell you're freaking out. So freak out all over the place, Briar."

"Of course I'm freaking out," I tell him through clenched teeth. "I just told you that I'm about to be an accessory to a huge theft. And you're just sitting there asking how my day's going!" I shake my head. "I'm not a good person, Jamie. I've never fucking been a good person. I don't know why you're even sitting in this truck with me."

I'm not sure what I expect Jamie to do just then, but it isn't what happens next. He slides across the bench seat of the truck, pulls me into his arms, and holds me.

Just holds me.

I melt into his body, feeling the worn cloth of his sweatshirt against my cheek and the pressure of his arms around my torso. I can't remember the last time someone held me like this. It was probably Gina, a very long, long time ago. Paul wasn't exactly a hugger.

"I don't deserve this," I mumble into Jamie's sweatshirt.

"Yeah, you do," he says quietly. "You deserve everything, Briar Nord."

I soak the words in as I soak in the beautiful heat of his body, and I try to decide if I believe them.

Eventually I get myself together and sit up, and Jamie starts talking again.

"What are you afraid of?" he asks me.

That's a loaded question, and it takes me some time to figure out the answer. "I'm afraid of Luke . . . of what he has the power to do, you know? I'm not quite sure how much Mr. Fletcher knows about my record and all that—I don't know exactly what DeShawn told him. And Louie and the other people at V and V definitely don't know any of that. I'm afraid of Luke outing me, I guess."

Jamie nods understandingly.

"And I'm always kind of low-key afraid of running out of money and ending up homeless again. Then I heard Mr. Fletcher talking about selling that book, and now I'm more afraid of that happening than ever. I'm afraid that the store's going to close and I'm going to end up screwed." I stop for a moment and try to put my next set of words together. "I guess I'm mostly afraid of losing what I have here. This is the best place I've ever been, you know? I don't want to lose all that."

"Yeah, I get that," Jamie replies softly.

He would. He's propping up an entire farm on a few hours of sleep and a prayer right now just to make sure he doesn't lose the place and the people who make up his entire world.

"I can't do it," I tell Jamie. "I know I can't. I can't do this to Mr. Fletcher or Tanner or any of them. I don't know what to do."

Jamie nods. "Hey, Briar? That night at the pizza place, the night Luke showed up. What did you think Lexy and Jeremy and I were going to do when he walked in?"

I frown as I think about it. "I'm not sure. I guess I was worried that maybe the three of you would like Luke or something. That you'd listen to him and whatever shit he said about me."

Jamie nods again. "Did that happen?"

"Okay, I see where you're going with this." And I do. I remember now, the shock that moved through me as Jamie and Jeremy and Lexy all stood up for me one by one. "I guess it didn't surprise me so much when you were there for me, since you know me and all. But Lexy and Jeremy had just met me."

"See, I think that's what you keep underestimating about yourself, Briar." Jamie's got one hand on my leg, and I sort of wish he'd pull me back into his arms again. That felt really, really good. "You don't realize that people see who you are right away—that we see the goodness in you, the kindness. You have so many more people in your corner than you think. And we're not all going to just disappear, even if the worst happens and V and V closes or something."

"Yeah? You think?" I ask.

"I *know*."

Jamie starts up the truck again, and we drive. We drive through Morse's Line and Fairlington and Jamie steers the truck back onto the highway, and neither of us says very much. We're halfway back to Burlington when Jamie brings up Luke again.

"I get why you're having a hard time walking away from Luke, Briar. I really do. You're not a bad person for wanting to have things."

"Are you sure about that?" One of his unruly curls has gone haywire by his right ear, and I itch to push it back into place. *What if one of the things I want is you?* The words rush through my mind so quickly that I barely stop them from spilling out of my mouth.

"Yeah. Look, I don't know what's going to happen if you talk to Mr. Fletcher or go to the police. I really don't. Maybe you will lose your job. Maybe the store will close someday. I can't tell you those things aren't going to happen. But I can tell you that *if* any of those things happen, I'm not going anywhere. I'll be your team. You know?"

The way he says the word *team* sends a charge of pure emotion right through me. That, I realize, is what I've been afraid of losing the most: the tiny little team I've built for myself here.

I wish we weren't driving down a highway right now. I want to crawl into Jamie's lap and curl up in his calm certainty. But I can't do that, so instead I just soak in the comforting warmth of his truck cab, and the smell of his shampoo, and I pull a croissant out of one of the bags Ellie gave us and eat it all in three bites.

I don't know what Jamie and I are going to be in the future, but somehow over the past few weeks he's become my team. I know his darkest fears and secrets. He knows mine. I know most of his body better than I know my own at this point.

I know who he is better than I ever knew Gina or Paul or Luke or anyone else who's been in my life.

"I need to talk to Luke," I tell the floor of the cab. "I need to tell him I'm going to the police if he doesn't get the fuck out of Vermont. I can't let him hurt V and V, Jamie."

Jamie nods. "Okay," he says. "Then that's what we do."

The word *we* echoes through my head long after we get back to Burlington.

23

WHERE JAMIE GETS A TEXT

Monday dawns bright and sunny, with forecasted highs of sixty-five degrees and a fifty percent chance of me and Briar getting ourselves killed.

I hope that's a huge exaggeration. It should be. All that's going to happen today is that Briar's going to tell Luke he doesn't want to be involved in his plan and that he's going to the police if Luke doesn't get out of Burlington. Simple, right? I'll just be there for backup. Briar says that Luke's never been the violent type—I guess he prefers blackmail and manipulation to fists and guns. Still, we both know this guy is unstable, and I'm still not sure we shouldn't have gone directly to the police.

"I think that's more dangerous," Briar finally decided. "We don't have any proof, so it would be our word against Luke's, and the police might not be able to do anything. And I don't know how Luke would react if I sold him out to the police like that. But if I just tell him to get lost and threaten him, the way he's been threatening me, I think he might get the message. Luke understands threats."

Still, as I catalogue books during my evening shift at the library, I can't help but check my phone every thirty seconds. Briar convinced Luke to meet up with him at his apartment tonight after we both get off work, and we're waiting to hear what time he's coming.

"Got a hot date tonight, killer?" Lexy appears at the checkout desk with Jeremy by her side. She nods at the phone sitting next to me on the counter. "You're watching that thing like it's about to blow up."

"I'm waiting to hear back from Briar," I tell her testily.

"Oooooooh." Jeremy plasters on a wide and wicked grin. "Are you finally going to make an honest man out of that boy and start dating him?"

"Right, sure." I grab the scanner to check Lexy's books out for her and try to keep my voice as low as possible. Because I'm a *good* librarian. "You, of all people, know I don't have time to date. I don't even have time to see you, and I live with you."

"Yeah, but I'm also not the one you moan about in your sleep."

"I don't moan about Briar in my sleep!" I hiss. Do I?

Jeremy's grin gets a little wider.

Lexy grabs her books off the counter. "You'd have plenty of time if you'd just talk to your dad," she whispers.

Like I don't already know that. I glare at her. "Briar doesn't want a relationship, anyway," I mutter. "And don't you two have anything better to do than bug me? Shouldn't you be studying or something?"

"I probably should be, yes," Jeremy says mildly, and Lexy sighs.

"You and Briar already have a more intense relationship than I've ever had with anyone I've dated," Lexy says. "Own it, okay? Whatever label the two of you decide to put on this, you are *not* just friends."

I'm trying to figure out a response to that when my phone buzzes. My heart sinks when the wrong name flashes across the screen: Dad.

911 EMERGENCY. Cows got out of north field. All over the road and in woods. Getting dark soon. Need help STAT.

"What?" I almost yell the word out loud—in a library. I catch myself just in time and manage to say it at a somewhat reasonable volume. "How the hell did they get out? What the fuck is wrong with that fence?"

"What's the matter?" Jeremy asks.

"Emergency at home," I mutter. "Somehow our stupid cows got out of the field. And they're all over the place and it's going to get dark soon." This isn't good. I have another hour on my shift at the library, and a quiz I need to study for, and I'm not sure when Briar and I need to meet up with Luke . . . but Lissie's away at some guitar thing right now, and Mom's not going to be able to chase them. Lissie was just texting me about how much her hip is bothering her. This is very, very bad.

"I have to find my boss and text Briar and . . . ."

Jeremy and Lexy glance at each other. "Or maybe," Lexy says softly, "you could tell your dad you can't go?" Jeremy nods.

I have no idea how to respond to that. "And do what?" I ask. "Leave my dad to chase a bunch of large animals all over the road and through the trees in the spring mud in the dark by himself?" Is she fucking crazy? "I have to go."

By the time I get back from talking to my boss, they're both gone. At least Darcy was cool and understanding—she grew up on a dairy farm, too—so I've got permission to leave early, and I jet to my truck as I call Briar. He doesn't answer, so I end up having to leave a voicemail.

"Hey. I've got to run to Morse's Line for a farm emergency. I'll be back as soon as I can. Text me what time Luke wants to come over and I'll make sure I'm back by then!" I'm not even sure any of that makes sense, but I don't have time to figure out if it does. Every extra second it takes me to get back to Morse's Line is an extra second something can happen to one of our stock. Or my dad.

It's moments like these when I miss Aaron the most. I wish there was some other person on the planet I could call right now who would get why I can't just abandon Dad. But would Aaron even get that these days? He abandoned all of us, didn't he?

I make it up to Morse's Line in record time and find Dad trying to coax a cow out of the road and through one of our pasture gates. The sun's already getting low in the orange and pink sky, and he tosses me a flashlight. "It's like whack-a-mole," he yells to me from across the pavement. "There's a hole in the fence somewhere. Every time I get 'em back in, more get out. Can you find where the problem is?"

"I'll find it," I assure him. *And I've got to do it quickly.* At least there haven't been any texts or calls from Briar yet. If we can just figure out what's going on with this fence, and I can just get back to Morse's Line before—

Oh shit.

I've found the hole in the fence, it seems. It's a large section of barbed wire that's been shoved to the ground. A few posts look like they rotted out, and somehow Dad and I never noticed. Three cows come charging toward me when I get to them, hoping for hay or treats. I nuzzle their noses. "Look what a mess you girls made," I chide them. This is going to take forever to fix. But I've found the problem, at least. If we can just get everyone back in, we should be able to temporarily fix it pretty quickly. I can still be back in Burlington in a few hours.

Darla, who never can resist begging me for food, nudges at my pockets. "I don't have anything for you," I scold her. She pushes on, her wet nose knocking at me incessantly while I study the fence post. "Listen," I tell her, "if you'll just let me finish this—"

Crunch.

The sound of something cracking grabs my attention, and I look away from the post just in time to see Darla step down hard on my phone, which she apparently knocked right out of my pocket.

"Darla!" I risk getting stepped on and dive under her to grab the phone away from her hoof. I've got a good phone case, but it's no match for that much weight and force. The phone is a goner. "Darla!" I shout, like yelling at the poor cow is going to bring my phone back to life. *"What did you do?"*

Immediately I start going into problem solving mode. I don't remember Briar's number, but I can use Dad's phone to call V and V. They probably have his number, right? In fact, Briar might even still be there. Yeah, that could work. I just have to get the cows back into the pasture and get back to Dad and—

And then, because my life is my life, Mr. Lewis appears in the falling light at the side of the fence. My heart drops into my stomach. Mr. Lewis is my old gym teacher from Morse's Line Elementary, and he lives next door to us. He wasn't a bad gym teacher, but he's an awful neighbor. Especially if you're a dairy farmer with cattle that occasionally wander into his garden patch. "Hey!" he screams. "Those animals of yours are on my property again!"

It must be all the years of yelling at little kids to do more push-ups, but Mr. Lewis has volume behind him when he speaks. His words boom into the pasture, and four of the cows startle at the sound of him.

The next thing I know they've all charged across the battered area of fence and into the darkening woods behind us.

Oh fuck.

Briar, please don't freak out when I don't answer your texts right away.

Briar, please don't meet Luke without me.

Briar, please don't think I'm abandoning you.

As I fall on my ass trying to grab Darla before she makes it all the way into the trees, I wonder if Jeremy and Lexy may have been right about everything they said to me back in the library.

24

WHERE BRIAR TAKES A STAND

It's nine forty-five, and there's no word from Jamie.

When I first got his message about the cows earlier, I wasn't all that worried. I hadn't even left work yet, and I hadn't heard from Luke. No big deal, right? How long could it take to get a couple of cows back into a field?

Then I got a text from Luke saying he'd be over around ten. No problem. Jamie had to be back in Burlington by then, I figured. I texted Luke back telling him to come over before I messaged Jamie with that info.

Then I spent the last hour of my shift at V and V checking my phone, waiting for a message back from Jamie. Louie tried to make jokes about me waiting for a hot date, and I sort of snapped at him a little. I apologized later, but I still feel shitty about it.

The problem is that about two seconds after I texted Jamie, I realized exactly how much I want him there when Luke comes over. I still remember the first time Luke talked me into doing something I didn't want to do. We were kids back in Hope House, and he wanted to steal some liquor out of Mr. Barnett's office, and I wanted nothing to do with the whole stupid plan. He kept calling me a baby, and I kept waiting for someone else in the common room with us—anyone—to back me up and be on my side. But everyone else sided with Luke. When Mr. Barnett caught us, I got in trouble too, even though I hadn't drunk a drop of the stuff.

No one's ever been on my side against the Lukes of the world before. Just knowing Jamie was going to be by my side today gave me this sense that maybe things would be different this time. Maybe I'd finally be able to hold my own against Luke and come out on top.

I pace the apartment, trying to decide what to do. Do I text Luke back and tell him not to come? That's probably what I should do. But what's the point? What if we reschedule for two or three days from now, and Jamie gets caught up in another farm emergency?

He warned you, says that obnoxious voice in the back of my head. *He tried to tell you he couldn't guarantee that he'd be there for you. He warned you over and over.*

Logically I know that the voice is right. Jamie's never been anything but honest and up front about where the farm sits in his list of priorities. Still, as each second ticks by and my text message alert stays silent, I start to feel resentment creeping through me.

"Fuck this," I tell my empty apartment. "This is why I don't like to depend on other people for stuff. You know?"

The furniture remains stubbornly silent.

"Maybe," I tell the couch, "I should change my mind. Just tell Luke I'll do it. It's not like Mr. Fletcher's going to put me first either. If V and V goes down, he's going to forget about me too. Just like Jamie. Right?"

There's no word of response from the cushions, and I throw one across the room at the wall at the exact same time there's a loud knock at the door.

Oh fuck.

My heart races uncomfortably in my chest as I try to get control of myself. I can't let Luke see that I'm even a little rattled when I open the door. Maybe I'm the only one here, but it's still just him and me. I can do this. I can say whatever I need to say to him.

Too bad I'm not sure what that's going to be anymore.

I wrench the door open, and—

Oh big fuck.

Luke's standing there with two guys behind him.

"Hey Briar." He grins wickedly at me. "Meet the guys who are gonna get rich with us."

These are the last people on the planet I want to do anything with—even get rich. All three of them look strung out as hell. Luke's eyes are blown so wide his pupils have almost disappeared, and one of the guys standing behind him is so fidgety he looks like he's about to crawl out of his skin. The other one's rocking on his feet and twitching his neck back and forth like a cartoon character. He's missing several front teeth.

But that's not what sends a wave of terror through me. Nope. That would be the gun that Twitch has holstered on the hip of his jeans.

"No guns in the apartment," I try to say, but my voice comes out more like a squeak. Luke just snorts and pushes past me, and his goons follow.

"This is Trace and Joe," he says, gesturing first to the fidgeter and then to the guy who's packing. "So. We're here. You got what we need to get into that fucking safe already?"

My hand automatically goes to my pocket. No vibrations whatsoever from my phone. *Where the fuck is Jamie?* I'm starting to think he was right—we should have gone to the police. I'm going to guess that Joe doesn't have the proper documentation for that handgun he's carrying.

Not that it matters. I'm stuck in an apartment with three guys who are tweaking out, and one of them has a gun. Whether or not he has the right paperwork for it is really the least of my concerns.

"So?" Luke jumps up on his feet slightly, clearly agitated. "Are we goin' or not? We got bills to pay, Briar, and I've been patient. You texted me, said you wanted to meet up today. We got ready." He takes a step toward me. "You're not chickening the fuck out on me, are you?"

"Luke," I say hesitantly, "I never told you I was going to—"

"Fuck!" Luke grabs onto a book that's sitting on the table next to him and sends it flying toward my head. His aim is terrible, though, and it hits the wall behind me, leaving a slight dent in the drywall. "You fucking didn't get what we needed, Briar? What the hell is wrong with you?" He advances on me, grabbing the front of my shirt in his hands. "What the fuck is wrong with you, asshole?" he screeches. "You think you can get away with messing with me, you little fucker?"

I'm frozen in place. I've seen Luke angry plenty of times before, and I've always known he messes around with meth and shit, but I'm never been around him when he's tweaking like this. I've never been this afraid of him before. Right now he looks angry enough to rip my head off with his bare hands. "Did you get it or not?" Luke yells.

He's loud enough that I say a silent prayer my neighbors will hear and call someone, but I know that's not likely. I'm on the very top floor of the house, and I've got it all to myself. That's one of the things I like about my apartment: I don't have to hear any of my neighbors, and they don't have to hear me.

"Luke," I say hesitantly, "I'm not trying to—"

Now Joe steps in, pushing the right side of his jacket slightly away from his body so that the gun there stays front and center in my vision. "Oh, you're not trying to do nothin'," he says in a low voice. "Except take us to that motherfucking store and get us into that safe."

Trace steps up beside him.

Joe pulls out the gun and presses it against my belly.

"Let's go," says Luke.

The ride to V and V is surreal. I'm sitting in the back of an ancient Ford Explorer with Joe, and the radio's playing soft rock. Apparently the last thing I'm going to hear before I die is Wilson Phillips telling me I just need to hold on for one more day.

The advice is both unironic and unappreciated.

I need to get a message to someone. Anyone. I keep one hand in my pocket, trying to figure out if I can text 911—is that even a thing you can do, can you text 911?—without anyone else noticing. But as jumpy and tweaky as Joe is, he's got his eyes everywhere, and they're on me every five seconds. This is not looking good.

Then I remember something weird.

Months ago, Louie was messing around with the voice command option in my phone, trying to teach me how to use it. I told him not to bother. When the hell was I ever going to need to use voice commands? I don't even drive. And I hardly had anyone to call or text then, anyway. I hadn't even met Jamie yet.

"You never know when you'll need to get in touch with someone while your hands are full," Louie told me. "Trust me, Briar, you'll be glad I dragged you into this century with the rest of your generation when that day comes."

My heart speeds up again—not that it's really gone down since we left the apartment. Could this idea work?

I've got to try. We're almost at V and V, and I'm almost out of time. Once we get to the store, Luke's going to see that the doors have a coded lock, and he's going to expect me to know the code. If I enter it, V and V is potentially fucked. If I don't, I'm probably going to die.

And you never even got to see Jamie one last time.

Fuck that voice in my head; I don't have time for it right now. "Hey, Joe?" I say. "Uh . . . should we use *Assistant, text Louie I need you at V and V right now bring police send* to make sure we get to the store the fastest way?"

Joe looks completely bewildered. "What the fuck are you

talking about? Who said anything about the police? He's talking about the police!" Joe booms into the front seat.

Luke nearly wrecks the car jerking the steering wheel. "What the hell, Briar?" he yells.

"No, never mind! I was talking about keeping the police away," I say quickly. "It was just a question. Never mind. Ignore me." And Joe is either stupid or high enough that he just eyes me suspiciously.

Thank goodness.

In my pocket, my phone vibrates quickly against my leg.

I have no idea what that means. Did the text go through? Did it go to Louie or someone else? Did what I sent even make sense?

Joe glares at me. "Don't say police like that again," he tells me, jabbing a finger toward my chest. "I mean it." He pushes the gun he's holding into the soft flab at the side of my stomach, and my heart beats in my throat.

Luke parks on one of the side streets near Church Street. My next hope is that someone sees us and realizes something's not right with the four of us. It's pretty early for a robbery, after all. Some of the restaurants and bars on Church Street should still be open. Even the V and V wine bar might still be open—I can never remember exactly when it opens and closes. Not to mention that there are apartments above the store and the bar.

Unfortunately, I know it's a long shot that anyone's going to notice I'm in the middle of being kidnapped. Church Street isn't exactly bumping at this hour on a Monday night, and if Luke's spent any time scoping out the bookstore at all, he should know it has its own loading entrance in the back. You can easily get to the alleyway where we load stock without stepping onto Church Street, and that area isn't visible from the bar or the other surrounding businesses. I'm not even sure you can see it from the apartments. If Luke takes us directly to that alleyway, there's a good chance nobody will notice us until it's too late.

I've only been inside a church a handful of times in my life, but I find myself praying hard that my text message to Louie went through.

Luke must have done some homework, because he knows exactly how to lead us through dark, silent alleyways to the back entrance of the V and V bookstore. For some reason all I can think of is the story Mr. Fletcher told me about the day a load of chickens arrived here. What I would give for a load of chickens to show up right now.

A coded lock sits by the door handle, haunting me with its blinking red light. "Okay, Briar," says Luke. "We're here, and we're not waiting anymore. Get us into that store." His blown pupils jump erratically, making him look like a character from an eerie horror movie, and I notice a skin sore on his neck I haven't seen before. Against all odds, I feel sorry for him.

I remember when he was just a kid trying to make a few bucks off candy bars and score some liquor to get drunk and forget the world. I remember all the sadness we both carried into that room where we shared bunk beds. That could be me standing there instead of Luke. It really could. But somehow he ended up with Fucknut and Asshole, and I ended up with the people at V and V. How did that happen?

But the answer is in the question itself. The answer *is* the people at V and V, and the people who led me here. The answer is Almont and DeShawn and Mr. and Mrs. Fletcher and Louie and, of course, Jamie. It's the million little things those people have done for me. They kept me far enough on the side of hope that I never resorted to what Luke's resorted to. Luke and I have both always wanted teams of our own so badly—that's all we ever wanted.

He just happened to find his in the worst way possible.

"Luke," I say, and it surprises me to hear that my voice is more of a croak. "Please don't do this. Please . . . please just don't."

"Is he going to help us or not?" Trace asks anxiously. He's shaking, and it's not all that cold out. That can't be a good sign.

Luke's expression looks familiar. I saw it right before the last time we got arrested together—the last time I was ever arrested. There was a car that kept parking in our neighborhood. Some old sports car, bright red. I know now that it probably wasn't worth more than a grand, but at the time Luke and I were fascinated by it. It was bright and shiny, and it looked so impressive. Luke got obsessed with it. He was going to drive that car one day, he said. I always laughed at him.

Until he dragged me to the car and told me to stand guard while he hotwired it. He'd been watching videos on YouTube, he said, and he'd figured out how. He had this look in his eyes that day, like nothing I could do or say would stop him. I didn't even try.

I didn't try then. But I can now.

"I'm not going to help you." I say the words as loudly and as clearly as I can, even though they stick in the back of my throat. "I'm not going to hurt these people. They're good people, Luke. Even if I did know the combination to the safe—which I don't—I wouldn't give it to you. I won't hurt these people like that. They've been great to me. Really great."

Luke advances on me, grabbing my shirt again the way he did in the apartment. "Are you fucking kidding me?" he snarls. "You string me along like this, making me wait, just to tell me you're not going to do this one fucking thing for me? After everything I've done for you?" There's a tiny click in the background, and I know Joe's just done something with his gun. "You know you're just fucking yourself over, right? I'm going to make sure they know all about you, Briar. You don't help me now, you won't have a job here tomorrow."

"He's not going to be alive tomorrow," Trace growls.

I've never believed that your life actually flashes through your mind before you're about to die. But a picture does appear in my mind just then: me and Jamie, lying in the field behind his farm, in that pet cemetery in the middle of a grove of cherry blossom trees. I wonder if it's weird to hope that you'll be buried next to someone's dog when you die. I wonder if it's weird to hope that you'll be laid to rest on the land of someone who didn't care enough about you to show up when you needed him.

Then again, I'm also grateful Jamie didn't show tonight. I wouldn't want him here with me right now. Jamie's innocent in all the ways I never got to be innocent, and I would never, ever want his life to be in danger because of my fuckups. If he'd been in the apartment when Luke got there, who knows what could have happened.

At least he's safe. That's what matters. Jamie is safe, and he's safe because he stayed away from me.

That thought is what gives me the strength to say, "It doesn't matter what you do to me. I'm not going to help you."

Luke's eyes widen, and then three things all happen at once.

One: Someone shouts "Police!" into the darkness, and a body appears in the streetlight just behind Joe.

Two: Joe makes a jerky movement with his arm, and a loud *crack* echoes through the air.

Three: Something strong and sharp hits my ankle, just below the calf, and hot, white pain blooms bright there.

I hit the ground as the world erupts in yelling and chaos.

Things drift in and out, and I think of Jamie. I think of cherry blossom trees and crullers and donuts and croissants and haunted schools and Alyssa Samuel and all the books we never got to read together.

It was so stupid of me to think that someone as good as Jamie would ever put me first.

It was such a good thing he didn't.

Because I think I've just been shot. And I would never, ever want Jamie to be shot.

My mind wanders. It would be nice, I think, if I could just see Jamie one last time. The pain in my leg is making it hard to concentrate, and I'm starting to think I'll never see him again. A strange face comes into view over me. "Sir?" says a voice.

"Tell Jamie," I whisper, "that he's even better than donuts.

And probably croissants. And tell him not to be sorry. I'm sorry."

That's the only thing I manage to say before everything goes dark.

25

WHERE JAMIE WAITS

"There are few places filled with more simultaneous sadness and hope than a hospital waiting room."

That's a line from the book *Lost Soul,* and it's all I can think about as I sit on a hard, plastic chair in the Emergency Room of Fletcher Allen Hospital. I can't stop jiggling my right knee back and forth. It's sometime after midnight, and Briar's still not out of surgery. Louie's sitting next to me, snoring lightly, and two men I hardly know are on the other side of him, whispering quietly to each other. Louie introduced them to me as Harrison and Tanner. Harrison owns V and V and Tanner runs the wine bar there.

I replay the events of the evening in my head for the thirtieth time, as if this time I might be able to finally change them. First I went to help Dad, and then Darla stepped on my phone and all hell broke loose when more of the herd scattered into the forest. Dad and I spent hours rounding them up in the dark. At one point I grabbed his phone from him and tried to call V and V to get in touch with Briar, but he'd already left. I asked for his cell number, but whoever was on the line said they had a policy against giving out an employee's personal information.

So once we finally got the cows back inside the pasture and into a secured area of the fence, I told Dad I had to go right away and I took off. Then I did the only thing I could think to do: I drove directly to V and V.

I'm still not sure exactly *why* that's where I went. Logically, I probably should have gone to Briar's apartment first. That was where we were supposed to meet Luke. But when I got off the highway, I found myself steering toward Church Street, and V and V is where I ended up.

The place was in chaos. There were blinking lights and cops and an ambulance, and no one would tell me what was going on. Louie was there, and he recognized me. He told me Briar got shot, and I lost track of time for a while after that. Somehow I ended up sitting in the hospital waiting room, waiting for Briar to get out of surgery.

Every time I go through the story again, I think of all the things I should have done differently. I shouldn't have gone to the farm. I shouldn't have dropped my phone. I shouldn't have chased after the cows before I tried calling Briar.

Shouldn't have shouldn't have shouldn't have.

But the one that I keep repeating to myself over and over again is the most obvious. *I shouldn't have gone.* I should have told Dad I had an important commitment in Burlington and I couldn't leave. I should have put Briar first.

Instead, I did what everyone else in Briar's life has always done to him: I let him be the second-place priority. And he got shot.

Someone in an EMT uniform comes into the waiting room. "Is anyone here with Briar Nord?" she asks.

Harrison, Tanner, Louie and I all spring out of our seats. "We are," Tanner says. "Is he still in surgery?"

"I think so, yes." She nods. "Is one of you named Jamie?"

The other three whirl around to look at me. "That's me," I say. My voice sounds like it's been dragged over sandpaper.

She nods. "I just wanted you to know that he passed a message along for you before he lost consciousness at the scene. He said to tell you . . . ." She cocks her head, like she's trying to remember the exact wording. "That you're better than donuts, I think? And something about croissants? He said not to be sorry. He said he was sorry."

My knees start to shake, and Louie has to lower me down into the chair as I lose it completely and start bawling my eyes out. Everything's starting to hit me now. Briar was *shot*. He was all alone, and he was probably scared shitless, and he was *shot.* And while he was on the ground, not knowing whether he was going to live or die, he was worrying about me and telling me not to be sorry about something that I *absolutely* should be sorry for.

"Jamie," says Louie, "the doctors said he's going to be okay."

They did. They said they were confident in their ability to heal the damage the bullet did to Briar. That doesn't matter, though. Tonight I just became one more person in Briar's life who let him down. One more person in a long line of people who haven't been there when he needed them.

So I cry. I cry and cry and I end up crying so hard that at some point Louie pulls me into a hug and I fall apart all over him, which should be embarrassing but I really don't care. Not even when his partner/husband/whatever shows up.

When I finally drift into sleep, it's welcome, even if it is across a row of hard, uncomfortable chairs.

"Jamie?"

I jerk upright, rubbing at my eyes because they're stuck together slightly. *You've been crying,* I realize. I eventually get them open and a quick look at the scenery around me brings everything back.

Briar. The cows. The shooting. The surgery.

Louie's there, staring at me with concern. "Briar's awake. He's asking for you."

It takes me a minute to put his words together in my mind.

"Oh," I finally say. "Oh. So . . . he's . . . ." I can't seem to finish the sentence. Louie smiles, a little sadly.

"The doctors say he's going to make a full recovery. He'll need physical therapy, but he shouldn't have any lasting damage."

The tension goes out of my body so quickly that it's a good thing I'm sitting down. If I was standing there's no doubt I'd fall the fuck right over.

"Do you want to see him?" Louie asks gently. I'm not sure what happened to everyone else who was there, but it seems to be just the two of us in the waiting room. I nod, and then I let him lead me blindly down stark, bright white hallways.

"You should talk to him alone," Louie tells me when we arrive at a door. "I'll wait here."

I nod again, more to the door than to him. Then I push the door open.

Briar's eyes are closed. He's lying in a hospital bed, surrounded by monitors and IVs, and there's a large lump under the covers where his right leg is. His eyes flutter open, just wide enough for him to see me, and he seems to push them open out of sheer will. "Jamie," he says softly.

"Briar." I choke his name out. "I'm so sorry. I . . . ."

I want to go stand by the side of his bed. I want to hold his hand and hug him and promise him that I'll never, ever let him come second again.

But that's a promise we both know I can't keep. I stay by the door.

"Don't be sorry," he says. His voice is even, his face somewhere between neutral and pained. "Please don't be sorry, okay? I'm glad you didn't come. If something had happened to you . . . ." He doesn't finish the sentence.

"But if I'd been there, I could have—"

"No." Briar's interruption is clear and very calm for someone who's just had their body cut open. "You wouldn't have been able to do anything. You probably would have just gotten hurt too. I'm glad you weren't there. And you always warned me, you know?

You told me right from the beginning that the farm would always come first. You always said it. I always knew the farm came first."

Everything he's saying is accurate, but the words are like a dagger slowly sinking into my stomach.

You told me right from the beginning that the farm would always come first.

I shake my head. "But I promised. I said I'd be there."

Briar's eyes are starting to close now. "It's okay, Jamie. It's okay. I'm not good enough for you anyway. I could have gotten you killed. And the farm is going to come first, right? That's how . . . it's . . . supposed to be." Briar's words start to slur, and I can see he's starting to drift into sleep. "You should . . . go. We were right. Maybe we can be friends. But that's it, you know? That's all . . . that's all we get. That's all I get. We can't be anything . . . more."

Part of me wants to shake him and beg him to stay awake so I can tell him that he's wrong—he's *too* good for me. I'm the one who's not good enough for him. I want to tell him I can put him first. I can get it right from now on. I won't leave him alone again when he needs me.

But I can't say any of that. Not without lying.

Briar's sleeping softly now, and I stay in the doorway, barely aware of where I am until I realize I'm shaking. At first I think I'm shivering because of sadness. Then I realize this isn't sadness that's coursing through me. This is anger. Red, hot anger. The kind of anger I don't think I've ever had before.

I watch Briar sleep. I watch him for a long time—probably longer than I should. I watch, and I shake. Then I shove my way out of the room and into the hallway.

"What—where are you going?" Louie asks me as I push past him.

"Morse's Line!"

The trip there is a blur. I have to take a bus back to my truck on Church Street, since Louie drove me to the hospital, but the ride barely registers in my brain. The long drive up I-89 doesn't either. It's just after six a.m. when I pull into the driveway of Tiny Acres

Dairy. The sun is only beginning to pull itself up behind the barn, but the lights inside the barn are burning bright, and I can hear the milking system running inside. Dad's doing the morning chores.

I walk into the barn on auto pilot.

"Jamie?" Dad's standing next to one of my favorite cows, Evie, with a milking machine in his hand. "Everything okay? Last night you said you had to get back to Burlington. It's six o'clock in the morning, son."

"Briar got shot," I blurt out, and Dad's eyes go wide. "Briar got shot, while I was supposed to be there to help him, but I wasn't. Because I was *here*, chasing some fucking cows in a field with you. Because that's where I always am when you call, Dad. *Here.* Even if I should be at the library or studying or hanging out with Lexy and Jeremy or *keeping Briar from getting shot,* I'm not. I'm always here. I have been ever since Aaron left, and I can't do it anymore. I don't care if you never talk to me again the way you won't talk to Aaron. I love this farm and I love you and Mom and Lissie so much, but I can't keep making choices like this. I can't keep putting everything else second. I can't keep giving up everything that matters to me."

Dad just stands there, staring at me, looking stunned. But I'm not done yet.

"I got offered a job this summer. It's at one of the libraries on campus, and I want to take it so badly. I've been afraid to tell you, did you know that? I've been afraid you'd let me go the way you let Aaron go, I guess. But I'm done being afraid, Dad. I can't be afraid that I'm going to lose you and Tiny Acres anymore. Last night I almost lost someone else—someone who means a lot to me —because I was afraid to say no to you. That's not on you—it's on me. But I'm not going to do it anymore."

Dad just keeps staring. Evie nudges gently at his leg with her nose.

And then I do the one thing I've probably needed to do for a long time: I turn around, and I leave.

26

WHERE BRIAR LEARNS STUFF

"You need to eat something."

Louie's just echoing what many medical professionals have been saying for hours, and logically I know he's probably right. It's been a full day now since my surgery, and broth and Jell-O and other clear, unappetizing foods have been arriving in my hospital room. The nurses keep prodding me to eat them. Apparently clear liquids are some sort of important step in my recovery plan? Just looking at them makes my stomach hurt. The doctors seem concerned that the antibiotics I'm on are having some kind of adverse reaction in my system, but I know it's not the antibiotics I'm taking that are the real problem.

The real problem is that Jamie walked out of my hospital room and hasn't come back. That makes sense, since I basically told him we were done with whatever the fuck it is we've been doing. But it still hurts.

The real problem is that Mr. Fletcher is coming to visit me in about five minutes. He knows everything that Luke told the police. So I'm definitely losing my job in about six minutes.

I think that would be enough to ruin anyone's appetite, even if they weren't coming off of major surgery.

Some people just don't get to have nice things, and I'm destined to be one of those people.

Louie's doing something on his phone. "Harrison's on his way up now," he says. He stands and stretches, and my stomach turns over again. I push away the plastic container of Jell-O that remains untouched on the tray next to my bed. "He's here already?" I ask.

"Yup!" Louie cheerfully slides the phone into his pocket. "I think I'm going to grab some coffee while you guys visit. That okay?"

Something strange dawns on me: Louie hasn't left the hospital once since I was admitted. At least I don't think he has. He was here when I woke up from surgery, and he's been here every time I've woken up since then, including when Jamie visited. I think he even slept here, on the weird pull-out loveseat thing that's set up near my bed. "Of course it's okay. You can go home, you know," I tell him. Doesn't Sam miss him? "You don't have to, um, stay here with me."

Louie just smiles. He looks tired, I realize. "I'm not going home. Sam and I firmly believe that no one should ever be in a hospital alone. Especially after they've just been shot." His face darkens slightly, just as there's a soft knock on the half-open door.

"Hello?" That's Mr. Fletcher's voice. The Jell-O suddenly looks grosser than ever, and my stomach turns over.

"C'mon in, Harrison," Louie calls. He pats my shoulder gently as he crosses the space to meet Mr. Fletcher in the doorway. "Hey, it's good to see you. I'm going to run down to the cafeteria and grab coffee. Do you want anything?"

I miss the rest of their conversation because I've got my eyes closed and I'm trying to get my breathing back under control. Is it my imagination, or is one of my monitors suddenly beeping louder and faster?

"Briar?"

I force my eyes open at the sound of Mr. Fletcher's voice. He's sitting on the loveseat, next to a white bakery bag and a giant basket filled with more items than I can identify. "I brought you donuts, but Louie said he's not sure if you can eat them yet. We can ask the nurse the next time she does rounds. The basket is from Mom. She wanted to come with me, but I convinced her we shouldn't crowd you. Expect at least ten text messages from her later." He smiles slightly. "How are you feeling?"

How am I feeling. I assume he doesn't mean spiritually or emotionally. "Okay. Mostly pretty numb right now. I think that's the meds, though."

Mr. Fletcher laughs. "Yeah, I hear they have you on the strong stuff. Listen, Briar—"

"I'm so, so sorry, Mr. Fletcher," I blurt out. "You don't have to fire me. I'm quitting. I know I almost got you robbed and this whole thing is all my fault and I don't deserve to keep my job. I love V and V and I really never meant for this to happen and—"

"Briar, stop!" Mr. Fletcher puts a hand on my arm, looking alarmed. "First of all, I keep telling you to call me Harrison. Now calm down, okay? Getting that worked up can't be good for you right now. And why are you apologizing? I understand from the police that you were shot because you were refusing to give up the code to the store. You stopped V and V from being robbed, Briar."

I shake my head. "Luke—the guy who was trying to rob the store—he's been around for a long time now. Like, weeks. I knew what he wanted. I should have told you. The police. Someone."

Mr. Fletcher's eyes widen with surprise, and he sits up slightly. I guess Luke left that part out when he talked to the police—and that's the most surprising thing I've heard in a long time. Was Luke trying to *protect me*?

That's definitely a question to examine later. Much later, when Mr. Fletcher's not staring at me with a mix of curiosity and confusion.

"Why didn't you tell me what was going on?" he asks quietly. "I talked to DeShawn and told him what happened. He sends his best, by the way. He said Luke's been getting you into trouble for a long time. You could have told me, Briar. I would have helped you."

"I . . . ." I can't look Mr. Fletcher in the eye, so I concentrate on staring at the Jell-O instead. "He offered me money. He wanted to steal that diary, the one you have in the safe?" Mr. Fletcher nods. "He offered me a cut to help him, and he threatened to tell you things about my past that would make you want to fire me. Then one day I heard you and your mom talk about selling the book, and I got worried that maybe the store was in money trouble and was going to close or something, and I was going to lose my job." The Jell-O is firm in its plastic prison, unmoving no matter how hard I stare at it. "I got worried about a lot of things, and I didn't handle stuff the way I should have. And then when I did try to handle it, I was too late." I can't look away from the Jell-O. I can't look at Mr. Fletcher. I can't watch his expression turn to something like disdain or disgust.

Everything's quiet for a few long moments. Then Mr. Fletcher says, quietly, "Briar, can you look at me?"

I force myself to move my gaze off the Jell-O and onto Mr. Fletcher. His eyes are soft with kindness. "I'm so sorry," he says, "that you didn't feel like you could come talk to me about what was going on. I could have told you that I don't care about your past. All I care about is that you're a great worker who loves books and makes my store better. I could have told you that V and V is doing just fine—we're not in any kind of money trouble, Briar. That's an area where Mom and I are very lucky." He smiles slightly. "I keep items like the diary around because I used to work with antiquities, and I enjoy dealing in rare books. Mom and I are thinking of selling the diary so we can reinvest the money into wine bar events and more bookstore staff. V and V is doing very well, and it isn't going anywhere, Briar. Neither are you. You're one of us."

I didn't cry when Jamie left last night. Maybe that's part of the reason I suddenly start crying and can't stop, since this doesn't seem like a normal amount of crying to do over a bookstore. I'm sobbing and sobbing and Mr. Fletcher grabs my hand and holds it, and he even makes these weird soothing noises like I'm an animal that's upset.

"I was so scared when Louie called me and told me about that text you sent him," he says. "Mom, too. And we weren't scared for the store. We were scared for *you*. Every single person at the store is worried about you right now. Don't believe me? Here." He opens up another small paper bag I didn't notice before and pulls something out. It's the copy of the book The Booklover Club is reading right now. "Open it," he insists.

I push open the front cover. On the inside, every single V and V worker has left a message or a signature—everything from Rainn's *Did you seriously get shot?! GET BETTER* to Tanner's slightly more serious *take care of yourself and we'll keep the donuts coming your way.*

I never even realized they knew how much I love The Maple Factory. Or that they'd all care this much if I got shot.

"I hope you plan to work at V and V for life," Mr. Fletcher says over my sniffles. "Because there's no way I'm letting someone go who literally got shot protecting my store."

And then I'm laughing but I'm somehow still crying, and I didn't know that was a thing a person could do but I guess it is. We talk for a little bit, mostly about books and the new store display window, and I only notice how long we've been talking when my leg starts to throb slightly.

Louie reappears at some point with coffee. "How long until he's discharged? Who's going to look after him when he gets out?" Mr. Fletcher asks Louie, like I'm not even there. In a way I feel like I'm not. I feel like I'm floating above my body, looking down on this strange, new Briar who has friends that stand in his hospital room talking about what he needs and who's going to take care of him.

"The docs think maybe tomorrow." Louie smiles at me. "Then he's coming home with me and Sam, if he'll have us, so Sam can force feed him homemade soup. You know how he gets when he's worried. I think he's made six pots of his butternut squash bisque already."

The thought of Sam's amazing cooking, along with the thought of the donuts that are now sitting next to my bed, has my stomach growling for the first time in what feels like days. "I'm going home with you?" I ask Louie.

"The doctor says you shouldn't be alone right now, and you've got all those stairs—is that okay? Briar?"

I can't answer because I'm crying again. I'm not sure I've ever cried as much as my entire life as I'm crying on this one day in Fletcher Allen Memorial Hospital.

It feels good, though. Like I'm washing years and years of loneliness and fear out of my brain and my body.

The only thing that won't seem to wash clean is the thought of Jamie. A memory of him by the cherry blossom trees stays with me long after Mr. Fletcher has finally left and Louie's snoring on the loveseat.

The memory follows me into my dreams.

27

WHERE JAMIE LEARNS STUFF

"Get out of this bed."

"No," I moan into my pillow. "I won't. You can't make me."

Covers disappear off the bottom half of my body, leaving me and my Holstein-themed black and white boxers exposed to the air. "You better fucking believe I can," Jeremy mutters. "Lexy, grab some jeans from his drawer."

"Lexy is here?" I push just enough of my face out of the pillow to see her rummaging through the built-in dresser in the corner of my dorm room. "What's Lexy doing here?"

Lexy pulls a pair of pants out of my bottom dresser drawer so hard that two other pairs come flying out with it. She leaves them on the ground and marches over to me. "I'm here because you're a mess who hasn't gotten out of bed all day, and Jeremy is worried as hell, and you're not answering your phone since that cow stepped on it, so now your mom's worried too and she's calling me."

"I'm fine." I bury my head back into soft cotton. The world is full of a family I can't deal with and a relationship I can't have. At least my pillow still loves me. "Tell Mom I'm fine." The words are muffled by the pillow, but it doesn't matter much anyway since Lexy rips the thing right out from under my head.

"What's wrong with you?" I sit up, rubbing my temple where I just banged it into the headboard. "Are you trying to maim me?"

"Nope." She throws jeans into my face. "Get dressed. We're going to Morse's Line."

"No, we're not." I toss the jeans back.

"Yes, we are." The jeans hit me in the chest this time.

"No, we're not."

"Yes, we—"

"Stop it!" The sound of Jeremy's yell freezes both of us in place. Jeremy may be the life of the party, but he is *not* a yeller. I think I've heard him yell maybe three times in the entire time I've known him, and drinking games were involved in all three cases.

"This. Stops. Now. Put your pants on." His voice is so authoritative that I immediately take the jeans when he hands them back to me. "Lexy is right. You're a mess, and I get why you're a mess, but Lexy and your mom have a plan to fix it. And you're fucking lucky to have a mom who does things like text your friends and try to fix your problems for you, *so put your damn pants on and get in the car with us.*"

Lexy and I just stare at him, mouths wide open.

"See?" says Jeremy. "I can be serious sometimes. Now put on your pants," he orders me. "We have places to be."

I pull on my jeans while Lexy hands me a Henley shirt. "You and my mom have been talking? What do you mean she has a plan to fix this?"

"No more questions." Jeremy pulls me off the bed. "You did good, Jamie. You did what we've been begging you to do. You talked to your dad."

"I yelled at him and then stormed out of the barn," I mutter.

"I agree that you could have shown a little more charisma in your approach." Lexy smirks. "But in your defense, the love of your life had just been shot in the leg."

She has a point.

"Anyway," Jeremy goes on, "you got the ball rolling, even if the circumstances weren't ideal. Now it's our turn to help you."

I let them steer me out of the dorm and through the parking lot into Jeremy's Audi, and I listen to them bicker about music options all the way to Tiny Acres. I don't ask what's going on, because I'm not sure it matters. Why would it? Dad hates me. The farm's probably going to go under without my help. And Mom couldn't fix things between Dad and Aaron, so how's she going to fix things between Dad and me?

"I should have just stayed in Burlington," I mutter as Jeremy makes the turn onto our road.

"None of that negativity," he says over the front seat. "Just promise you won't freak the fuck out when you see who's at the farm."

"Why would I freak out? Is . . . ." I can't bring myself to say the thing I hope for most: *Is Briar there? Is Briar at Tiny Acres?*

I know that's not possible, though. There's no chance he's even out of the hospital yet. So who could Jeremy be talking about?

He pulls the Audi into the farm's driveway, and I know the answer right away.

Parked in front of the milkhouse is an older, black Jeep—a Jeep I haven't seen in a very long time.

"Aaron's here?" I whisper.

"Good, you're not freaking out," says Lexy cheerfully. "C'mon. Your mom planned a family conference. I just agreed to get you here. And I brought some ideas, but—"

"Jamie!" One hundred pounds of tween hits me right as I get out of the car. "Lissie," I say into my sister's hair. At least I haven't lost her—not yet. She's right here, in my arms.

"You jerk," she hisses into my neck. "You haven't been answering your phone! Were you just going to stop talking to me like *he did?*"

Oh, crap. "I'm sorry," I tell her. "Darla stepped on my phone, and I haven't gotten a new one yet. I should have borrowed a phone. I shouldn't have disappeared on you."

"I shouldn't have either." The quiet, low voice behind Lissie has my head up in seconds—because it's a voice I haven't heard in a very long time. Months. So many months.

There's Aaron, standing just a few feet behind Lissie.

Looking at Aaron has always been a little like looking into a distorted mirror. He's a slightly taller and more muscular version of me. He's got the same curly hair, though he keeps his cut close to his head, and the same eyes and the same cheekbones and chin. Mom used to dress us in matching outfits when we were kids.

Lissie steps slightly away from me. "He came back," she mutters. "But I'm not speaking to him yet."

Aaron winces. "You have every right to be mad, Lissie," he says softly. "And you do too, Jamie." He sighs. "I should never have taken off like that and just left you both behind." He glances at the barn off to one side of us and the house on the other. Jeremy and Lexy have disappeared, but I have a feeling they're not far. "I should never have left this place behind like that. I was mad, but that's no excuse. Mom called. She told me . . . she told me things were bad for you. Really bad. I knew I couldn't stay away anymore. I knew I had to come home."

I'm still digesting the fact that Aaron is standing in front of me when Mom appears at the side door of the house. "Jamie, is Briar all right?" she calls across the driveway.

Now it's my turn to wince. I start the walk to the house, Lissie clinging to my side. Aaron falls in step behind us. I let myself go as I bury myself in my mom's arms on the doorstep of the house I love. She smells like beef stew and hay, and I almost start sobbing right into her sweater. "He's going to be okay. But we're not."

I'm not sure what Briar and I ever were, if we were anything at all. But I know that we're not okay.

"Oh, hon." Mom smooths my hair and holds me tight. "Sweetie, I know it's not too late. Let's fix things here, okay? And then you can go fix things with Briar."

I lift my head up for a moment and realize Dad's standing behind her. I expect his expression to be one of anger and frustration—the same expression he wore the day Aaron left. But he just looks sad.

Immeasurably, horribly sad.

"Come inside," he says softly. "All of you. We need to talk."

The five of us end up sitting together in the den on the two old couches that live there. Jeremy appears with a tray of tea, which is weird. I didn't know Jeremy could even boil water. Lexy is with him, and she leans over to whisper something in my mom's ear. My mom nods and squeezes her hand, and then Lexy and Jeremy disappear again.

I take a sip of the tea, just because it's there. It's good. I should get Jeremy to make me tea more often.

Aaron sighs. "I think I need to talk first here. I owe all of you an apology. After Dad and I had our fight last August, I should have stayed in contact. I shouldn't have just cut you all off like that. I was hurting, and I didn't know how to make that hurt stop, so I tried to do it by forgetting all of you instead." He shakes his head. "Not only was it impossible, but it just made everything worse. For me and for all of you. I'm sorry."

"What did you fight about?" Lissie asks anxiously, and I'm instantly glad she did. We all know broadly what that fight must have been about, and I'm guessing Dad's told Mom all the gory details, but Lissie and I have never known exactly what Dad and Aaron said to each other the day Aaron left.

"What we've always fought about," Aaron says miserably. "What we owe to this place. What we owe to each other." I haven't seen him and my father make eye contact once since we sat down, but now Aaron looks at my dad long enough to lock eyes with him. "I said some shitty things. I told Dad I couldn't be tied to his dreams anymore, which wasn't fair. This place has given me so much, and I love it here. I've always loved it here. I love the land and the animals and working with all of you, and I love that this place helped pay for me to go to college so I could get into law school. But I was mad that day, and I was tired, and I said a lot of things I regret now."

"Me too, son." Dad's words are soft but firm in the warm room. This is the same room where we put up the tree and open presents every Christmas, the same room where we used to curl up together and watch TV after chores and dinner, and watching my dad and Aaron apologize to each other here feels like the rightest thing in the world. "I panicked that day; I won't pretend I didn't. We were in a bad way with milk prices then, and my knee was acting up again. I wasn't ready to retire, and I couldn't see running this place without you, and I got angry instead of listening to you." Dad shakes his head. "Son, I've always been so proud of you. Proud of all those As you always brought home on your report cards, and I was so proud of you for getting into that school early the way you wanted. But I wasn't ready to quit. I'm still not ready to quit." Mom leans over to squeeze his hand, and I notice a tear in the corner of one of his eyes.

I'm not sure I've ever seen my father cry before.

Farming is a true labor of love, and the most unforgiving part of that love is that it takes your body apart long before your mind. Your joints and bones give out while you still have so much more you want to do. I've never been able to picture my father without this farm. I'm not sure what that visual even looks like.

I'm guessing he doesn't either.

Dad clears his throat. "I said some terrible things that day," he says to Aaron. "Unforgiveable things. I called you ungrateful. Lazy."

Aaron frowns. "I said some terrible things too," he replies. "I don't even want to repeat the things I said."

"You two and your tempers." Mom shakes her head. "You could have come back to the house to talk with the rest of us, you know. We could have figured this out as a family. We've always figured things out as a family!"

"I'm so mad you didn't do that." Lissie crosses her arms and huffs, and for a moment she looks like the tiny little girl in pigtails that used to hide under the kitchen table during dinner. Aaron tugs her into his side.

"Sorry, Giggles," he murmurs. Lissie groans at the sound of her old nickname, but there's also a small smile on her face.

"We both owe everyone some apologies," Dad says. "All of you. We drove a crack in this family, and there's no excuse for that. But Jamie, maybe we owe you the biggest apology of all."

I have no idea what to say.

Aaron shakes his head. "You've been doing all of it, haven't you? Farming and going to school and trying to work at the library . . . ."

"And he got a boyfriend!" Lissie blurts out. Then she frowns. "But did you break up with Briar, Jamie? Is that why you left too?"

The pressure of all of them staring at me is starting to feel like a vice around my chest. I still don't know what to say or how to say it. "This place," I finally whisper. "I wish I loved it enough to be a farmer forever. Because it means so much to me, and you mean so much to me, Dad, and I can't lose it or you. But I just don't want to be a farmer. I never did."

Dad nods. "I know. I always knew that Aaron was going to go off and be a fancy lawyer or businessman, and I always knew you'd do something with all your books, and Lissie would do something with her music. I always knew that. I just haven't been ready for any of it."

"I could still change my mind!" Lissie nearly shouts. "I could maybe not like the guitar as much and want to farm instead?"

Mom laughs. "Baby, you were born with a guitar in your hand. And that's good." She looks over at Dad. "We have something to tell the three of you. I called Lexy yesterday, looking for Jamie. She and I have been making plans. Lexy," she calls out, "can you come in here?"

Lexy appears in the room right away. It's clear she and Jeremy have been waiting outside, and they've probably heard everything we've been saying. That's kind of a relief. At least I'm not going to have to relive this conversation for them on the drive back to Burlington.

"So!" Lexy clasps her hands together the same way she does when she's corralling Jeremy and me. "I was talking to my sister Mindy, and she reminded me that she did a farm study program at the high school here before she decided to drop out. I forgot the program even existed. But then she mentioned it might help all of you, and she explained it to me."

I'm not sure exactly where Lexy is going with this, and I have no idea what program she's talking about, but I just nod like I do. With Lexy, I've learned that it's best to just nod and follow her lead.

"Here's how it worked. Mindy got to work at my parent's place in exchange for school credit since she was learning how to run the farm. She was thinking that there must be other kids around here who want to be farmers and join that program, but maybe they don't live on farms like Mindy did." Lexy grins at me. "So I called Fairlington High and talked to some people, and it turns out that Chrissy Brighton's little sister—Jamie, do you remember Chrissy? She graduated with us?—really wants to own a farm someday, and she's been trying to find a farm study placement!"

"I met with her for coffee this morning," Mom says. "And I think she'll work out perfectly here. She's very motivated, and she clearly loves dairy farming. She's spent a lot of time on her uncle's farm, and she knows the ins and outs of a barn. She'd like to take on as many hours as she can this spring and summer."

"Jamie!" Lissie squeals. "That would be so good for you!"

"I don't know why we didn't think of that program before," Aaron says, looking stunned and slightly annoyed.

Dad sighs. "I did think about it once, actually. Right before you boys started college. But I was hesitant. This has always been a family operation." He shifts uncomfortably. "Your mom reminded me that maybe I need to start expanding my ideas about this place some. This Chrissy seems nice. And she wants to farm."

"Exactly," agrees Mom. "There are no guarantees, of course, and we both know that. It could work out, or it might not. But I think we owe it to everyone here to try. I think we owe it to Jamie."

Dad's look softens. "You could take that job. The one at the library." He sighs again and shakes his head. "I wanted this to be a place where we could raise you kids in peace. Make you happy. I never wanted it to be a burden."

"Dad!" The last thing I want him to think is that I consider this place, and him, to be a burden. "I *am* happy. I always have been. This is home, Dad." The words come out more harshly than I expect them to. I so badly need him to understand that I mean every single one of them.

He looks at me, and then Lissie, and then Aaron, studying us each one by one.

"How'd we get so lucky?" he asks Mom. "How'd we get these three, out of all the kids in the world?" He smiles at me. "Take that job, Jamie. We're going to find a way to make this work. And Aaron, I better not see you miss another Christmas this year." He stands up. "Now who's going to help me out in the barn?"

Mom starts crying, and Lissie announces she's going to change into her barn clothes. Aaron leans over to hug me around the neck.

"Missed you, little brother."

They're the best four words I've heard in a long time.

We get back to Burlington late in the evening, and I ask Jeremy to stop at Fletcher Allen Memorial.

I knock on the same door I knocked on less than forty-eight hours ago, and Briar calls for me to come in. The sound of his voice is like a light guiding me home, but the tension in my body doesn't lift as I open the door.

I've come to tell him that I can put him first now. But I have a terrible feeling I'm too late.

"Jamie?" Briar tries to sit up on his elbows when he sees me in the dim light, and I can tell from his grimace that the movement hurts him.

"Lie down," I urge him as I move across the room to stand next to his bed. "How are you feeling?"

He's studying my face like he's never seen it before. "I missed you," he says.

It's like the vice from earlier is back around my chest. "I bet I missed you more." I pull in a long breath. "Briar, I did it. Well, Lexy did it, but I did it first. It's a weird story. I talked to my family, and Aaron's home. I'm taking the summer internship. I'm going to live in Burlington, and Dad's getting someone else to help on the farm."

Briar's eyes brighten. "Jamie, that's amazing. The library will be so lucky to have you."

He brought up the library first. That's not a great sign. "Yeah, I'm excited about that. But I also thought maybe you and I could . . . try again. Try to be together. I can make sure you come first. I can do it now."

I know the answer before Briar speaks—it's written all over his face. "I don't think so, Jamie," he says.

The vice pulls so tight that for a moment I feel like I can't breathe. But I expected this. I knew it was probably coming.

"It's because you don't trust me, isn't it?"

Briar hesitates before he answers. "I get why you didn't show up," he says softly. "I'm even *glad* you didn't show up—who knows what would have happened to you if you had. But . . . ."

He doesn't finish the sentence. He doesn't need to. I know the rest of it.

"But I was just one more person not showing up for you when you needed me," I finish quietly.

Silence fills the room, and I know I'm right.

"Okay." I turn to leave, but Briar's voice stops me.

"Jamie?"

"Yeah?" I don't turn back around. There's no chance I can look at him right now and still make the rest of the walk out of this room.

"Thank you. Seriously, thank you. You'll never know everything you did for me."

I'm grateful to have at least that from him, even if I can't have what I really want. "You deserve it all, Briar," I tell him. "Never forget that."

You deserve better than me.

28

WHERE BRIAR HEALS

It's amazing how many romance novels you can read when you don't get out of bed for a week.

The doctors say my leg is healing really well, but they've been advising me to keep my activity level low, and it also turns out that Louie's husband Sam is a total mother hen. I've learned that a stay-at-home accountant who did a stint as an army nurse really *will* pick you up and carry you back to the guest bedroom if you try to go to the bathroom yourself without their permission. And then they'll tell their husband on you when he gets home.

It's weird being clucked and cooed over like this. Between Louie and Sam and the regular visits I'm getting from V and V people and the members of The Booklover Club, I'm starting to wonder how I ever thought I could possibly leave this place and these people. The therapist Mr. Fletcher and Louie hooked me up with (who I've been seeing over Skype because there's no way Sam would let me out of bed for my appointments) says I'll probably always have issues with abandonment and worrying that I don't belong or fit in or whatever. But she's giving me things to do and work on when that happens. It feels good.

Now if only I could stop thinking about Jamie every time I finish another novel. The end of Alyssa Samuel's latest, *Lost Love,* nearly killed me. It came out the night after my melee with Luke, and I keep wondering if Jamie's read it yet. I've almost called or texted him at least six times since he came to visit me in the hospital. But I've forced myself to put down the phone every time.

I asked my new therapist if that was the right choice. "Well, Briar," she said, "you have to choose where to set your own boundaries." Sometimes I wish she'd do a little more of my work for me.

"Yoo hoo!" The face peeking around the door of Louie's guestroom right now isn't at all surprising, since Mrs. D mentioned she might drop by today. "Briar, love, Sam let me in. Are you decent? I have a new stack of books for you and a fresh batch of donuts."

I think I've eaten fifty maple donuts this week—people just keep dropping them off. But my stomach manages to growl at the word anyway. "C'mon in, Mrs. D." I pull myself upright in bed, just to keep a hint of my dignity. I don't think I look too terrible. I took an awkward shower earlier, and I'm wearing a pair of Louie's sweatpants and one of my V and V t-shirts. I even combed my hair. Not too bad for a recovering invalid.

Mrs. D sweeps into the room in Birkenstocks and a long, patterned skirt. Her trademark purple lipstick is neatly in place, and her graying hair is pulled back into a ponytail. "You look even better today!" she says, beaming. Her enthusiasm is so contagious that I grin right back without even thinking about it. I didn't have the best experiences in elementary school, and I sometimes wonder if I would have liked it better if I had a teacher like Mrs. D.

She fusses over me as she sets up a pile of books on my left bedside table and the donuts on the right table. "And, of course, coffee," she announces, producing a tray with two cups on it. "Straight from V and V, of course. A little bird told me that Sam makes terrible coffee."

"Yeah, it's awful," I whisper, just in case Sam's nearby. I'd hate to hurt his feelings. The guy is this brilliant cook, but he makes the worst coffee I've ever tasted. Louie doesn't drink coffee, so I guess he's never noticed. But I mentioned something about craving decent coffee to Rainn the last time he stopped by. Apparently word gets around.

"So!" Mrs. D plops into the giant recliner Louie put next to my bed a few days ago and picks up one of the cups of coffee. "How's tricks?"

It takes me a few seconds to figure out that she's asking me how I feel. "Okay, I guess. I read a few more books yesterday."

"Do you think you'll be well enough to make it to our meeting this Saturday?" she asks. "We're discussing that new Alyssa Samuel, *Lost Love*. Lucia scowled but went along with it because you're injured and she felt sorry for you."

"We'll see!" Sam's voice echoes from the hallway. "It depends what the doctor says at his appointment tomorrow."

Mrs. D smiles approvingly. "Louie and Sam continue to take excellent care of you, obviously."

"Yeah." I pick at a thread popping out of the corner of the bedspread. "They do. I've never really had people do that. Not that I remember, anyway."

Mrs. D just nods. I've realized over her last few visits that the best thing about Mrs. D is how she always seems to know when to say something . . . and when not to. I end up talking a lot when she's around, and my therapist seems to think that's a good thing.

"Louie's leaving V and V," I tell her. "His art is taking off right now, and he only really ever worked at V and V for fun and to make extra money or whatever. I was kind of panicking when he told me. He's been so great ever since I moved here, but especially this week. I think I thought—I thought . . . ."

"If he left V and V, you'd never see him or Sam again," Mrs. D finishes the sentence for me, just when I need her to. She really must be some kind of magician.

"Yeah. My therapist told me to tell him I was worried, and I did." *That* was weird. The new definition of "awkward" in Webster's is going to be a picture of me trying to discuss my emotions with someone. But I got through it, and Louie didn't even laugh. "We talked. He and Sam want me to come over for dinner once a week, on Thursday nights after my shift, once I go back home. Sam says he needs to make sure I'm following my recovery plan."

Mrs. D laughs. "Oh, Briar," she says. "Are you finally starting to realize how much we all want to keep you around?"

I blush *hard*. "Yeah, maybe. Maybe."

Mrs. D hands me my cup of coffee. "Here. Drink. I'm about to make you talk about feelings again."

"Did you put any Bailey's in it, then?"

"I was worried Sam might shoot me, so no. Darling, I saw Jamie when I dropped by the store to pick up more books for you. He was sitting in our book club corner, sipping at the loneliest, saddest cup of coffee you ever did see. I asked him if he was planning to attend our meeting on Saturday, and he said he wasn't sure you'd want him there. Then he clammed up like a bull with digestive issues and jetted out of the store as if the place were on fire. I think the woman nearby thought I'd come onto him or something, can you even imagine?" She shakes her head. "What happened between the two of you?"

"I really need Bailey's if I'm going to tell you this story."

"Well, you'll just have to make do with dark roast."

I sigh heavily. Clearly she's not going to let this go. "Fine. The night I got shot—Jamie knew Luke and I were meeting. He was supposed to be there with me. Be my backup, you know? But something went wrong on the farm, and he never made it." I take a long, deep sip of the coffee. It's delicious, but it doesn't help. I don't think anything's ever going to make it easier to tell this story. "I know he blames himself or whatever, and he shouldn't. I'm glad he didn't come. He might have gotten hurt too, or worse. But when he came to see me to apologize, all I could think about was how I felt when he didn't show that night. How much that hurt."

"Why did it hurt so much?" Mrs. D asks.

"What are you, my therapist?" She ignores my snark and waits patiently for me to answer her. "I don't know. I guess because it was the first time I really expected someone to show up for me. Since I met him, Jamie's been this one constant *good* in my life. He makes books better. He makes donuts taste better, even though he's dumb and he likes crullers. He makes pet cemeteries good places to be, for crying out loud. Who can do that? He made me try a croissant, and it was amazing. So was ice wine. Everything with him is always just . . . better. I thought he'd be there—I really did. I thought he'd make things better that night, I guess, the way he's made everything else better."

Mrs. D nods thoughtfully. Great. We're in full-on pseudo therapy now. I wonder if I can get out of my weekly Skype session if I tell Dr. Koski that I met with a nosy book club grandmother instead of her this week. "I'm sorry Jamie disappointed you," she says.

I open my mouth to tell her that's not it—and then I stop. That's exactly what the problem is, I realize. *Jamie disappointed me.*

And I can't seem to let it go.

"I can tell you've been disappointed by a lot of people. That must have been hard."

I sip some more coffee so I don't have to answer her.

"Briar," she says, "do you feel Mr. Fletcher did the right thing by giving you a second chance at the store?"

I jerk my head up because I think I might know where this is going. "Um. I don't know. But I didn't expect him to."

"Of course you didn't, silly. But he did because you, Briar Nord, are a lovely human being. A lovely human being who made a mistake that he won't make again."

That's for sure. Nothing like the pain of a gunshot wound to remind you not to stay involved with criminal ex-friends.

"I don't want to tell you what to do here, Briar. I can tell you've been hurt badly before, and sometimes pain leaves us with deep, deep scars. But I will say this: Jamie Morin is also a lovely human being who made a mistake. And if what I saw in that bookstore today is any indication, it's not a mistake he'd ever make again. If he were given a second chance, of course."

A lump rises in my throat. I'm on pace to cry more this week than I've ever cried in my entire life.

"People make mistakes every day," Mrs. D goes on. "Books about relationships are filled with conflict, and relationships in real life are filled with conflict. Happy endings, in books and real life, are always just stopping points before the next conflict comes. You know that, don't you Briar?"

I can't answer her. I'll probably turn into a ball of tears if I even try.

"And that's okay," Mrs. D goes on. "That's why books have sequels. That's why people do, too."

She leans over to kiss me on the forehead, and then she sweeps out of the room, coffee cup in hand and skirt flapping madly behind her.

For a long time I just sit there in that room. The sky outside darkens, and Sam calls out something about dinner.

I sit. I sit and I think. And I wonder.

I wonder a lot about happy endings.

At some point I reach for my phone and open up my text messages.

I've spent a lot of time believing that happy endings don't exist for me. But I'm finally realizing that I've never tried to write my own.

29

WHERE JAMIE GETS CRULLERED

I've got to be a masochist.

That's all I can think as I pull into a parking garage on Church Street the Saturday after my family's big reunion. I definitely wasn't planning on attending The Booklover Club meeting today. As if it weren't bad enough that Briar ripped my heart out in that hospital room the other day, the group is talking about Alyssa Samuel's new book, *Lost Love*. For days I've wanted to text or call Briar and see what he thinks of it. It got so bad that at one point I even tried listening to some of it on audio with Jeremy so I could talk about it with him.

We made it five pages in before he asked if reading this book was going to help him get laid more. I gave up.

I had big plans for this Saturday afternoon: I was going to curl up on the couch in my dorm room and spend so much time playing Madden on Jeremy's PlayStation that I couldn't possibly think about book clubs or V and V or perfect, scruffy blonds who like the same books I do. I swiped a few beers from Mom and Dad's fridge for the occasion and everything. But then, this morning, Jeremy and Lexy came charging into the room together and started throwing clothes at me again.

"You're going to that meeting," Lexy announced. "We're not

going to let you huddle in this room like the sad sack that you are. You love that club. You're going."

"Yeah. I don't want to talk about books with you anymore," Jeremy added. "It's bad enough profs make me do that in class. And if you don't go to that meeting, I have a weird feeling you're going to keep making me do it in my free time."

I tried to argue with them, but I've never been the best at fighting Lexy on anything, and Jeremy was doing that thing again where he actually looked serious. Somehow I ended up getting into my truck and driving down to Church Street for what could be my first encounter with Briar since he let me go in that hospital room.

You can do this, I chant in my head as I force myself out of the parking garage and onto the street. *Just focus on talking about the book. Don't pay attention to Briar. Pretend he's not there or something. Maybe he won't be. He's barely out of the hospital, right? Maybe he'll stay home today. You can do this.*

I seriously consider saying fuck it and going into The Maple Factory instead of the bookstore, but the display case of donuts and crullers in the window twists a knife into my gut and quickly changes my mind.

You can do this. Just walk into V and V.

So I do. I take a deep breath and push open the door.

It takes me a moment to register how strangely quiet it is. Usually there's plenty of noise bleeding over into the store from the wine bar, and there are always at least a few voices in the place, even when it's mostly dead. I look around and realize that there's no one there—the entire place is empty. No one behind the counter. No one sitting on the couches. No one behind the coffee bar area.

No. One.

What the hell is going on? Did they kick me out of the club and not tell me? And why was I able to get into the store if it's closed?

Just when I'm starting to feel like I've been dropped into one of those crazy dreams where everyone else has clothes on and you don't, all the lights go off, and the store plunges into darkness.

"What the fuck," I whisper. My eyes attempt to adjust to the dim light around me as I try to process what's going on. There's a faint giggle from somewhere and the sound of feet shuffling, and before I can even move again, the lights spring to life and the bookstore flashes back in front of me.

Standing there is Briar. He's leaning heavily on a crutch and holding out a plate of crullers. Behind him are all the members of The Booklover Club—and every single one of them is holding up a plate with a cruller on it.

"Well?" yells Betty. "You figure it out yet?"

My eyes move back to Briar, who's smiling slightly. And then it all comes together.

This is a scene from *Lost Key*. It's one of the last scenes of the book, where Porter professes his love for Lance by gathering some of their favorite people in their favorite place and filling it with carnations, Lance's favorite flower.

Briar's filled our favorite place with some of our favorite people. And crullers.

"It's *Lost Key*," I croak out. "You made *Lost Key* for me."

"Yeah," Briar says softly. He moves forward to grab one of my hands and manages to somehow keep his balance. I fight the urge to tell him to sit down before his leg gives out. Everyone's standing there, staring at us, but somehow this scene doesn't feel in any way creepy or strange. It just feels *right*. It feels right that these people, who have all been such an important part of bringing Briar and me together, should be there for whatever's happening right now. Just like it felt right in Alyssa Samuel's book.

"Jamie," says Briar, "I know I'm kind of weird, and I don't really get why you think crullers are so much better than donuts, and I'll probably always be a little messed up in the head or whatever—"

"Stop with that kind of self-talk," Lucia hisses from behind him. Briar laughs.

"Okay, okay. Sorry. I'll start over. *Jamie.* I know I'll mess stuff up sometimes if we're together." Lucia groans again. "*But,*" Briar goes on, "I want to try this with you. I want to try being an *us,* you and me. I want to go out dancing with you again, and I want you to take me to weird Vermont festivals and call me your boyfriend. I want to chase cows with you—once I can walk again, anyway—and I want your dad to teach me to milk cows like he said he would, even though that sounds really hard." There's a snort from somewhere in the room. "I want to be with you. If you want that too, I mean."

What's ridiculous is that I start crying a little. There's no way I should be crying—this is everything I wanted. Everything I thought I'd lost. "Of course I want all that too, you dumbass. Will you sit down so I can kiss you?" I beg him. "I'm afraid I'm going to knock you over if I try to do it while you're standing up."

There's soft laughter behind us, and then clapping, and someone says, "Thank goodness!" We end up on the couch where Briar sat at our first club meeting while I tried not to stare at him. And my lips find his, and everything in the world that's been tipped upside down in the last week suddenly rights itself.

There's more clapping, but I barely hear it. All I can see and feel is Briar.

Eventually I come up for air and wrap my arms tightly around his neck. Everything about this moment feels surreal, and I need to make sure that this isn't some dream I'm stubbornly refusing to wake up from. "But you deserve better than me," I whisper in his ear.

Briar holds my arms in place around him. "No, that's not true. Before I met you, I didn't think I deserved anything. But you showed me I was wrong. I deserve *you,* Jamie Morin. You've done so much for me. More than you'll probably ever know. This is me going after what I deserve. This is me finally writing my own happy ending."

His next kiss is better than any cruller or donut could ever be.

30

WHERE BRIAR GETS HIS HAPPY ENDING (OR STOPPING POINT)

I recognize that recreating a scene from a romance novel in the middle of a bookstore while you're recovering from a gunshot is ridiculous.

In fact, when I first talked to Mrs. D and Louie about making the whole thing happen, both of them asked me if I was on too many painkillers. And maybe I was, because Old Briar never would have even thought to declare his feelings for someone else in front of a bunch of people. It's probably the biggest risk I've ever taken. What if the book club refused to help me? What if Jamie rejected me in front of them?

But I've taken a lot of risks in my life, and most of them have been the wrong ones. This one felt right. So I went for it. And right now, sitting on this couch, I can't regret a thing. Even if I am surrounded by crullers and there's not a single donut in sight.

I still can't believe this all happened the way I pictured it. Mr. Fletcher closed the store for a few hours for a "private function," even though I never asked him to do that, and Sam and Louie picked up the crullers for me. Then a whole lot of people let me sit down comfortably on a couch with my leg up while they set Jamie up for probably the weirdest surprise moment ever staged in a bookstore. And now here the two of us are, sitting together like some low-key version of royalty, while the club floats around us, drinking coffee and eating crullers and discussing the symbolism and metaphorical quality of the scene we just reenacted.

At some point Jeremy and Lexy drop by. I never could have pulled this off without them—there's no way Jamie would have come to the store today if they hadn't talked him into it. "I love you guys so much," Jeremy announces, as he stoops to grab us both in an awkward hug. "Briar, this is the most extra thing I've ever heard of. I didn't think anyone could out-extra me. Good job, bro."

Lexy sighs and leans over to kiss my cheek. "Jeremy, please don't try to one-up him out of boredom. I know it's tough to have a perfect life completely devoid of problems, but please just throw a dorm party or something, okay?"

For a moment Jeremy's face clouds over at those words—but then he's immediately back to his usual grin.

Bart tells us he's glad to see we "finally got our heads out of our asses," and Lucia informs us that she felt *Lost Love* was awfully vapid, though she may have a new appreciation for Alyssa Samuel and *Lost Key*. "This scene is quite the grand gesture, I suppose," she concedes. Emily gives Jamie a hard and quick hug and smiles at me sadly before she disappears from the party.

I don't blame her. If anyone understands how hard it can be to let go of a crush on Jamie Morin, it's me.

I do a quick toast thanking everyone for their help. It's less than twenty words, and I barely get through it without blushing, but I want to make sure these people know how much I appreciate them.

At some point Jamie's phone chimes with the Facetime signal. "It's my parents," he says. His eyes narrow as he looks at Jeremy and Lexy. "They didn't happen to know this was going on today, did they?"

Jeremy and Lexy both try to look innocent.

Jamie answers the phone. His entire family appears on the

screen, including a tall guy I've never met before who looks exactly like Jamie. It can only be one person: Aaron.

"You knew about this?" Jamie demands. "Did everyone know except me?"

"That's how surprises are supposed to work, hon," his mom answers.

"Hi, Briar. I'm Aaron. Can't wait to get to know you better," the Jamie lookalike says. "If my family thinks you're good enough for Jamie, you must be pretty damn amazing."

"Why does he get to swear and I don't?" Lissie whines.

"You can swear when you're in grad school," Frank informs her seriously.

"When you're well, Briar," says Ellie. "I'd like us all to get together at the farm." Her glance over at Aaron as she says it makes it clear that she means *all* of us.

"Absolutely," says Aaron.

I've clearly got a lot of Morin family news to catch up on.

We end the call pretty soon after that, with Jamie promising to follow up about dinner plans. I try to help with cruller clean up, but Jamie leaves me on the couch with coffee and demands that I sit still. Then Mr. Fletcher shows up, and we talk about me returning to work. "I think the doc will clear me to work next week," I tell him. I don't like the idea of everyone at V and V covering my shifts. I don't like the idea of not pulling my weight. But Mr. Fletcher insists that I shouldn't rush it. "We're excited for you to come back, but we're doing fine," he says, patting me on the shoulder. "Come back when you're sure you're ready. And *please* start calling me Harrison."

"And please start calling me Audrey!" Mrs. Fletcher appears next to us. "Now, when am I having you and Jamie over for lunch?"

For some reason I don't feel anything in my stomach when she says that. Not a single churning sensation or butterfly. "Soon," I answer.

She smiles like I've just handed her a new Caldecott winner.

When it's time to leave, Jamie tells me that he and Louie have been texting, and he's going to take me back to Louie's place. "I guess he and Sam want to go out for a few hours," he says. "I was going to see if you wanted to come back to the dorms with me, but Jeremy will be there, and your place has all those stairs . . . ."

Louie and Sam obviously want to make sure Jamie and I have some alone time. It's the kind of thoughtfulness I'm still not used to, and I almost open up my mouth and tell Jamie not to worry about me or stairs or whatever.

But I stop myself the second I feel Jamie's hand come around the back of my neck and squeeze gently.

He helps me crutch my way out of V and V and onto the street. The end of the afternoon is giving way to the evening light. "I'm going to go get the truck so you don't have to walk," Jamie says as he sits me down on a bench. "Be right back."

He disappears up the street, and I notice someone standing next to The Maple Factory. Someone tall and lanky, wearing a coat and a Red Sox hat I've seen before.

Luke. It's Luke.

I grab the phone in my pocket out of instinct, not even sure what I plan to do with it. Call Jamie for help? Call the police? I can't even believe he's out of jail already after what he did—did he make bail? How? *What does he want?* The voice in my head screams.

But then I remember that Luke never told the police or Mr. Fletcher what had happened in the weeks prior to the break-in. He never gave me up to them. I remember, and I stay still.

Luke nods once in my direction. He lifts his right hand to his forehead and makes a gesture like he's saluting me. Or maybe he's saying goodbye. Or maybe both.

Then he turns the corner and disappears around the building, just like he was never there.

I know, deep in my gut, that I won't see him again.

"I don't want to hurt you."

Jamie's words, whispered in my ear as he holds me tightly in his arms, are soft and sweet, and they seem to stay in place in the warm air of Louie and Sam's guestroom. The window's open, and a Vermont spring breeze has given the room as much of a fresh lift as Jamie's presence.

"We can be careful," I insist. I need Jamie so badly. I need to feel every inch of him inside of me. I need to remember how perfectly we fit together. How right the whole world feels when he controls my body with his.

His movements are slow as he undresses me and himself and then traces his hands down my body. He stops when he gets to the bandages just above my right ankle. "I'll never stop wishing that I'd made a different choice that day," he says.

I tug at one of his curls. "Don't say that, okay? We've both done things we'd do over differently if we could. But we're here now, making plans for the future. Mrs. D says happy endings are just stopping points anyway. So let's have as many of those as we can. Do you know what I mean?"

Jamie traces a hand over my cheek. "Yeah. I think I do." He leans over and sweeps my mouth up with his, and he takes my cock in his hand and strokes it until I'm nearly at the brink. He stops and holds me while I shudder and beg, and then he takes me in his mouth and brings me right back to the edge. Over and over and over.

"Not going to last much longer," I finally croak out. "Please, Jamie . . . ."

I'm propped up on my side, my injured leg carefully placed by Jamie on a high stack of pillows. He gently preps me, sinking one finger after the next into me until I'm begging for him, begging for his cock, begging to have him inside of my body.

"Are you comfortable?" he asks urgently. "Are you sure you're not in pain?"

It's like the whole world is a cloud, and I'm floating in its perfect softness. "I'm better than I've ever been. I love you," I choke out, before I can stop myself from saying the words.

I've never said that out loud to anyone before. But nothing feels strange or wrong about those words as they fall out of my mouth. Every single syllable feels right.

"Fuck, Briar. I love you too. So much." And then Jamie eases his way into my body, every hard inch of him owning a piece of me. He thrusts softly at first, then a little more intensely, then more gently again, all the while moving his hands up and down my body and back and forth across my cock. He pushes all the way in, and it's like our bodies are merged, as if we've joined at some kind of a cellular level. I can feel the heat and excitement humming in him, dancing in time with the same heat and excitement that's moving through me, and I grab his hand that's teasing and tugging my dick.

"I wanna do this forever," I choke out. "But I'm not going to last."

He laughs in my ear. "You don't need to. We can do this over and over and over again. I'm not going anywhere, Briar. I'm not."

He thrusts into me one more time as he says the words, and I come all over the place where our hands are joined together. I feel him coming inside of me, coming undone, and our mouths meet in the kind of kiss Alyssa Samuel can only dream of writing about.

I'm not going anywhere.

For the first time in my life, I hear those words and I believe them.

We sleep. Then we wake up and make love and sleep some more and wake up and make love again. And then we lay in each other's arms, forgetting the past and creating the future.

"I need a place to live this summer," Jamie says. "I've got to start apartment hunting."

For the first time, it registers in my mind that Jamie and I are going to have the whole summer in Burlington together, and hopefully a whole lot more months after that. Even years. A conversation I had weeks ago that I'd forgotten all about comes back to me. "You know what? When I paid my rent this month, my landlord mentioned that the people who live on the second floor are moving out. Their place is bigger than mine. It's a two bedroom."

"You think we need two bedrooms?" Jamie teases.

"We could make one into an office space. For you to study. And maybe for me to use too? I've been thinking about starting a book review blog on the V and V site. Louie suggested it, and Mr. Fletcher thinks it could bring more web traffic to the store. They both really like the reviews I write and post up around the shelves."

Jamie clasps his arms a little more tightly around my body. "Briar, are you asking me to move into that Pepto-Bismol-colored abomination you call a house with you?"

I grin as I snuggle into his arms. "Fucking right I am. We'll have donuts every single morning. Maybe I'll let a cruller into the place once in a while. Maybe."

"Mom and Dad will keep us supplied with croissants too, no doubt. Especially after Dad and I teach you how to milk cows and he talks us into a few five a.m. shifts together."

I don't think I'd want to get up that early every single day, but doing it once in a while doesn't sound so bad. I like Frank and Ellie and Lissie a lot, and I suspect I'm going to end up liking Aaron a lot too. And spending some Vermont sunrises with Jamie in the quiet calm of Tiny Acres could never be terrible. "Sounds great to me. Are you in?"

"Well," Jamie says, "I should warn you that Jeremy claims I'm a crappy roommate."

"The guy who locks you out of your own bed four times a week thinks *you're* a crappy roommate?"

"I never dust. And I guess I snore. And I've never lived with someone who wasn't my family or Jeremy before, so I might be terrible at it."

"I leave books all over the place and I hate doing dishes, if that makes you feel better. And the only thing I know how to cook is eggs, so I eat them like six times a week."

"Luckily for you Ellie Morin taught me her secret meatloaf recipe."

My mouth waters.

"Yes, Briar Nord," Jamie whispers into my ear. "I'd love to move in with you. But only if you promise to make my biggest fantasy come true."

My eyes widen as I try to imagine exactly what Jamie's biggest fantasy is. "Tell me?" I croak.

Jamie nips at my ear. "Briar Nord, some men dream of seeing their perfect lover strutting around in hot lingerie or tiny speedos. I dream of my perfect lover naked, with a stack of books strategically placed in front of them."

I laugh so hard that for a moment I worry I'm going to pull out some stitches. I don't, luckily, and Jamie and I are still wrapped up in each other's arms, laughing and making plans, when the sun comes up a few hours later.

It's the best happy ending and beginning I could ever imagine for myself.

31

WHERE ALYSSA SAMUEL WRITES A LETTER

Dear Briar and Jamie,

I don't have time to respond to every email I receive, but I wanted to make sure I responded to yours. I've spent a great deal of my life reading and writing stories of love and happy endings, and few stories have touched me the way yours did. I very much enjoyed the pictures of your *Lost Key* moment. I was honored to see my storytelling was part of a day that clearly meant so much to both of you.

I immediately looked at Briar's book blog, *Booklover,* and I can now say that I might be *your* biggest fan, Briar Nord. The way you review books is thoughtful, considerate, and manages to be kind and honest at the same time—I hope you know how incredibly talented you are. I especially enjoy the guest appearances Jamie makes on the blog from time to time with his "Librarian's Corner" column. The two of you have created quite the space for your shared love of reading!

Sometimes, I know, it can be tempting to believe that real love will never live up to the kind of scenes we read in romance novels. So much of real love is just the everyday: the load of laundry you do for someone, or the walk you take around a neighborhood together. The way you put up with a partner who is moody or sullen. Sometimes we lose sight of that fact. The way you two write together on your blog, and the lovely email you sent me, suggests neither of you is likely to forget what real love and romance is anytime soon. A couple that milks cows together in order to spend time with family is, I suspect, a couple that is likely to stay together. Briar, I hope your father-in-law continues to be impressed by your growing farm skills!

I wish the two of you nothing but the best in your future together. I've enclosed two signed copies of my newest book, *Found Dreams*. I look forward to reading your reviews.

Best,
Alyssa Samuel

THE
END

ACKNOWLEDGMENTS

I've jokingly said that *Booklover* is a love letter to my home state, but in many ways that isn't a joke. I was raised on a small dairy farm in northern Vermont very similar to the one Jamie lives on. My childhood was full of morning milkings and trips across the border for croissants and pet cemeteries in back pastures. I left Vermont when I was eighteen, and I miss it greatly. I will forever be grateful to Sarina Bowen and her amazing team for opening up the True North world and inviting me to join it. This is a world I have read in happily for years, and writing in it has allowed me to explore a beloved part of my life.

I am equally grateful to the team of people who lifted me up while I was writing this book. Shantel Schonour, Riley Stouffer, and my mother, Dianne, all gave incredible insight and feedback on the original manuscript. Karen Bradley offered so much support as I worked on this project. My editor Kari Shafenberg cheered on the story from the very beginning and worked tirelessly to ensure the book reached its fullest potential. My fellow authors in the True North universe have been there for me every step of the way, offering ideas, wisdom, help, and feedback at the drop of a hat. They have made this book infinitely better, and they have made this entire experience great fun.

And then there is my partner, Travis. He never stops believing in the possibilities of my writing, never stops encouraging me, and never minds when I lock myself away in my office for hours on end. Our love is in the everyday, and every single day I am grateful for it.

Ultimately, this story would not exist without the wonderful cast of characters I was raised around who inspired it. None of them appear here, of course—this book and all the characters in it are entirely a work of fiction—but they all had a hand in making me who I am today: a Vermonter through and through, who loves books and words and cows (though I prefer not to milk them twice a day anymore). My father, mother, and brother, who I spent years milking cows and eating maple cream with, have always been my greatest supporters. I am thankful for them every single day.

I am also eternally thankful for maple donuts. Sorry not sorry, Jamie.

Made in the USA
Columbia, SC
02 December 2021

50277454R00137